THE WINTER KING

The death of an unpopular nobleman brings trouble to Sir Josse's family, in the latest Hawkenlye mystery.

All Saint's Eve, 1211. An overweight but wealthy nobleman, desperate for an heir, dies at a celebration feast. The death seems natural, but healer Sabin is beset by doubts. There is only one person Sabin can turn to for help: fellow healer Meggie, daughter of Sir Josse d'Acquin. But what she requires of her is dangerous indeed...

Recent Titles by Alys Clare

The Hawkenlye Series

FORTUNE LIKE THE MOON
ASHES OF THE ELEMENTS
THE TAVERN IN THE MORNING
THE ENCHANTER'S FOREST
THE PATHS OF THE AIR *
THE JOYS OF MY LIFE *
THE ROSE OF THE WORLD *
THE SONG OF THE NIGHTINGALE *
THE WINTER KING *

The Norman Aelf Fen Series

OUT OF THE DAWN LIGHT *
MIST OVER THE WATER *
MUSIC OF THE DISTANT STARS *
THE WAY BETWEEN THE WORLDS *
LAND OF THE SILVER DRAGON *

* *available from Severn House*

THE WINTER KING

A Hawkenlye Mystery

Alys Clare

Severn House Large Print
London & New York

This first large print edition published 2014
in Great Britain and the USA by
SEVERN HOUSE PUBLISHERS LTD of
19 Cedar Road, Sutton, Surrey, England, SM2 5DA.
First world regular print edition published 2013 by
Severn House Publishers Ltd., London and New York.

British Library Cataloguing in Publication Data

Clare, Alys author.
  The winter king. -- (A Hawkenlye mystery)
  1. D'Acquin, Josse (Fictitious character)--Fiction.
  2. Helewise, Abbess (Fictitious character)--Fiction.
  3. Great Britain--History--John, 1199-1216--Fiction.
  4. Detective and mystery stories. 5. Large type books.
  I. Title II. Series
  823.9'2-dc23

ISBN-13: 9780727897268

Severn House Publishers support the Forest Stewardship Council™
[FSC™], the leading international forest certification organisation. All
our titles that are printed on FSC certified paper carry the FSC logo.

MIX
Paper from
responsible sources
FSC® C013056

Printed and bound in Great Britain by
T J International, Padstow, Cornwall.

In memory of my mother,
Joan Harris,
8th August 1917–3rd July 2013
with my love

PROLOGUE

All Saints' Eve, 1211

In the dark years, the last day of October was reserved for the honouring of the dead. The coming of the churchmen meant that the name had been altered; craftily, they grafted a new feast day on to one that the people would have been celebrating anyway, and they dedicated it to their endless panoply of saints.

The fat man presiding over his own feast in his own hall suppressed a belch and reflected that, call it what you will, people always flocked to the promise of free food and drink. If he'd said he was honouring the devil himself, they'd still have come, and they'd still have raised their mugs and goblets when he called for the toast.

The fat man let his intense dark eyes run slowly along the double row of tables that lined his hall, either side of the central hearths. Each table was flanked by benches, and they were so tightly packed that you couldn't have found space for a sparrow. His gaze moved on, lingering here and there, and with part of his mind he totted up the approximate cost of what he had supplied for the men and women tucking so single-mindedly into their dinners.

He reached for his goblet – it was a beautiful piece; solid silver, gracefully shaped, decorated around the base with gemstones – and, discovering it was empty, he gestured in irritation for the nearest serving boy. With a nervous smile, the lad half-filled the goblet. The fat man took the slender wrist in a savage grip and, forcing the boy's hand, made him tilt the wine jug until the silver goblet overflowed.

Now which one of the arse-lickers in my hall, he mused, *had the audacity to tell my own servants how much of my own wine I was to be allowed?*

Once more, he moved his eyes down the long lines of revellers. He had his suspicions; not a few of the important lords present depended on the fat man, in more ways than one, and he was not deaf to the mutterings and whisperings that spread the pernicious rumours of his failing health. His narrow obsidian gaze fixed on two likely culprits. *Him? Or what about him?*

From somewhere nearby he heard a light, fluting laugh, swiftly suppressed. He put up a hand, as if to wipe his brow – it was very hot in the hall – and beneath it turned his eyes to the beautiful young woman in the rose-pink silk dress. He liked to observe her when she was unaware of his gaze; it gave him a sexual thrill, for he perceived that, in some way, it symbolized his power over her. He had made a spy hole in the wall of the small space where she performed her ablutions. Sometimes, watching her, he had to stuff his fist in his mouth to stifle the sounds that would otherwise have burst out of him.

Tonight she was placed to his left, in what would have been a position of honour, except that the table where she sat was not on the elevated dais upon which his own throne-like chair stood. He, in fact, was the only person present to have that honour, and he had bestowed it on himself.

My hall, my feast, my meats and my wine, the fat man thought. *I'll seat my kin and my guests as I please.*

Openly now, his eyes bored into the young woman in rose-pink silk. Her gown was low-cut and savagely laced – she was, he observed, having difficulty drawing a deep breath – and the white flesh of her breasts swelled out above the neckline. She was clearly embarrassed by this, for she kept putting up her hand to try to raise the gown a little higher. He'd tell her about that, later. He'd inform her that the damned gown was intended to display her, and he'd administer a reminder or two to force the lesson home; women, in his view, were like puppies, and needed regular physical punishment to teach them to obey without question. And those plump breasts were, after all, his to do what he liked with.

Later...

Deliberately he conjured up an image of her naked body, spread out for him on the furs of the wide bed, pale flesh turned gold by the fire in the hearth. He closed his eyes, emitting a soft groan of desire, and, just for an instant, he felt his flesh respond.

Then the moment was gone.

He stared down at the great swell of his belly.

9

Somewhere beneath the jutting overhang, his useless manhood lay, pathetic, small, soft. He swore, quietly, repeatedly. He *had* to have a son; what was the use of all this new wealth – the jewels, the garments of fine wool and smooth silk, the glossy furs, the supple leather work, the pure-bred horses, the swift hounds, the food, the wines, even the extensive improvements to the very dwelling in which he now sat – if there was no heir to pass it on to?

His first wife had died in childbed, together with the girl child she was trying to bring into the world. The second had done better, although only slightly; her infant son had survived two winters, then died, together with his mother, of a sudden springtime fever. After that, he'd found it harder to find a woman prepared to take him on – God alone knew why – and he'd been alone for too many years, growing older, fatter, unhealthier. Then this heaven-sent opportunity had come and, like many other men who kept their wits about them and their eyes wide open, he had found it all too easy to make the money come rolling in. It had quite surprised him how many mothers and fathers were suddenly eager to throw their daughters at his feet.

The girl in rose-pink silk was his wife of three months. She had come unwillingly to the marriage bed and, despite his initial efforts to persuade her with *very* generous gifts, her reluctance had only increased. He had managed to consummate their union – a feat he'd repeated twice – but, recently, everything he'd tried, or made her try, had resulted in the same dismal failure.

His heavy brows drew together in a ferocious scowl as he recalled the humiliation of his attempt to find advice. He had not wished to broadcast his shame to his own household; to a man and to a woman, they were terrible gossips, not deterred for long even when he made an example of one or other of them with a brutal beating. Instead he had gone, stealthily, at dusk and alone, to consult the infirmarian who tended the Augustinian canons in Tonbridge. The word was that the best healers were to be found among the nuns up at Hawkenlye Abbey, but he could not face discussing his problem with a woman, even if she hid herself behind veil and habit.

In the end, he wondered if that would have been the better option. The monk he saw – a tall, broad-shouldered, well-muscled fellow who didn't look as if he'd ever have difficulty getting and maintaining an erection, and wasn't *that* ironic? – made him drop his hose, and then proceeded to inspect him minutely, humming to himself as he did so. Then, as if he were addressing some lowly serf, the damned man had said, 'Your trouble is that you carry far too much weight. The blood that is required for the task you have in mind is too busy keeping you on your feet to do anything else. You eat too much, and your body is constantly working to digest the intake. Do you get breathless? Do you sometimes feel your heart's trying to burst out of your ribs?' Before the fat man had a chance to respond, the monk had answered his own questions. 'Hmm, yes, I thought so. Your swollen,

11

discoloured nose and that purplish tinge to your face are reliable signs.' He frowned. 'You also drink too well, and drink is known to be the sworn enemy of potency in a man.'

As if those bitter words had not been sufficient, the wretched man had smiled. Then he'd added, 'If you really wish to know how to bed your new wife and get a son in her, my lord, I suggest more exercise – rather a lot more – and a great deal less on your plate and in your cup.'

The fat man, trying to gather his shreds of dignity around him even as he laced up his hose and straightened his tunic, had ventured to ask if there were not some herbal concoction he might take, or some more exotic substance ... was there not some sort of magical horn from faraway lands which, ground into a mug of wine, made a man regain his youthful vigour?

The infirmarian had given a hearty laugh. 'Oh, my lord, if there were an easy way out of your little problem, don't you think everyone would take it?' Still chuckling, he had turned away to wash his hands in a basin. 'No, take my word for it,' he added over his shoulder, 'restrict your diet and get yourself moving, and those rolls of fat will drop off you. Then, anything will be possible – you'll see!'

The fat man had tried. Oh, he'd tried, all right. To no avail. He might have succeeded in tightening his belt a notch and, once or twice, he'd experienced a definite twitch in his loins, but that was all.

And there was that ripe girl, *his own wife*, his for the taking, and he could manage no more than a *twitch*...

Impatiently the fat man reached again for his goblet. Once more, he found it empty. This time, the serving boy filled it to the brim. It afforded the fat man some satisfaction to see that the lad's wrist was dark with bruising.

He drank deeply. The kitchen women were sending in more food and, eagerly, the fat man watched as they piled his platter high. He might not be able to service his wife, he reflected, his mouth so full that he could barely chew, but, by God and all the precious saints, he could still eat and drink. *And, damnation take it, I shall*, he thought, *while I am left up here in peace.*

He stuffed a honey cake between his lips. It tasted good, so he had another.

For, soon, the eating would be over. The tables would be cleared of the debris, and then it would start. One by one, they'd come sidling up to him, smiles stuck on their greasy faces, hands clasped over their wine-splattered garments, and they'd all have some variation of the same refrain. *A sumptuous feast, my lord, and may I say what an honour it is to be here?* Then, hard on the heels of the sycophantic words, while their echo still filled the air: *Might I be forgiven, my lord, for taking this opportunity to ask one small favour?*

The fat man sighed. He wished he did not have to endure it, but there was no choice. He was making money, yes – a great deal of it – but he could not do it alone. Although he hated to admit it, he needed these men. His extravagant wealth and high position had not come without making enemies, and, apart from his men's other uses,

13

he required their strength of arms for protection. He must at all costs keep them loyal, and if that meant listening to their ingratiating little speeches and waving a careless hand to grant their pathetic little requests, then so be it.

Soon they'd come, mounting the dais one by one, leaning over him, whispering in his ear, so close that he'd breathe in the fumes of garlic, onion, half-digested meat and sour wine issuing out of their foul mouths.

The fat man gave a sigh and reached for another honey cake.

It was nearly over. Soon he would be alone again. Almost all the petitioners had returned to their seats, and the pot boys were busy replenishing the mugs, tankards and goblets. Ale, mead *and* wine; perhaps he had been *too* generous...

Suddenly he felt a pain. Oh, *oh*, not a pain – this was *agony*; stopping his breath, shocking his whole body, his entire being, with its intensity.

His heart laboured. It beat once, twice ... then the pain doubled. He could not be sure, but he thought he might have cried out.

Then something inside him seemed to burst.

He sat in his great chair, his head back, his eyes half-closed, his hands clasped across his stomach. Most of the people in his hall were at least a little drunk, including the pot boys and the serving men and women, for there were always opportunities for a quick swig when no one was looking.

Here and there along the length of the tables,

14

one or two pairs of eyes glanced surreptitiously up at the fat man on his dais. Otherwise, his guests – all too aware of his lashing tongue, his unreasonable and swiftly roused temper, his cruelty – preferred to leave well alone. If the fat lord was content to let them go on drinking at his expense without demanding anything in return, they weren't going to argue with him.

In time, guests began to take their leave. In ones and twos, and in family groups, they approached the dais, bowed to their lord and backed away. Nobody thought it odd that he failed to respond to them. It was his habit to ignore those who stood below him, unless there was really no alternative.

The young wife in the rose-pink silk, appreciating all of a sudden that the hall was now almost empty, gave a small, sad sigh of resignation. Wishing a polite goodnight to the two men still seated near her, she got to her feet and, moving with her usual grace, approached the dais.

'Have I your permission to retire, my lord?' she asked politely, risking a quick look at him from under her long eyelashes. 'I am rather tired and have a slight headache,' she added, more in hope than in expectation; very occasionally, if she said she had a headache, he left her alone.

He did not reply.

She took a step closer. 'My lord husband?'

Still he neither spoke nor acknowledged her.

He must have fallen asleep. She was tempted to slip away and leave him to be woken by one of the servants, but he wouldn't like that. He'd probably tell her she'd dishonoured him by her desertion, and by allowing someone other than her to wake him up, and then he'd find some way of making her pay. Whatever it was, she knew it would hurt or humiliate her, and probably both.

She reached up a timid hand and grasped the hem of his tunic, pulling at it. 'My lord!' she said, speaking more loudly.

His hands slowly unclasped. One of them, dropping by his side, touched hers. Considering how hot it was in the hall, the flesh felt rather cool. Clammy, even...

A sudden wild hope surged through her. Could it be? Oh, surely not, she had only hoped to...

Eager now, the fierce joy threatening to burst through her carefully maintained self-control, she leapt up on to the dais. Crouching beside him, she stared down into his face. The full lips and the swollen, bulbous nose still had their usual deep reddish-purple colour, but otherwise his skin was ash-grey.

She put her cheek up to his open mouth. She waited. Then she slid her hand inside his tunic, feeling for the heartbeat.

Nothing.

Nothing!

Remembering who and where she was, she held herself firm. Looking around, she caught sight of her husband's steward. He stood at the far end of the hall, and his deep, hooded eyes were on her. She beckoned him.

When he was close enough for her to speak in the quiet, respectful tone that the circumstances

16

demanded, she said, 'Fetch help, please.'

His eyes asked the unspoken question.

'I am afraid,' she said, her voice carefully toneless, 'that his lordship is dead.'

ONE

In King John's England, suffering the results of the monarch's petulant squabble with Pope Innocent and under an interdict these four years, several diverse elements were slowly moving together. When, inexorably, they would collide and combine, the outlook was stormy.

It was a time of frightening portents. In the royal hunting preserve of Cannock Forest, a herd of deer had been discovered with a terrible disorder of the bowels. The wildest of the rumours claimed the deer had fled halfway across the country and thrown themselves into the sea at the mouth of the River Severn. A two-headed, eight-legged animal had been born and, although nobody was entirely sure what sort of animal it was, or where this abomination had occurred, everyone accepted it as a sign of nature's – and, far more importantly, God's – extreme distress at the ways of the world. The moon had been observed coloured deep red, as if bathed in blood; a sure sign, if ever there was one, of strife. War, or at least some terrible disaster, it was generally agreed, must surely be coming...

In a small Kentish village a dozen miles up from the coast, an elderly woman was basking in sudden notoriety. Some said she was a witch; others that she was just plain daft. She had an uncertain grip on reality, but this was possibly no more than a clever act. She appeared to be even more agitated than most by the alarming portents that were regularly occurring and, one mild autumn evening, according to witnesses, she emitted an ear-piercing scream and fell into a deep and very public trance in the middle of the village green. In her trance state – and opinion was equally divided between her being inspired by God or the Devil – she began to proclaim frightening and dangerous predictions.

'Darkness will prevail all the while this Winter King rules,' she began.

'Winter King? Who's that, then? What's she on about?' her audience muttered.

As if she had heard – possibly she had – the crone obligingly elucidated. 'The Oak King rules in the months of light,' she wailed, 'and the Holly King takes over at the autumn equinox, for he is made of darkness and belongs to the winter.' She paused, her wide, pale eyes ranging round her audience. 'He is the Winter King!' she cried. A few flecks of spittle dotted her lower lip.

'Does she mean King John?' a bold soul demanded.

'His peers will try to bring him down,' the old woman went on, her tone high and quivery, and not, according to witnesses, her normal speaking voice, 'demanding that he signs a great document that will call him to account, but it will be to no avail. He will suffer disaster on the water, losing all he holds most dear. He will die an

20

untimely death, leaving his realm in grave jeopardy, beset by the enemy from across the seas.'

The crone's eyes were wide and staring. Once or twice she put a hand up to her brow, as if her head pained her. It seemed to some that she was listening to words that nobody else could hear.

A nervous frisson went through the villagers. Men and women turned to each other, searching for reassurance. On the outer edge of the now sizeable crowd, men looked anxiously over their shoulders. It did not do to be observed listening to such dangerous talk, and Heaven help the poor sap making the comments. One man, more sensible than most, hurried off to find the most respected of the village elders.

'His successor will be weak and untrust-worthy,' continued the crone, either unaware of or ignoring her audience's unease, and well into her stride now. 'He will extract vast sums from his people to pay for ultimately fruitless wars—'

'Just like this one, then,' put in some humorist, raising a few half-hearted guffaws.

'—and he will reign for half a century, although it will seem longer,' went on the old woman. 'Only on his death will a great king emerge, one who will provide strong leadership against England's enemies and, at long last, permit his people a stake in their own lives.'

'What's she talking about? Stake in our own lives? When hell freezes over!' her fellow villagers protested, howling their derision.

A burly man – the village blacksmith – approached the old woman. His intention was un-

21

clear: perhaps he was going to demand an explanation, or perhaps, for her own good and theirs, he would attempt to stop her. Behind him, hurrying to catch up with his long strides, came the village elder, accompanied by the man who had run to fetch him. But they were too late to reason with or silence the old woman. With a dramatic cry, her eyes rolling back in her head, she fell into a swoon, and neither burnt feathers waved under her nose nor several quite hard slaps on the face could revive her.

That might have been the last anyone heard of Lilas of Hamhurst, for the village would probably have soon forgotten the event, or else saved it up as an amusing tale of the odd ways of folk, to relate on a dark evening. Unfortunately for old Lilas, however, one of those who heard her was no local man but a lord, and a member of the king's court circle to boot. As he silently slipped away from the crowd encircling the prostrate figure on the grass, he was committing to memory every last one of her pronouncements. He had an idea that certain men of his acquaintance would be very interested to hear them.

Nobody knew who he was. He had arrived by boat in Dover that afternoon, and was putting up overnight in the village inn, having made landfall too late in the day to complete his journey before dark. Even a wealthy, well-fed, strong lord carrying both a fine sword of Toledo steel, and a wickedly sharp dagger with which he was ruthlessly efficient, hesitated to travel by night

22

nowadays. Especially when, for reasons best known to himself, he rode alone. Especially when, as now, he had gone to considerable effort to make himself look like any other impoverished traveller, the sword and the dagger carefully concealed from the eyes of the curious.

He saw no reason to reveal to the sots and the slatternly serving women in the Hamhurst tavern where he had come from and where he was bound, and when a drunk in the taproom ventured to ask him, he said, with a ferocious scowl, 'Mind your own business.'

Retiring early to the dirty cot assigned to him in the far corner of the sleeping quarters (he kept all his clothes on, including his boots, in the hope that he would thus deter the other living things that dwelt in the bedding) he wondered if he would have done better to go on his way after all. But it had been a long day, and he was exhausted.

His journey had begun before dawn, far away in northern France. He had been away for a long time – too long, he thought wearily – and the various tensions of the past few weeks had worn him out. He had travelled on the least-known lanes and tracks, sleeping under hedges or, at best, putting up at the sort of mean, rough, dirt-cheap tavern he was staying in that night. He had lost count of the number of days it was since he'd had access to hot water or changed his linen. He knew he stank, but comforted himself with the fact that to reek like a peasant was a good way of disguising his identity.

His mission to France had been both dangerous and delicate, and, for both those reasons, absolutely secret. Only a handful of men knew where he had gone, and why. Those men would even now be anxiously waiting for him, desperate to know what news he brought, whether or not his mission had been a success.

They will just have to wait another day, the man thought sourly. He turned over on the hard, mean cot, trying to get comfortable. His stomach ached, and the throbbing inside his head did not abate even when he closed his eyes and tried to relax. He had spent too long eating bad food and, to cap it all, the violent swell in the Narrow Seas had turned his guts inside out. He had vomited almost all the way from northern France to the south of England, leaning over the rail of the small boat bobbing her way through the heavy seas and wishing, at times, that he could just die and bring the misery to an end. The inn at Hamhurst was no haven of comfort and warmth, but even such a filthy hole was better than nothing. And, if he hadn't stopped when he did, he would not have been standing on the edge of that avid crowd of villagers when the old crone started her rant. He smiled grimly – a mere stretching of his thin lips. Perhaps some helpful deity was watching over him, keeping him from harm and ensuring that he'd been in exactly the right place at the right time...

All things considered, he decided, yawning so hugely that he heard his jaw crack, it was far better to risk a few flea bites than sleep in some ditch. Who knew what starving wretch, driven to desperate measures by King John's rule, might have seen his chance to kill off one more poor traveller, grabbing what he could from the corpse to sell for whatever he could get?

And that, the man reflected as sleep finally took him, would have been quite ironic...

Half a day's ride from Lilas's village, another voice was speaking out against King John's rule. The voice was that of a passionate, idealistic and naive young monk named Caleb, and he lived at Battle Abbey.

Bemused, innocent, and not a little deranged, Caleb believed fervently that King John's rule and its attendant hardships were a punishment from God. In private, Caleb had been taking secret measures – fasting, self-flagellation – to try to appease the terrifying version of God that he had been taught to believe in, hoping thus to move the Almighty to have pity on the people of England.

Although it was hard to say how it came to happen, Caleb had heard whispers concerning the happenings in Hamhurst. One whisper in particular – the strange new name that Lilas, in her trance, had bestowed upon the king. Now Caleb, too, deep within the confines of his monastery, began to refer to John as the Winter King.

Caleb's superiors, however, were not in the least happy at the young monk's growing notoriety. Battle Abbey had recently paid the vast sum of fifteen hundred marks to the king, in order that he should confirm the abbey's ancient privilege of being answerable directly and only

25

to him, and not to the bishops who would otherwise have had control over the abbey and its life. It was not the moment for one of their congregation – even a young, innocent and slightly daft one – to upset the king by complaining that his rule was so terrible that it could only be a punishment from God.

The bishops were not at all pleased with the new arrangements at Battle. Not that it mattered very much; since the interdict had begun, English bishops had been steadily leaving the country, and their displeasure was thus largely irrelevant. The climate in England was not good for senior churchmen, for the uncompromising terms of the interdict were making people question if they really needed the church after all. Give or take the odd marriage service or funeral rites, they seemed to be managing quite nicely without it. The muttered grumbling was becoming gradually louder. *Why do we have to pay tithes and taxes to the church when it doesn't lift a finger to help us in our time of need?* People were, moreover, unconcerned at seeing the king continue to extract all that he could from the church and the religious houses. King John, the rumours said, needed chests full of money for some campaign he was mounting against the Welsh. *Well, if he gets what he needs from the church*, men muttered, *he won't have to tax the people so heavily*.

The insuppressible Caleb, who refused to be turned from his God-ordained path by threats or cajoling, was now saying that King John was not fit to rule. Perhaps this was another phrase that

26

the young monk had overheard; it was, or so it was claimed, the view of the church's most senior figures. The Pope, should he finally lose patience with this king upon whom both excommunication and the imposition of the interdict had had so little effect, might well conclude the same, and then he would formally depose John of England, and release his subjects from the duty of allegiance to him.

By some strange mechanism of fate, Caleb appeared to be saying just what the people of England wanted to hear. His fame spread, and men and women flocked to Battle hoping to hear him speak. They were disappointed, for, having experienced just what happened when the young monk was allowed out, his superiors now kept him firmly within the abbey walls. But in every tavern in the town, there was only one topic of conversation; so loudly and frequently were Caleb's pronouncements repeated that few visitors came away unaware of exactly what the young monk had said.

These included the three nondescript merchants who, as the spell of fine weather finally ended and the cold November rains began, prepared to leave Battle and head back for where they had started from. They did not speak as they set off on the busy road from the coast to the capital. There was no need: they had what they'd come for. Now, urging on their mounts, their sole aim was to hurry back to the men who had sent them on their mission and give their report.

In the narrow, rectangular hall of a large and

rambling old manor house, an elderly man sat by the huge fire that blazed in the hearth, stretching out his long legs to its warmth. The house had been well sited, sheltered as it was in a fold of the northern slopes of the High Weald. It was not affected by the insidious damp that crept up from the wide river valley to the north, and the higher land at its back kept off the worst of the prevailing south-westerly winds. But the old man had seen too many winters, and he hardly ever felt warm between October and April.

He sat in a costly oak chair, its arms, legs and back beautifully carved, a cushion stuffed with goose feathers on the seat to comfort his bony backside. Before him, on a large board balanced on two trestles, was a wide scatter of parchments, some still rolled and bound, some spread out and weighted at the four corners to hold them down.

So much information, the old man thought.

He sat back in his chair, slowly turning the huge rock of citrine set in heavy gold that graced the middle finger of his right hand.

Events were falling out just as he would have dictated, had it been possible to do so. At long last, not one but two people had found the courage to stand up and speak aloud what so many others murmured in secret. Yes, one was a wild-eyed crone and the other a naive young monk, but that did not matter. They had spoken out; they had done the unimaginable. Added to that, there were all the portents and omens; it was as if nature itself was eager to underline the message.

28

The old man's hard mouth twisted in a grimace of wry amusement. He did not believe there was any deep and worrying supernatural cause behind the two-headed, eight-legged deer, for he had long resided among living, breathing, breeding creatures, and had observed for himself what abominations sometimes slid from a dam's womb when something had gone awry with her offspring. But he was a keenly intelligent man, and fortunately for him and his companions, most of the population were wonderfully gullible and highly susceptible to fantastic rumour.

He leaned forward again and, picking up a quill, dipped it in ink and began to draw on a scrap of vellum. Under his slim, skilled fingers, a shape gradually emerged: a two-headed axe enclosed by a maze. It was the symbol they had adopted, he and his companions. Once again, the old man smiled. His companions, even those closest to him, believed the axe was simply a weapon, and that the surrounding maze represented the secret, concealing web which they were weaving around themselves and their activities.

The old man could have enlightened them, only he didn't choose to. It was not an axe but the labrys: butterfly symbol of transformation and rebirth. Inside his head, the old man regularly walked the twists and turns of the maze that enclosed it, for they would lead him to the ultimate insight.

Then, he had no doubt, he would know exactly how to complete the task that had now begun.

His drawing complete, he looked at it for a

29

long time. Then he screwed up the piece of vellum and tossed it into the fire.

He sat back, relaxed, patient.

Soon, he knew, it would be time for action.

TWO

Sabin de Gifford, wife of the sheriff of Tonbridge, had no need of the widely repeated rumours of omens and portents to make her feel deeply uneasy. It was all very well for the wide-eyed townspeople with nothing more pressing to worry about to scare themselves with such tales; Sabin's problems were far more acute and considerably more terrifying.

And it had all begun with the desire to *help*...

She had just spent a sleepless night and, deeply dispirited at the prospect of another one, came to the difficult decision that she had to *do* something. But what? Talk to Gervase? She shrank from that: her husband was a decent, if rather too ambitious man and, all things considered, her life with him was sufficiently happy for her not to regret the decision to accept his offer of marriage. That had been fifteen years and three children ago, and, in general, they had been good years. Gervase had not protested when she had insisted on carrying on with her work as apothecary and healer. *But then why should*

30

he, demanded the Breton peasant blood that ran in her, *when my fine reputation adds to his prestige, and the money I earn adds to his wealth?*

No, Sabin did not regret her choice of husband. But the matter that was so deeply affecting her was really not for discussion with Gervase.

The morning was advancing, and the November day was surprisingly mild. Gervase had gone out early, and the only one of the children still living at home, eight-year-old Alazaïs, was at her needlework lesson, in the house of the elderly widow who was patiently trying to teach her. For an hour or so, Sabin was alone. Perhaps, if she thought through her problem calmly and logically, a solution would present itself. With an anxious frown, she sat down at the hearthside and went back in her mind to the moment when she had first begun to suspect that something was badly wrong.

The urgent summons had come from Canon Mark, one of Tonbridge's Augustinian Canons. He was Sabin's favourite of the brothers, in fact; over the many years since she had made herself available to help the canons with patients whose care and treatment were beyond their considerable skill, Mark had always been her friend. The Augustinians had built their house too near the river, on a patch of damp, claggy ground that everyone with experience of Tonbridge, and the problems associated with the town's lower-lying areas, usually avoided. Coughs and colds, sprains and broken bones, the canons' infirmarian could deal with himself; for the end-less variety of fevers, shivers, joint pains and pestilences which occurred all too frequently, the brothers usually turned to Sabin de Gifford and her apothecary's art.

Sabin had realized something out of the ordinary had happened as soon as she saw Mark's expression. He had come hurrying across the yard to where she stood on the steps up to her door, black cloak swept back to reveal the white surplice, his broad, honest face sweaty with exertion. His short, stocky frame was not really built for speed, and he had obviously been running.

'What is the matter, Canon Mark?' she asked, going down to meet him. 'Please, come inside and catch your breath!'

He stopped, panting, and waved a hand. 'No time, Mistress Gifford, thank you just the same.' He paused to take a breath. 'I need your help, if you please. Can you come with me straight away?'

'Yes, of course,' she replied. 'I will fetch my satchel and my cloak.' She hurried back inside, returning in moments. Opening her leather bag, quickly checking the contents, she said, 'Can you think of any particular remedy we'll be requiring?'

Canon Mark gave a sound between a snort and a laugh. 'No remedies needed at all, Mistress. The patient is dead.'

She stopped in the middle of her inspection, eyes flying to meet his. 'Then why do you need me so urgently?'

'Because,' Mark said heavily, 'the dead man is – was – Lord Benedict de Vitré, of Medley Hall.'

'Lord Benedict?' She felt she understood. Everything. And with comprehension came the first sharp anxiety. Hurriedly buckling up her satchel and putting it back inside the house, she said, 'It will take a few moments for my horse to be saddled, and then I shall come at once.'

Canon Mark must have left orders for the horses to be prepared while he ran to fetch Sabin, for by the time they reached the Augustinian house, a mare and a gelding stood saddled and bridled. Recognizing the handsome, well-built young canon holding the two sets of reins, Sabin called out a greeting to him.

'Canon Stephen, good day to you!' Then, taking in the significance of *two* horses, she added, 'Are you coming with us to Medley Hall?'

'I am, Mistress Gifford.' Stephen's mouth twitched in a grimace. 'Lord Benedict recently came to me for ... er, for advice of a personal nature, and Canon Mark felt I should attend the inspection of the body.'

'You gave him advice?' Already Sabin was wondering whether the two canons' evident consternation was to do with guilt over some dreadful wrong diagnosis. If that were so, then...

As if Stephen read her thoughts, he said swiftly, 'The advice amounted to nothing more than that he should eat and drink less and exercise more.'

Despite her fear, Sabin smiled. 'If someone had convinced Lord Benedict of the good sense of that, then perhaps he would still be alive. I have always suspected a labouring heart beneath all that f—' She stopped herself. *Fat* wasn't perhaps tactful, when speaking of a man so recently dead. 'Er, all that bulk,' she substituted.

Canon Mark was mounting the mare. 'We should not prejudge,' he admonished gently. 'Come, let us be on our way – it is a considerable ride to Medley.'

The trouble was, Sabin reflected as she rode along between the two monks, that barely anyone who knew Lord Benedict de Vitré, either personally or by repute, would be all that sorry he was dead. Lord Benedict was universally recognized to be a close friend and confidant of King John and, of late, he had been busy supervising the collection of the endless taxes and tithes which the king demanded from his subjects. Also universally recognized was that Lord Benedict was getting wealthier and wealthier: either the king was very generous in rewarding those who did his work so well, or else Lord Benedict was creaming off a portion of all that he amassed for the king, and keeping it for himself.

Such was Lord Benedict's reputation for ruthlessness, arrogance, bullying, and cold-hearted cruelty, however, that nobody – apart from the king, were he to suspect it – would dare to suggest such a thing.

Lord Benedict had resided in the extensive manor of Medley, which was centred upon a hump of higher ground amid low-lying land to the south-east of Tonbridge. There he had lived

34

well, by most people's standards, even before the work he undertook for the king had started to bring him such generous rewards. Now, however, it seemed he had been determined to make his formerly modest residence into a veritable palace. It was no secret that he had been busy building extensions, setting out gardens, constructing fine stables for his beautiful new horses, and furnishing the living quarters to the very height of expensive luxury. Perhaps, Sabin mused, suppressing a grin, King John had been told of this sudden excess of spending and, suspecting its cause, had had Lord Benedict murdered.

Of course he hasn't, she told herself. *Kings don't behave like that.*

Presently they reached the summit of a long, steady climb. Canon Mark, in the lead, waved a hand and called back, 'Medley Hall!'

The manor house was heavily guarded. A ditch had been dug right round the collection of dwellings and the many outbuildings that encircled the yard, and the excavated earth had been piled up on the inner side of the ditch, forming a bank. On top of the bank was a wooden paling fence, the tips of the palings sharpened into spikes. For a moment, Sabin wondered why Lord Benedict de Vitré had elected to defend himself so very carefully. Then, recalling his reputation for efficiently and ruthlessly collecting revenue on the king's behalf, she understood.

There were many armed men in evidence; no less than six on duty at the single entry point,

35

where double gates stood closed. Six pairs of eyes were fixed on Sabin and the two monks as they approached.

'We are summoned to attend Lord Benedict,' Canon Mark called out. 'This is Canon Stephen, and I am Canon Mark. With us is Mistress de Gifford, apothecary and healer of Tonbridge.'

One of the guards leaned over to his companion, and Sabin caught the tail end of a muttered comment: '...late in the day to attempt to heal him.'

A broad-shouldered man with a broken nose had stepped forward. He glared at the man who had spoken, then looked up at Canon Mark. 'Aye, we were told you'd been summoned,' he said. He stared at all three of them for several moments. 'You'd better go on in,' he finally acceded. He nodded to two of the guards, who heaved at the heavy gates, opening them just enough for Sabin and the two canons to ride through into the courtyard.

A lad ran out to take their mounts, nodding in the direction of the lord's dwelling house, a large, rambling building showing signs of recent expansion. A flight of stone steps led up to the main entrance. Coming down the steps was a tall, slim man with dark, hooded eyes who introduced himself as Lord Benedict's steward. He seemed to know why they were there; undoubtedly, Sabin thought, because it had been he who had summoned them. Silently he led them across the great hall, along a passage, down a short flight of steps, along a further passage and, finally, down a wide spiral stair into a large, cold cellar. Wooden racks lined two of its walls, many of them loaded with barrels of wine. There were several huge wooden vats – of ale, perhaps – and big joints of smoked meat hung from hooks in the enormous beams which supported the stone slabs of the ceiling.

'This must be part of the original house,' Sabin whispered to Stephen. 'It's quite diff—' She shut her mouth hard on the words that had almost come out.

'Quite what?' Stephen whispered back.

'Quite dark and frightening!' she hissed. 'And so cold!'

She thought he gave her a brief, quizzical look. She hoped very much that she was wrong.

Her heartbeat gradually slowed down. Oh, but she must be more careful...

Lord Benedict had been laid out on a trestle table and covered with a length of deep-red velvet. He lay on his back, his hands crossed over his breast. The great hump of his stomach rose up, round and hard as that of a pregnant woman. Torches flamed in sconces on the wall behind him, and eight lighted candles, set in tall iron holders, had been set in pairs at the four corners of the trestle.

Whoever had undertaken the task of closing his eyes had not done it very well; there was a slit between the upper and lower lids, and the candlelight seemed to catch a glitter from the dark, dead eyes.

Canon Mark addressed the steward. 'Did anything unusual happen on the night Lord Benedict died?' he asked. 'Did he vomit, for example?

37

Was there a flux of the bowels?'

Sabin fought to suppress a gasp of horror. *He suspects poison...*

The steward's mouth twisted, as if he found the question distasteful. 'He did neither, as far as I know,' he said coldly, smoothing back his long hair with a graceful hand. 'He ate and drank as enthusiastically as he normally did, with every sign of enjoying all that he consumed.'

Sabin let out the breath she'd been holding.

'Thank you.' Canon Mark turned to his brother in Christ and said, in a matter-of-fact tone that Sabin found immensely reassuring, 'If you would begin, please, Stephen?'

The steward retreated to a dark corner of the cellar as, with swift, deft hands, Stephen folded back the velvet cloth and unfastened the dead man's tunic. He untied the hose, rolling them down the legs and off the feet, and then removed the undershirt. Lord Benedict de Vitré lay ready for their inspection.

There really was not much to see. He was vastly overweight – even more so than it had appeared when he was clothed – and there was a definite blueish tinge to the flesh of his face and jowls. Beneath the huge belly, the genitals appeared small and shrunken. Thick, purplish veins ran down the insides of both legs, tangling into knots in the calves and at the ankles. After a while, and with considerable effort, the two canons turned the dead man on to his front. The two vast buttocks shuddered as the body settled in its new position, and the sudden pressure on the corpse's belly made it emit a loud and prolonged fart. The flesh of the back – white and unpleasantly greasy – was dotted with several pimples, one of which the man must have been scratching at before death, for it was crowned with a large bead of dried blood.

For some time, Sabin and her two companions stood looking down at the corpse. Then, as if some signal had been given, the canons took hold of the body once more and returned it on to its back. Then they replaced the garments, finally drawing up the dark-red velvet and pulling it right up over the face.

Sabin, well used to dead bodies, was nevertheless very grateful to be spared the further sight of the narrow, glittering eyes.

Canon Mark turned to where the steward stood in his corner. 'We have finished,' he said quietly.

The steward moved forward, swiftly and silently. It was as if, Sabin thought, he was gliding across the flagged stone floor. 'What is your conclusion?' the steward demanded.

Canon Mark looked enquiringly at Sabin. 'Mistress Gifford? Would you care to speak first?'

Sabin's heart was thumping again. She drew a breath to steady herself, then said, 'This man was too heavy, and I conclude from his colour that his heart troubled him. I suspect that, during times of excitement, stress or sudden activity, he would become breathless, and his heart would have fluttered in his chest. Its beat would be irregular, and I imagine he probably felt some pain.' She hesitated, deliberately calmed herself, then concluded firmly, 'It is my opinion that a particularly severe spasm could well have caused his death.'

'Thank you,' Mark said. 'Stephen?' Turning to the steward, he said, 'I ought to have told you before, Canon Stephen is our infirmarian. I apologize.' He gave a little bob of a bow. The steward nodded impatiently.

'It is my conclusion also that Lord Benedict died from a spasm of the heart,' Stephen said. There was a pause, and then he went on: 'Perhaps I should not mention this, although, under the circumstances, I cannot see the harm.' Turning to the steward, he said, 'Lord Benedict came to consult me recently concerning a personal matter, and I suggested he should try to reduce his considerable weight by eating less and exercising more. I believe I made it clear to him that his general health, and in particular that of his heart, would improve if he followed my advice.'

The steward nodded again. Sabin was watching him closely, but his face gave nothing away, and she could not tell if Lord Benedict's visit to Canon Stephen's infirmary was news to him or not.

'Thank you, Stephen,' Mark said. 'I am not a medical man,' he added, addressing the steward, 'and I bow to the wisdom and experience of my two colleagues. I believe that the late Lord Benedict's widow and his kin, your good self and the household may accept what Mistress Gifford and Canon Stephen have said. Lord Benedict was at a feast when he died, I understand?'

40

'He was. The feast of All Saints' Eve,' the steward replied.

Canon Mark spread his hands and raised his eyebrows, as if to say, *Well, then!* 'It was a hearty meal, I dare say? You have already told us that he ate and drank well.'

The steward gave a grunt of assent.

There seemed nothing more to say. Hoping that it would prompt her companions to follow, Sabin began to edge away towards the steps leading up out of the cellar. At first it seemed that all was well, for they followed her and soon all of them were mounting the stair. They went on down the passage, up the further flight of steps, and were approaching the heavy door when Canon Mark turned to the steward and said, 'Perhaps we should speak to the widow before we go? Lady Richenza, isn't it? She has just suffered the loss of her husband, after all, and I believe she is but a young woman, probably not previously acquainted with grief.'

Sabin's heart seemed to stop for a few seconds. When it resumed, its beat was so rapid that she thought for a moment she would pass out.

But, thank the good, merciful Lord above, the steward shook his head. 'Lady Richenza has given orders that she is not to be disturbed. I will undertake to pass on to her what you have told me.'

Then, with a very definite air of finality, he ushered them out of the door and closed it firmly behind them.

Sabin leaned forward and poked at the fire. She

felt shivery, and clutched her warm shawl more closely around her. She had been so relieved, on the ride back from Medley Hall to Tonbridge, that she could have sung. *It's all right!* she had wanted to shout. *It was his heart that killed him, his heart made feeble by his own sinful gluttony!*

It was only later that the guilt had begun.

What should she do? Someone else, she was well aware, would be sharing her dreadful suspicions. But, under the circumstances, that someone was the last person she should seek out. If her suspicions were wrong, there was absolutely no need to muddy the waters by drawing attention to them. If they were right, then...

If they were right. Sabin pressed her fisted hands to her breast, sick with fear. Oh, dear God in heaven, if her suspicions were right, then what had she done?

She went on sitting there by her fireside, her muscles tight with the terrible tension of fear and indecision.

Eventually, the whirl of her thoughts edged towards a conclusion. The two brothers had found no evidence of what she so dreaded. Nor, come to that, had she. But the canons had not known what they should be looking out for. Sabin knew, but she had no idea how it would have manifested itself.

What she needed was a trustworthy friend whose knowledge of herbal remedies, their intended effects and their possible *unintended* effects was as good as – no, better than – her own.

She stood up. She knew what she must do. It was not yet noon; there was plenty of time.

Thrown into action, she set about the many tasks she must do. Issue orders to her kitchen servants to prepare a meal for Gervase and Alazaïs. Tell Gervase's manservant to fetch Alazaïs home from her needlework lesson, when the time came. Leave a message to tell Gervase she'd been summoned out to ... to what? Where? Frantically, she tried to think. Then she stopped. Oh, what did it matter? It really wasn't important; anything would serve. She would just say she had been called to a sick patient, and leave it at that. Gervase didn't like her to go out without being escorted by one of the servants, and would like it even less if he had any idea how far and where she was bound, but that was just too bad.

Soon, warmly dressed, well-mounted and carrying her apothecary's leather bag, she was on her way. Putting everything else from her mind, she concentrated on muttering, over and over again: *Please, please, let me find her*.

THREE

Josse d'Acquin, taking advantage of an un-
expectedly fine and warm morning, had decided
to ride out to Hawkenlye Abbey to see his old
friend Brother Saul, who had been ill with a
ferocious cough for a fortnight and now, by all
accounts, was on the mend. Josse and Saul had
known each other for a very long time. It did not
do, Josse reflected as he urged Alfred into a
sprightly canter, to pass the chance of wishing an
ageing old friend well. You never knew if the
chance would come again.

Settling comfortably in the saddle, happy at
the prospect of the ride before him, Josse made
a start on the same task he always seemed to do
on the few occasions he found himself alone. As
a devout man might tell his rosary beads, Josse
went through the names of all those who were
dear to him, pausing for a moment to think about
what they might be up to and always finishing
by sending an affectionate – or, for those closest
to his heart, a loving – thought their way.

He went through his own personal rosary in no
particular order. This morning, it happened to be
his son Geoffroi who came first, largely because
Josse had belatedly realized he'd left the House
in the Woods without saying goodbye. Not that

44

it really mattered, for he wasn't planning to be away long, and he doubted Geoffroi would even have noticed the lack of farewell. The lad was now twelve, and more like his father every day. To look at, anyway – for Josse, admiring and even awestruck at his son's uncanny abilities with any living creature from a bull to a mouse, had to recognize that the boy didn't get those skills from him. He smiled to himself. As any responsible parent would, he went on trying to encourage Geoffroi to lift his eyes above his own horizon. 'There's a big, wide world out there, son,' he would say, 'with all sorts of amazing things in it, and it would be most suitable for a boy like you to go and spend a few years in some knight's household, where you'd learn a thing or two that nobody here can teach you.'

Every time he made the suggestion, rephrased a dozen ways, the response would be the same. His son would look at him, smile and say, 'But I'm happy here, Father.'

He was; any fool could see that. And, deep in his heart, Josse would recognize that Geoffroi was his mother's son too, and Joanna had abandoned the world and almost everything in it to live out in the wildwood. It was, he had to admit, not all that likely that her boy would truly find satisfaction or joy in training to be a squire.

Josse's thoughts progressed to his adopted son, Ninian – also Joanna's child, but not by Josse. Ninian and his new wife Eloise – known as Little Helewise until Ninian had returned from his long travels in the Midi and renamed her –

had taken to married life with touching delight, first in each other and then, quite soon after their marriage, in their baby daughter, born at midsummer. They had named the child Inana. Josse, never having heard the name before, said innocently to the proud new father, 'Is that really a name?' To which Ninian, with a flash of hard steel in his bright blue eyes, had responded, a touch defensively, 'My mother used to speak of someone very powerful and beautiful named Inana.'

The child – who was indeed very beautiful, like her mysterious namesake – was, after all, Joanna's grandchild; great-granddaughter to old Mag Hobson, who, if all Josse had ever heard about her was true, had been one of the most powerful of the forest people. Josse had said no more; it seemed more than likely the name was highly suitable.

Ninian and his new family had set up home in a newly-built extension to the House in the Woods, affording them both the security of living close to an established household, and a degree of privacy. It was interesting, Josse mused as he rode out of the woods and into the sunshine, that nobody had suggested the newlyweds might care to live either with, or near to, the bride's family. Not that her father, Leofgar Warin, was the problem. Helewise's elder son was a rich and powerful man now, moving, it was said, on the fringes of court circles. His daughter loved him dearly, and Ninian appeared to like him well enough; it was clear that he respected him. No: the problem would have been Eloise's mother. Rohaise had not yet forgiven her daughter for having 'allowed Ninian to have his way' and, before wedlock, 'behaving like a married couple'. Rohaise was good at euphemisms. Useless for Eloise to try to explain that it had been her will just as much as Ninian's, or to protest that, with England still under the interdict, you couldn't marry there even if you wanted to; Eloise and Ninian had made their vows at Josse's family home in northern France.

Josse let out a sigh and, because he was alone except for Alfred, he vented his feelings by calling the increasingly stiff and starchy Rohaise a few choice names. *It's her loss*, he thought sadly. *It's she who is robbing herself of the huge joys of grandparenthood, while we at the House in the Woods enjoy them more with every day.*

He sighed again. Living in contentment as he did, he preferred it when everyone he cared for was as happy as he was. Eloise, despite everything, often looked as if a shadow of sorrow was darkening her lovely face.

Lingering with her, Josse sent her his love.

His thoughts moved gently on, through his household – Will, Ella, Tilly, Gus and their children – then progressing to Helewise's younger son, Dominic, and his family. Dominic, too, was steadily becoming a wealthy man (*these Warin men have a talent for it*, Josse thought) and in his case, the money was coming in through wool. Dominic farmed New Winnowlands, the manor that had once belonged to Josse, but prosperity had allowed him to expand his sheep pastures until he had all but doubled them. With young Geoffroi's help, Dominic had instigated a programme of animal breeding that seemed to have resulted in the sheep best suited to New Winnowlands' acres. The beautifully fine wool was much in demand among the weavers of the Low Countries, whose skill ensured that it was a particularly soft, strong and luxurious fabric that eventually made its way back to England.

Dominic had never forgotten that his house had once been Josse's. To show his gratitude, he encouraged Josse to graze his own growing flock on the same pastures. Situated on the edge of Romney Marsh, the New Winnowlands acres afforded land out on the saltmarsh for summer grazing, and up on the higher, drier ground for the remainder of the year. If nothing turned up to overturn the hay cart – Josse removed one hand from the reins and crossed his fingers – then, for the foreseeable future anyway, none of them need worry too much about money.

On his imaginary rosary, he had now reached the bead dedicated to Meggie. She had recently returned from Brittany, just as she had promised. 'I'll be back in the autumn,' his beloved daughter had said, and, of course, she was.

Josse had missed her sorely and worried about her constantly, yet he'd recognized that she was old enough to live her own life and, hopefully, sensible enough to live it wisely. Or, if not wisely, then at least without too much risk to her safety and happiness. Moreover, she had gone off with her dark-skinned Breton blacksmith, Jehan Leferronier, and within only a few days of meeting the man, Josse had sized him up as tough and resourceful. He was also, Josse couldn't help but notice, deeply in love with Meggie.

It had given him quite a shock when Meggie had turned up without Jehan at the House in the Woods – he had believed theirs was a relationship set to last – but Meggie had swiftly explained. Jehan, she said, had received word of friends of his who had come to England the previous year and, before coming to join her, he was going to see if he could track them down.

Josse was trying very hard not to think about that. He knew what Jehan's friends had had in mind when they'd set sail for England; knew, if it came to it, what Jehan too had been planning...

'Don't dwell on it,' Helewise had advised. 'What Jehan does or does not do is quite beyond your influence or your control. Do not spoil your happiness at Meggie's homecoming by entertaining worrying thoughts which are probably quite without foundation.'

Now, her words echoing in his ears, he did his best to heed her wise advice. Aware suddenly that Alfred's pace had slowed to an amble, he tightened the reins, put his heels to his horse's sides, and broke into a smart trot.

I am a very lucky man, he told himself – as, indeed, he told himself most days. And, as the crown on his good fortune, there was the very woman he had just been thinking about: Helewise.

They had come to an understanding, over in

49

France earlier in the year. Josse had kept his word, and thrown his efforts behind her as she set about building the little sanctuary she had dreamed of. It was situated a hundred paces or so off the high road that curved around the forest; hidden away behind the outlying trees, yet easily found by those who had been instructed how to find it. According to Josse's sole stipulation, it was some distance from the House in the Woods. 'We are secluded here,' he had said to Helewise, 'and largely overlooked, since only ourselves, our kin and our close friends know of our exis- tence. I am more than willing to support you in your new endeavour, but not at the cost of putting at risk our precious privacy.'

She had bowed her head and agreed.

The sanctuary had been in operation since the summer. Word had quickly spread, and now most days people in desperate need found their way to the place where help would be given. Tilly and Ella prepared bread and nourishing soup, and several times a week Will drove a cart loaded with food and firewood from the House in the Woods to the sanctuary. Tiphaine fre- quently turned up, bearing herbs and potions, ready to prepare remedies for the sick and the ailing. Helewise admitted to knowing full well that the herbs came from Hawkenlye Abbey, where Tiphaine had long been the herbalist, and she suspected it was with the knowledge and approval of Abbess Caliste. One day, Josse be- lieved, Helewise was going to overcome her scruples about going back to the Abbey; she and Abbess Caliste were, after all, working for the same thing, and he thought it would help both women to discuss how best to help the vast and increasing numbers of England's poor, destitute, sick and desperate.

Many who came to the sanctuary thought Helewise was still a nun. Her dark robes and veil, and modest white headdress, tended to support the illusion. For the eyes of the world, perhaps, she was still abbess of Hawkenlye. For him, she had slipped into a different identity.

Even his own household did not know the truth, for he and Helewise were extremely discreet.

Without being aware of having covered the distance, all at once he found himself at the point on the road where it diverged, the right-hand track leading down the hill to Tonbridge and the left to Hawkenlye Abbey. A smile on his face, he urged Alfred to a special effort for the last couple of miles.

Both for courtesy's sake and because he was very fond of her, Josse went first to see Abbess Caliste to exchange the latest gossip.

'They say Lord Benedict de Vitré is dead,' Josse said, settling comfortably on the chair which Abbess Caliste kept for visitors. It was, in Josse's view, a vast improvement on the little stool that her predecessor had deemed quite sufficient.

'Yes, so I heard,' the abbess replied. She glanced up and met Josse's eyes, but discretion kept her from speaking further.

Well, after all, she's a nun, Josse thought. He

decided to say what he was sure they were both thinking. 'The man was a vicious bully who abused his position and preyed on the weak,' he stated firmly. 'While I would not have actively wished him dead, I cannot truly say I regret his passing.'

The abbess closed her eyes briefly. Then, presumably indicating the closure of that particular topic by a firm change of subject, she said brightly, 'We seem to be honoured just now with many important visitors to the area, Sir Josse. The de Clares, down at Tonbridge, are reported to have a clutch of the great and the good of the realm within their walls, and only yesterday a couple of very well-dressed young men, riding expensive mounts, stopped at our gates to ask directions to the dwelling of Lord Wimarc of Wealdsend.'

'Lord Wimarc?' Josse queried. 'I understood he was a recluse.'

'So did I,' Abbess Caliste agreed. She smiled. 'He will not thank those bright young men, for advertising the fact that they were bound for his manor, and thereby reminding us all of his existence.'

Josse, barely registering her remark, grunted agreement. He was thinking; trying to piece together what he knew of Lord Robert Wimarc. The total did not amount to much. The old man was rarely seen outside his own stout walls, and was reputed to repel would-be visitors with total ruthlessness. Josse resolved to seek out Helewise and ask her if she could add to these sparse facts, since it had been she who had told him of the old man in the first place.

He glanced up, to see that Abbess Caliste was watching him. The look in her eyes surprised him: he could have sworn she was nervous. Frightened, even. He had known her a long time and, although she bore a heavy burden, he had rarely known her to be distracted out of her usual serenity.

He leaned towards her. 'What is it?' he whispered.

She shook her head. 'Oh, probably nothing.' She managed a small laugh. 'I should not listen to idle tongues with nothing better to do than spread alarming rumours!'

He dropped his voice still further. 'What rumours?'

She frowned, began to speak, then stopped. Abruptly she got up, came right up to him and, leaning down to whisper right into his ear, breathed, 'They do say that those who congregate with the de Clares in Tonbridge Castle are no great supporters of ... of...'

He put up a hand to stop her. 'Do not speak it, my lady,' he advised. 'Safer that way, for both of us.'

They went on to speak of mundane matters. But presently, as Josse took his leave, he caught a shadow of something in the abbess's expression. He might have dismissed it, except that the same emotion was fighting to make itself felt within himself.

Both of them were apprehensive, and the apprehension was deep enough that it bordered on fear.

* * *

It was not easy, after that, to go on to see Brother
Saul with the appropriately cheerful demeanour
for visiting the sick. He was, however, much
encouraged to find his old friend propped up in
bed and clamouring to be allowed up and back to
work.

'I shouldn't be lying here abed, Sir Josse,' Saul
said, fretfully pleating and re-pleating the fresh
bed linen. 'Not when there's so much work to be
done, and all too few hands to do it.'

He was right, Josse knew. Another pernicious
effect of the interdict was the absence of young
men and women asking to enter the abbey as
novice monks and nuns, or even, like Saul, as lay
brethren. It was all too understandable, Josse
reflected, but the abbey was suffering, nevertheless.

It was not, however, the moment to further
depress poor Saul with such morbid thoughts.
'You'll be far more use to the abbey if you do as
you're told and stay here till you are fully well,'
he assured his old friend. 'I am sure it won't be
long now.'

He was further reassured when the infirmarer,
Sister Liese, confirmed that Saul truly was on
the mend. 'I'm only keeping him in here another
day because I know full well he'll go straight
back to doing three men's work,' she whispered
to Josse as he left, 'and he's not as young as he
was.'

Which of us is? Josse thought as he went to
fetch Alfred. Brother Saul could not be much
older than Josse; did that mean people saw

Josse, too, as being on the brink of old age?

It was not a particularly welcome image.

There was a sure-fire way of recalling the happy mood of the morning: on his way home, he would make a detour and go to visit his daughter.

Meggie was enjoying a few precious days alone, in the little hut in the forest which had been her mother's, and in which she had spent the first few years of her life.

Although she missed Jehan all the time, nevertheless it was wonderful to be back within the hut's four stout wooden walls. It was so full of memories – of her mother, of course, and, more recently, of Jehan, for it was the place where they had met.

Stop thinking about him, she told herself firmly. She was busy digging, turning the soil, pulling out a summer's worth of weeds (nobody had tended the hut's herb patch for months) and preparing the ground for the spring. *I must fetch a few sacks of chalk*, she thought. She did not know why, but the soil of the forest, consisting as it did almost entirely of leaf mould, did not nourish good growth in her herbs unless she dug in a good quantity of chalk. It had been one of the forest people who told her that, and, on the morning that he offered the advice, Meggie had experienced a sudden, vivid memory from early childhood: her own small, pudgy hands playing with a lump of chalk while Joanna dug. Exactly where Meggie was digging now.

Her back and shoulders were beginning to

ache, and the faint hope that she'd had of subduing her body's longing for Jehan by making it work like a slave seemed not to be working. She paused in her digging, wiping a hand across her sweaty brow. Those summer weeks in Brittany, deep within the secret forest of Brocéliande, just the two of them living out there alone, had been magical, and getting to know each other's bodies, naked under the trees, had been like—

'Meggie! Are you there?'

Hastily she dragged her thoughts away from making love on the soft green grass, pushed back her hair, straightened her robe and, with a smile of welcome, turned to greet her father.

He jumped down from his horse and came hurrying across the fresh-turned earth to put his arms round her and wrap her in a rib-creaking hug. Laughing, she hugged him back.

'It's lovely to be greeted so warmly, Father,' she said, still grinning, as he released her, 'but we saw each other only four days ago. Anybody would think it had been months!'

'You were off carousing in Brittany for months,' he pointed out reasonably.

'Yes, I know, and *you* know I wasn't carousing,' she replied. 'Jehan has agreed to come to England for my sake, because I don't really want to go and live in his country, and I felt the least I could do was to accompany him while he went about severing his ties over there.'

'Aye, my love, you explained your reasons to me before you went.'

She hesitated. There was something she

56

wanted to tell him, but she feared it would open old wounds. She stared up into his eyes.

And, as he quite often did, he read what was at the forefront of her mind. Very softly, he said, 'You went to the Brocéliande. I think you must have done,' he added in a rush, 'because I know that's where Jehan comes from.'

'I did,' she agreed.

'You know you'd been there before?' He had turned away and she could not see his face. 'With ... with your mother and me?'

'Yes, I know.' She paused, thinking how to reply so as to give him a moment of remembered happiness, rather than the sudden sharp pain of lost love. 'I'm not sure I really recognized any of the places Jehan and I went to,' she said slowly, 'but I had the strongest sense that it wasn't the first time I walked under those huge, ancient trees, or lay snug on the leaves of centuries, inside the bend of a stream with the sound of the rushing water to lull me to sleep.' She thought she heard him give a sort of gasp. 'I felt there was something there that recognized me and welcomed me back,' she whispered. 'It was love, I believe; yours and my mother's.'

She gave him a few moments. When he turned to face her again, his eyes were bright with unshed tears. 'It was a good time,' he said gruffly, 'although not without considerable peril.' Then, beginning to smile: 'Your mother fought like a cornered bear.'

One day, she vowed to herself, *one day when it doesn't hurt him so much, I'll ask him to tell me about it.*

57

It was time for a change of subject. Slipping her arm through his, she walked him round the small clearing beside the hut, showing him what she was doing, and telling him what she was planning.

He nodded. 'You'll want to live here, when Jehan comes to join you?' he asked.

'Some of the time, yes.' That was not strictly honest. 'Well, most of the time, I expect.' Quickly, before he should be hurt, she went on, 'Jehan will need to work, and I told him about the spot beyond the old charcoal burners' camp, where once there was a forge. There's water there, where the stream runs down a short fall, and, of course, endless wood.'

'It's Hawkenlye Abbey land,' Josse remarked.

'Yes, it is. I'm going to see Abbess Caliste, to ask her what she thinks about having her own blacksmith on the doorstep.'

'We could do with a forge here,' he said.

She smiled to herself. She'd been rather hoping he'd see it that way. 'So, if the idea is acceptable to the abbey, then Jehan will need to live close by, and I – we thought maybe we'd repair the old smithy's cottage, and sort of divide our time between there and here. Oh, and of course we'd come often to see you all, at the House in the Woods.'

He was silent for quite a long time. Then he said, 'I keep forgetting you're not a girl any more.'

She guessed that was acceptance, in a way, of her right and her need to make her own life in her own home. She reached out for his hand, clasping it in both of hers. 'I'm still your girl,' she said softly. 'Always will be.'

He was frowning, and she wasn't sure if he had heard. 'I still don't like it that your Jehan let you come all the way back here from wherever it was you landed in England!' he exclaimed suddenly. 'It's not safe on the roads nowadays for a woman on her own. He should have brought you back, before he set off on this – this – whatever it is.'

She felt the anger surge up inside her. She drew a breath, then another. She thought she heard a quiet voice in her head say: *He is your father. It is his right to be concerned for you.*

She said calmly, 'Jehan doesn't *let* me do anything, Father. I have made him no promise of obedience, and he respects my ability to make my own decisions.' Before he could reply, she hurried on. 'As for not being safe on the roads, I totally agree, which is why I didn't travel on the roads.' His sudden intake of breath suggested he understood, but she explained anyway. 'The route by which I travelled home, from the little port where our boat dropped us, passes largely through woodland and forest. For those who know the hidden ways, it's easy. And I met friends along the route – so, you see, I was perfectly safe,' she finished.

He grunted, and she decided to take it for assent.

They walked together back to where he had tethered Alfred. She sensed he was still not entirely happy, and wondered which of the things they had discussed was on his mind. *It hurts me when he's sad*, she thought.

59

Acting instantly on the idea that had just popped into her head, she hurried over to her hut, checked briefly that all was in order inside, and grabbed her cloak. It was a present from Jehan, made of fine, soft wool, deep silvery-grey in colour, and the hood was lined with reddish-grey fur. Jehan had told her the fur was vair, and came from the squirrel's thick winter coat. He also confessed that the garment wasn't actually new, but had once belonged to his grandmother, who had missed the warmth of her native land. New or not, Meggie loved it.

She ran back to Josse. He looked at her enquiringly.

'The sky's clear, so it'll be cold tonight,' she said. 'I haven't got very much firewood till I have the chance to collect more. May I come back to the House in the Woods with you?'

His grin seemed to split his face.

Sabin had arrived at Josse d'Acquin's house to be met with the distressing news that everyone was out. The glum-looking man who had given the information stood in the yard looking up at her, as if waiting for her to make the next move.

'It's really important!' she said.

He seemed to consider the matter for quite a long time. 'You're the sheriff of Tonbridge's wife?'

'Yes.' She had already told him, and surely he knew anyway?

'You can wait within,' he said eventually. Having made the momentous decision, he seemed to soften a little. 'I'll tend to your horse, Mis-

60

tress. Go you on in, and I'll get Ella to mend the fire.'

Quite soon, she was sitting in Josse's hall, in a big carved chair that she guessed was his, with her feet in front of a blazing fire that was really too hot for the mild day and a mug of very good ale in her hand. Now, all she could do was wait.

They were good people, Josse's household, she realized some time later. The servants had made her welcome – a woman who said to call her Tilly had brought her some cakes, and a man called Gus, whom Sabin was sure she recognized, appeared from time to time to make sure she was all right. Then the family began to return: Josse's son, Geoffroi; Ninian and Eloise; Helewise. Each of them greeted her warmly.

None of them was the person she was so desperate to see.

When at last Josse came into the hall, he was speaking over his shoulder to someone following him in. Forgetting her manners in her huge relief, Sabin leapt up, gathered up her skirts and rushed over. Virtually ignoring Josse's courteous welcome, she took Meggie's hands in hers and hissed, 'I've got to talk to you! I think I've done something *terrible*.'

'What do you think she's doing here?' Josse said.

The rest of the household had retired for the night. He and Helewise were sitting beside the hearth, sharing the last of Tilly's jug of spiced wine.

'I have no idea,' Helewise replied calmly. 'To

61

be honest, I'm not really much concerned.'

'Not like you,' he observed. 'Usually you want to know every last thing about everyone's comings and goings.'

She smiled. 'Perhaps I'm learning to be less nosy.'

He considered that. 'I wouldn't say you'd ever been *nosy*.' He glanced across at her. 'Bossy and inclined to believe you knew best, maybe.'

'Ah, when I used to be an abbess, yes. Now that I'm not, I no longer have to be omnipotent.'

A companionable silence fell. A log settled in the huge hearth, sending up a glitter of little sparks. 'You did right to get Gus to ride down to Tonbridge when you discovered Sabin had turned up,' Helewise said after a while. 'I don't know why,' she went on, lowering her voice, 'but I have the distinct feeling that, until he got your message, Gervase wouldn't have known where his wife was.'

'I thought that, too,' Josse murmured back.

'It was Meggie she was so keen to see,' Helewise mused. 'You weren't here, but, without being actually rude, Sabin managed to make it perfectly clear that the rest of us were of no more use to her than the flags of the floor.'

Josse thought about that. 'They both follow the same calling,' he said. 'In all likelihood, Sabin wants Meggie's advice as a fellow healer.'

'If so,' Helewise said slowly, 'then it must surely be a difficult or an important case – perhaps both – for Sabin to have come hurrying up here to seek out Meggie, without being sure she would even *be* here.'

62

'You're right,' Josse said, frowning. 'In fact, had I not decided, on a whim, to call and see Meggie, and had it not promised to be a cold night, Sabin's mission would have been in vain, because Meggie would have been at the hut.' He paused, then said, very quietly, 'I wouldn't dare tell even a friend such as Sabin de Gifford where Meggie's hut is, unless Meggie told me I could.'

'Oh, neither would I!' Helewise agreed. 'Goodness, I'm not even going to imagine her reaction if we did!'

They sat for a while, happily silent. Then, remembering his conversation with Abbess Caliste, Josse said, 'A name cropped up today that is not often spoken: Lord Robert Wimarc of Wealdsend. You know of him, I believe?'

Slowly Helewise nodded. 'Indeed. Many years ago, I even met him briefly. One of his kinsmen was treated in Hawkenlye's infirmary – by Sister Euphemia herself – and the man must have been important to the old lord, for he rode down to the abbey to thank the nuns for their good care.' She smiled. 'He gave a generous donation, too.'

'What did you think of him?'

'Oh, Josse, we only exchanged a handful of words, and it was, as I said, a long time ago. He was stern, unsmiling, with little joy about him, yet I had the impression that he was a man of strong morality. A...' She paused, frowning. 'A straight man, if that makes sense?'

'Aye, it does,' Josse said. 'How did he come by his manor?'

'They say his forefather fought with the Conqueror, and, like so many, was rewarded with a house and estate that had formerly belonged to one of the conquered. There had long been a stronghold at Wealdsend,' she went on, more fluently now as memory returned, 'right back into the ancient past, for it is well placed, on the northern edge of the High Weald. The prudent men who originally built a dwelling place there sited it wisely, for, whilst it is itself sheltered in a fold of the hills, its tower commands a view right over the valley.'

'You speak as if you had seen it for yourself,' Josse remarked.

She glanced at him. 'I did visit, yes, but that was even further back in time, when I was wed to Ivo. Lord Robert was still in his prime then.' She sighed. 'As was I,' she murmured.

Josse picked up the jug, leaning across to her. 'Oh, you're not so bad, even now.' She gave a quiet chuckle. 'Help me with the last drops,' he said, sharing them out between their two mugs. 'Then I reckon it's time for bed.'

Sabin, offered a comfortable cot set close alongside Meggie's, waited until the house appeared to have settled. Then she hissed into the darkness, 'Are you still awake?'

She heard Meggie sigh and roll over. 'Yes.'

'Will you help me?'

'You haven't told me yet what you want me to do.'

Quietly, muttering so fast that she wasn't entirely sure she was making sense, Sabin explained.

When she had finished, Meggie gave a low

whistle. 'Dear God, Sabin!'

'Oh, I know it's nothing to do with you, and I've no right to involve you,' Sabin said, her panic rising again, 'but I don't know where else to turn. I thought you might be willing to give me the benefit of your experience, but if not, tell me, and I'll—'

'Stop,' Meggie interrupted gently. 'I *will* help you, Sabin.'

Sabin breathed a quiet prayer of thanks.

'So, what do you suggest we do?' Meggie asked.

Now that the moment had arrived, Sabin faltered. It was such a lot to ask, and, after all, she didn't know Meggie that well. They were certainly not what could be called close friends. But she'd been over and over it, and had come to the conclusion that this was the only sure way.

She took a deep breath and told Meggie exactly what sort of help she wanted from her.

FOUR

As darkness fell at Hawkenlye Abbey, Abbess Caliste sat in her great chair with her head in her hands, overwhelmed with troubles. Apart from the endless problem of how to run an abbey meant to *help* people when there was no money, she was deeply anxious at the frightening, unnerving rumours, which, just then, were all anyone seemed to want to talk about.

A soft tap on the door halted the long trail of her depressing thoughts. Relieved at the interruption, she called out, 'Come in!'

Sister Liese stepped into the little room, closing the door quietly behind her. She did everything quietly, Caliste reflected absently, as if she was perpetually considering the comfort of a sleeping patient. 'What can I do for you, Sister?' she asked, smiling. 'It's late, and you should surely be abed.'

'The same observation might be made of you, my lady abbess,' Sister Liese replied, returning the smile.

Caliste sighed. 'Yes. I will retire soon.' She raised her eyebrows enquiringly.

Taking the hint, the infirmarer came a step closer. 'There's a new patient who I'm very worried about,' she began. 'I need your advice, my lady.'

'*My* advice?'

'Oh, not concerning the treatment, although, in the dear Lord's name, I hardly know how best to help...' She stopped and, with a brisk shake of her head, resumed. 'The truth is, I am very afraid that this patient brings grave danger with her. If I may, I will tell you all about her, and why her presence here worries me so much.'

Concerned, for it was rare for Sister Liese to seek her out to discuss a patient's care, Caliste indicated the visitors' chair and, when the infirmarer had settled, said, 'Now, please explain.'

Sister Liese paused, presumably arranging her words, then said, 'Her name's Lilas, she's old and quite frail, and she comes from a village called Hamhurst that's on one of the main roads leading up from the coast. Apparently she had some sort of a vision – or maybe a visitation, I don't know exactly – and she stood on the village green shouting something about a Winter King who was doomed to early death, and how the evils in the land wouldn't come right till he was gone, and that all the omens we keep hearing about are God's way of telling us that we're all cursed for generations to come.' She paused, shaking her head again as if in dismissal. 'I'm not sure of the details, but whatever old Lilas was saying, it was dangerous talk. The headmen of the village were apparently on the point of stopping her when she collapsed in a swoon.'

'It sounds as if that was just as well,' Caliste

said. The thought of someone saying such things aloud, with witnesses, was highly alarming.

'Indeed, my lady. Anyway, it seems Lilas wasn't quite right when she came out of her faint. Sometimes she spoke sense, but there were times when she apparently went back into her trance, and the villagers became frightened. They...' Again, she broke off. 'To cut a long story short – and, believe me, my lady, it is a *very* long story; probably the most exciting thing that's ever happened in Hamhurst since Noah was a lad, and they're all making the most of it – in short, the village elders decided Lilas needed help, and they've brought her to us.' She smiled grimly. 'It's a long way to come from Hamhurst, but, even in the state to which these times have reduced us, apparently folk in grave need still follow their instincts and turn to Hawkenlye.'

'Can you help her?' Caliste asked.

'We can feed her, clean her, tuck her up in a bed and keep her safe while she raves and rambles, but if you mean can we heal her, the answer's no, my lady.'

Caliste, aware of her infirmarer's generous heart and strong instinct to care for all those brought into her care, was surprised at her tone. 'You sound ... If I did not know better, Sister Liese, I would say you sound almost out of patience with this woman.'

Sister Liese sighed deeply. 'I am sorry, my lady. The truth is, I cannot for the life of me decide whether or not these wild words come from a true trance, or whether old Lilas is playing a clever game.'

'A dangerous game, surely?' Caliste said. 'To voice such harsh criticism of – of the current situation, without the excuse of being deeply disturbed in one's mind, is tantamount to inviting arrest and imprisonment.' *At the very least*, she added silently.

'Yes, I know,' Sister Liese said, her face wrung with anxiety. 'I keep telling myself that Lilas's visions must be genuine. Then, when I'm with her, sitting holding her hand while the poor soul speaks all those dreadful words, her eyes wild with passion, sometimes I have the strange idea that she's watching me – watching us all – and trying to gauge the effect she's having.'

Caliste frowned. 'I bow to your experience, Sister,' she said, 'and if you have doubts about this woman's veracity, I will take them seriously.' She stood up, and the infirmarer instantly did the same.

'My lady?' Sister Liese said. 'Are you going to bed, at last?'

Caliste looked at her in surprise. 'No, Sister! I'm coming with you to see your patient.'

The long infirmary was dark and quiet as the two nuns slipped inside. A nun sat at the far end, a single candle illuminating the area immediately around her. She stood up as Caliste and Sister Liese walked towards her, and the infirmarer motioned her to sit down again. Sister Liese led the way to a curtained recess at the far end of the room.

Caliste stood looking down at Lilas of Hamhurst. The old woman was awake, lying quite

69

still with her eyes fixed on some point on the wall to her left. Caliste sat down on the edge of the bed.

'What do you see?' she asked softly. 'Do your visions disturb you, Lilas?'

Lilas turned her head. 'Who are you?' she whispered. There was fear in her eyes.

'My name is Caliste, and I am abbess here,' Caliste said.

Lilas shot out a hand and grasped Caliste's wrist. 'I've been bad, my lady,' she whispered. 'I did have a vision – as God's my witness, I *did*, I saw ... I saw...' Her face crumpled, and she whimpered in terror. 'I saw terrible things, and the voices, they went on and on at me, telling me what would happen, saying the land was gone to the bad because we were all sinners, and the greatest of us were the worst sinners of all, and then – oh, I'm sorry, my lady!' She pulled Caliste's hand up to her face, kissing it over and over again.

I would send for a priest, if I could, Caliste thought. *Here is a soul in torment, yet the solace of confession is not available to ease her suffering*.

She would just have to do her best.

'What have you done, Lilas?' she asked quietly.

The old woman shot her a look. 'I may have exaggerated a bit,' she muttered. 'I liked the attention, see. My neighbours, they all fussed round me, making me feel I was something special, and I thought, why not? I'd had one vision – I swear before God, I did! – and I

70

reckoned that if I just repeated what I'd seen, and made as if I was under the spell again, the rest of the village would be impressed like my neighbours. Only ... only...' A sob broke out of her, shaking the narrow frame.

'Only what?' Caliste prompted.

'Only, soon as I started on my pretend trance, the real one came back,' Lilas whispered hoarsely, 'and then it came on me, far worse than before, and I lost myself, my lady; I had no memory of who or where I was, nor what I was saying, and when they told me, afterwards, like, I didn't recollect a word of it!'

Caliste held the bony old hand in both of hers. She glanced up at Sister Liese, standing quietly at the foot of the bed. The infirmarer gave a faint shrug.

Caliste turned back to the old woman. 'Lilas, I—' she began.

But Lilas interrupted her. 'Oh, my lady, help me!' she whimpered. 'I'm so frightened!'

'You're safe here,' Caliste soothed. 'We'll—'

'Not safe! Not ever safe!' Lilas hissed. *'They* heard, see? And now – oh! *Oh!* Now they say I must go with them, I must repeat what I've been saying, and they'll ... they'll...'

But what *they* would do was apparently beyond her. With a soft little cry, Lilas removed her hand from Caliste's, turned her face to the wall and curled up into a tight little ball.

Silence fell.

Slowly Caliste rose to her feet. 'She needs rest,' she murmured. 'Sleep, preferably.'

'I will prepare a soporific,' Sister Liese whis-

71

pered back. 'Don't worry, my lady, we'll look after her.' She paused. 'Do you think she's putting it on?' she said, her words all but inaudible.

'I don't know,' Caliste admitted. 'She is very disturbed, I believe. *Something* has happened to her, and, in addition, she is very afraid.'

She and Sister Liese walked slowly back the length of the infirmary. Caliste was thinking hard. By the time they reached the door, at the far end, she had made up her mind.

She did not know how to help someone as deeply distressed as Lilas, and, on her own admission, neither did Sister Liese. But Caliste believed she knew of somebody who might...

As she bade Sister Liese goodnight, she resolved that, as soon as she could spare someone, she would send for the one person who might be able to reach inside the damaged mind of Lilas of Hamhurst.

Helewise woke after a good night's sleep, eager for the day's work ahead. She was usually one of the first to rise, and today was no exception. Only Tilly had preceded her, and she was already warming water on the fire as Helewise went into the kitchen. A heavy pot, its base blackened from long use, hung beside it, steaming gently.

Tilly glanced over her shoulder. 'Porridge is on, my lady,' she said. 'It's dry but cold outside, and something hot will warm you for your walk out to the sanctuary.'

The household knows my daily routine well,

72

Helewise thought. *They all know that little short of death will keep me from what I feel so driven to do.*

Driven, she reflected as she ate her porridge (delicious, as were most foods prepared by Tilly) was not really the right word, implying as it did something you didn't really want to do. During her years as a nun, she had been taught that a good deed was not truly pleasing to God if the person performing it derived satisfaction and happiness from their action. Helewise had asked the priest who was instructing her if that meant it was pointless to do any good deed, a question that had earned her a rigorous punishment. It had been very early in her noviciate, and she had almost decided there and then to walk out of the abbey and never return.

Now, older and, she hoped, wiser, she thought about the conundrum again. She still didn't know the answer.

The day passed swiftly. The weather was definitely getting colder, and the usual crop of cold-related illnesses was beginning. Cold- and also hunger-related, Helewise reflected, trying to feed a mouthful of gruel to an elderly woman so far gone in hunger and despair that she had all but lost interest in everything, including the food that might just save her life.

For much of the day, Helewise had worked alongside one of the others: first Ninian, who had carried over some supplementary supplies and stayed to help her with the first few visitors, and later Tiphaine, who had come armed with a precious supply of her special white horehound cough remedy. It was special because, aware that many of those needing it would be children, Tiphaine sweetened it generously with honey. As the afternoon began to darken and the evening advanced, however, Helewise found herself alone. She tidied the little building, rinsing out the wooden bowls and stacking them ready for the next day, and then did her best to sweep up the mud, the muck and the dead leaves trodden in by twenty or more pairs of feet.

It was fully dark inside the shelter now. She lit a taper from the fire in the hearth, setting it to the wicks of a couple of oil lamps. As the gentle light spread through the room, the outside immediately appeared blacker. *I am less than a mile from home*, Helewise told herself firmly. *My family know where I am, and, in any case, I have never once felt fearful within the sanctuary. It is a good place, and God protects those who visit and work here.*

But she felt fearful now.

She went to the door, opening it further to peer outside. The sanctuary was set back from the track that ran round the bulge of the forest, secluded within a grove of trees, most of which were pine and yew. Even in the leafless months, the sanctuary was hidden from unfriendly eyes. All those who needed the succour it offered, however, somehow managed to find out where to go.

Helewise stared out into the darkness of the woods all around the little clearing. She strained her ears as she listened to the silence: had there been some sound that should not be there, so that now she was alert and fearful?

She heard a faint rustling, as if some creature was moving through the litter of dead leaves. She felt the hairs on the back of her neck rise up. *It's just a fox, or a hare*, she told herself.

The sound came again. And again; this time, it was accompanied by a low groan of agony.

Helewise picked up a lamp, shot out of the door and hurried in the direction of the moan. 'I am here!' she cried. 'I will help you!'

She did not know which way to go. She stopped abruptly, listening again. Nothing.

'Do not be afraid,' she said into the darkness. 'I am Helewise, and I tend the sanctuary on the edge of the forest. If you can, call out, and I will find you.'

She waited for what seemed a long time. Then, very faintly, she heard a voice say, 'Help me.'

It was over to her right, in the direction of the narrow path that wound through the trees to meet the road. Gathering up her skirts, she hurried along it, almost tripping several times on the roots that twined like raised veins just beneath the ground.

She almost fell over him.

He was lying on his right side, and the front of his tunic was dark with blood. Holding the light over him, she saw that there was a cut on the left side of his brow, deep and pouring blood. His eyes were huge in his deathly pale face. He opened his mouth and said again, 'Help me.' But this time, had Helewise not been standing right over him, she would not have heard.

'I must get you to the sanctuary,' she said, as much to herself as to him, for his eyes had closed and she thought perhaps he had slipped into unconsciousness. 'Although I do not know quite how...'

She prayed for help. *Please, dear Lord, you must know that one or other of the good people at the House in the Woods usually sets out at dark fall to find me if I am not home. Inspire them now, please, Lord, and send them to help me with this poor man.*

She knew she could not lift a grown man on her own. To drag him over rough ground would undoubtedly make his terrible injuries worse. There was little she could do but wait.

Putting down the lamp, she crouched down beside the man, wishing she had paused to snatch up her cloak, or even a shawl. All she had to warm him was her own body. She stretched out on the cold ground, her chest to his back, her legs bent up behind his. She wrapped her arms round him, clasping him to her.

Eventually, after what seemed an age, she heard footsteps: two people, at least. A voice called out her name. *Josse!* She sent up a prayer of thanks.

'I'm here,' she shouted. 'On the path leading up to the road. There's a man, gravely wounded. Come quickly!'

The footsteps began to run. In a moment, Josse and Ninian were upon her.

The man was young, slender and – before agony, despair and the marks of someone's fists had

76

distorted his features – had clearly been handsome. In the light within the sanctuary, Helewise could see his glossy fair hair, fashionably cut, and the costly garments that must once have looked so fine. Josse helped her to cut away the blood-soaked emerald green tunic, while Ninian added cleansing herbs to the pot of simmering water that always hung suspended over the hearth. The smell of lavender filled the little room.

The young man's wounds were grievous. Apart from his battered face, a deep, wide cut had opened up his throat, nicking the great vessel that rose under the skin beneath the ear. His torso was bruised and beaten. Both hands were bloody across the knuckles, and a long slash ran down his right forearm.

'He fought hard,' Josse whispered.

Helewise pointed to the cut in the throat. 'If that had been only a little deeper, he would have been in no position to fight at all.'

Josse did not reply, except to go, 'Mmm.' He was, she realized, thinking very hard.

Ninian brought the water, and she squeezed out a cloth and began to bathe the wounds. Blood was still flowing from the young man's throat, so, not knowing what else to do, she padded up the cloth and pressed it hard against the wound.

This cut should be stitched, she thought. Aloud, she asked, 'Is Meggie home?'

'Not when we left,' Josse replied. 'She went off with Sabin, and she said they'd probably be gone all day. They were going to see that mystery patient, no doubt.'

Suddenly the young man's eyes opened. He looked up, first at Helewise, then at Josse. His face filled with terror.

'I didn't tell!' he cried, starting to thrash around on the narrow cot. 'I swear I didn't! We were lost, and did not know how to find our way to you, but we didn't say anything! Oh, you must believe me!'

'Hush,' Helewise soothed. 'You must rest, and we will...' *We will what?* she wondered. She did not know what to do. Tentatively she raised the edge of the linen pad to check on the bleeding. She thought the flow might have lessened a little.

The young man closed his eyes again.

Josse leaned over him and, speaking softly, said, 'What is your name, and what's your business here? Who did this to you?'

The man's eyes flew open again. He did not seem to have registered Josse's urgent questions. 'I didn't tell, before God, I didn't!' he cried, his anguish painful to watch. 'He – they – he came for us, for Symon and me, although I do not know how he found us, and they fell on us, with their terrible, sharp weapons, and he ... he ... he *slew* Symon, my own cousin, right there before my eyes, and as he wielded the knife, he said, "You are not to be trusted", but he was *wrong*, my lord, for Symon and I are resolved, and we have sworn to – we have sworn...' He swallowed, the Adam's apple rising visibly beneath the padded linen that Helewise still pressed to his throat. Then, his voice weak and barely audible, he said, 'Accept my sword, my lord. *Please.*'

There was scarcely a sound in the little room except for the young man's gasping breaths.

Ninian crouched beside Josse. 'He's dying,' he said very quietly. Helewise met his eyes, frowning, and shook her head. It was surely not right to let a man know he was about to die. Besides, all the time the heart beat and the mouth drew breath, death had not yet won.

She looked down at the young man. His lips were as pale as his face, and the flesh of his cheeks seemed already to be shrinking.

As if he felt her eyes on him, his opened. 'I'm so cold,' he said. 'Are there no blankets here? No furs?'

There were no costly furs in the sanctuary, but Helewise had made sure of a good supply of fine woollen blankets, all of which were now piled on the wounded man.

'Father, we have it in our hands to let him die content,' Ninian said, right into Josse's ear: Helewise could only just make out the words. She was moved, for Ninian only referred to Josse as Father in moments of extreme emotion.

She did not know what Ninian had in mind, but it didn't matter, because Josse did. He looked up at his adopted son with a brief smile, then, bending once more right over the dying man, he said, clearly and firmly, 'I accept your sword.'

A look of huge relief eased the young man's tense features. With a great effort, he moved his right hand, the fingers opening and closing as if trying to grasp something.

Now Helewise understood. 'His sword, I think,' she murmured.

Ninian shot her a swift look, blue eyes bright in the firelight, and drew the young man's sword from its scabbard. The blade was filthy, coated with mud and blood. Ninian put the leatherbound handle in the dying man's hand, and, shaking with effort, the youth held it up to Josse. 'My sword, my allegiance, my life,' he said. His voice was suddenly strong again.

Helewise was watching Josse. He was scowling deeply, and she guessed he was seeking for the right words with which to send the young man through the gates of death.

Josse's expression cleared. He held out his hand to Helewise, pointing to something – the simple wooden cross she wore around her neck. Swiftly she lifted its leather cord over her head and handed it to him.

With his left hand on the young man's sword, Josse pressed his right to the young man's chest. He drew a breath, then said gravely, 'We place this cross on your breast that you may love it with all your heart, and may your right hand ever fight in its defence and for its preservation.' He paused. 'May God have mercy on your soul.'

The young man's hands closed over Josse's, still holding the sword, and his deadly pale, gaunt face stretched into a smile. He whispered, 'Thank you, my lord. Symon and I will not fail you.'

They crouched around him, Helewise, Josse and Ninian, and Helewise hoped that their vigil gave him comfort. Presently, he drew a deep, ragged breath, letting it out on a soft sigh.

Helewise put her hand over his heart. Then she leaned down so that her cheek was against his mouth. She waited, just to be sure.

Straightening up, tears falling from her eyes, she said, 'He's dead.'

They covered the face with a linen sheet. Ninian made to remove the blankets, but Helewise grasped his hand. 'Please, leave them,' she said. Ninian raised his eyebrows. 'He was so cold,' she muttered.

It made no sense, and she felt foolish, but Ninian seemed to understand. Bending down, he tucked the soft wool more closely around the still body, as tenderly as if he were comforting his own little daughter.

They would return to him in the morning.

Helewise prepared hot drinks for the three of them, adding herbs from what they all referred to as 'Meggie's heartening brew'. Whatever was in it – and Helewise still was not sure – it always worked. Apart from anything else, as soon as the mixture met the hot water, a warming, calming aroma issued from the ingredients, stilling the mind even in the most trying of circumstances. Looking round at her companions, Helewise observed that their tense expressions had eased.

'It was a fine gesture, to accept his service and speak so fittingly,' she said to Josse. 'It comforted him, just as Ninian said it would.' Josse grunted a response. 'I watched you as you sought in your memory for the right words. From where in your life did you recollect them?'

81

'I don't know,' Josse admitted. 'They just came into my head.'

Ninian looked up. *I* know,' he said quietly.

'Then I wish you'd tell me,' Josse replied gruffly.

Helewise studied his face, illuminated by the soft lamplight. His expression was profoundly solemn.

'It is the oath taken by a Knight Hospitaller when first he is given his cross,' Ninian said. 'You chose well, Josse, for a man on the point of death.'

FIVE

Early that same morning, Meggie and Sabin had set out from the House in the Woods, bound for the manor of Medley, perhaps an hour, two hours' ride away. Meggie had borrowed Helewise's mare, Daisy, not having a mount of her own, and she was looking forward to a decent ride in the crisp sunshine. As to what would happen when they reached their destination, that was another matter.

Although Sabin had begun to protest, Meggie had insisted on giving at least some explanation to her father of Sabin's presence, and, indeed, of where the two of them were off to that morning. Aware of Sabin furiously shaking her head out of Josse's line of sight, Meggie had taken his hand

and said quietly, 'Sabin is concerned about a matter of some delicacy, and I have undertaken to give her my opinion.' It was the truth, more or less. Josse, bless him, had not asked any awkward questions, but simply bent to kiss her on the top of the head and then wished her well.

'Do you always have to account to your father for your comings and goings?' Sabin said quite sharply as they left the courtyard. 'This is meant to be secret, Meggie!'

'It *is* secret,' she had replied. 'I told him nothing that would give us away. As to accounting for myself to him, I do it not because he orders me to, but because I love him and he worries. All right?' She kicked her heels into Daisy's sides and trotted on.

She had spoken rather more sharply than she had intended. However, it had the benefit of shutting Sabin up, for which she was quite grateful.

Her offer of help the previous night had been instinctive, given almost before she'd had a chance to think it through. Now, although there was no question of withdrawing the offer, she was well on the way to regretting it.

She drew rein slightly, allowing Sabin to come up beside her. 'Go through it again,' she said. 'The body is in a cellar, but you think we might be able to get down there without anyone seeing us?'

'Oh, they'll *see* us,' Sabin relied, 'and there is no way we can avoid it, for the manor is heavily guarded. My hope is that our arrival will not arouse curiosity. They will recognize me,' she muttered, as if reasoning with herself, 'but that is probably to the good.'

Meggie waited. When Sabin did not elucidate, she said, quite sharply, 'Well? What do you plan to do?'

'I'll just have to tell them I've become uneasy about my diagnosis of the cause of death,' Sabin replied, frowning, 'and wanted to consult you.'

'So now that's two canons from the Augustinian house in Tonbridge, the town apothecary and a forest healer,' Meggie remarked, not without irony. 'Won't Lord Benedict's household start to be suspicious?'

'Oh, I think they already are,' Sabin said grimly. 'That's why ... why...'

'Why you want to be absolutely sure that suspicion can't fall on you.' It was, Meggie thought, high time for some blunt words.

Sabin hung her head. 'Yes.'

Meggie sighed. 'Very well. Come on. The sooner we're done, the sooner you – and I – can relax.'

They rode up to Medley Hall to find the place eerily silent. It stood alone on its low rise; the surrounding land was marshy, dotted here and there with watery areas of bog, for they were deep in the valley here. Whoever had sited Medley up on its mound had chosen well.

As Sabin had predicted, the men on guard duty at the gates recognized her, and accepted without question her explanation that Meggie was a fellow healer. They were permitted to pass through the gates with nothing worse than a few ribald comments.

Meggie, looking round, noticed that there was a large, central house made of mellowed old stone, with two new-looking wings running out on either side. There were faint sounds of sawing and hammering from somewhere out of sight, and a voice yelled out something, followed by gruff male laughter, abruptly cut off. Lord Benedict, it appeared, had been in the process of extending his dwelling when death had interrupted.

Sabin called out – not very loudly – and after a while a young stable lad came to take the horses. It did not appear to be part of his duties to ask their business or usher them inside, for he did neither, simply leading the horses to a corner of the yard, where he tethered them before ducking back inside whatever building it was that he had just emerged from.

'What now?' Sabin asked in an anxious whisper.

You're asking me! Meggie thought, amused. 'We'd better go inside.' She strode across the courtyard and up the steps to the imposing front door, which was made of oak banded and studded with iron and looked new. It stood slightly ajar. She pushed it, and it opened on to a wide hall in which a fire smouldered in the hearth. The hall was hung with beautiful tapestries, their glossy sheen and the faint, woolly smell they emitted suggesting that they, too, were brand new, and there were some heavy pieces of fine oak furniture along the walls of the hall.

And then Meggie remembered exactly who

Lord Benedict was, what his job had been, and the likely source of his sudden wealth. She almost blurted it out to Sabin, before realizing that, if Sabin didn't already know Lord Benedict had been as close with the king as a flea to the hound's back, then now wasn't the time to tell her.

Feeling even more apprehensive, she stepped into the hall, Sabin on her heels. She called out softly, 'Hello? Anyone there?'

At first there was no reply. Then there was the sound of hurrying feet, and an ample woman in the middle years came puffing up from a passage off to the left. 'Her Ladyship's not receiving callers and the steward's out the back with the builders,' she said breathlessly. 'What do you—' She caught sight of Sabin, standing behind Meggie. 'Oh, it's you again. Thought you'd finished last time. Come to lay him out, have you?'

Meggie dug her elbow hard into Sabin's ribs. Sabin gave a sort of squawk and said, 'Yes.'

The serving woman turned back down the passage. 'Help yourselves. You know where he is. He hasn't moved, as far as I know.'

Her coarse laughter echoed back along the passage.

'Not exactly pining for him, is she?' Meggie whispered.

'He was an awful man,' Sabin hissed back. 'He—'

'Hush,' Meggie said. 'Not now. Anyway, I know his reputation.'

Sabin, looking intrigued, opened her mouth as

if to pursue the comment, so Meggie gave her a nudge to stop her. 'We'd better do as that woman said,' she said firmly. 'Where's this cellar?'

'Down there.' Sabin broke into a trot, hurrying off down a second passage which, presently, began to descend. Soon they were in the cellar; Meggie drew her cloak more firmly around her and wished she had something to press against her face.

They stepped up to the trestle table and looked down on the body of Lord Benedict de Vitré. Working together, they quickly removed his garments, and Sabin stood back while Meggie inspected him from head to toe. Then Sabin helped her turn him over, and she did the same to his back.

'Bring that candle nearer,' Meggie whispered. Sabin obliged. Meggie removed it from the holder and, with the flame close up to the corpse's back, leaned right over the body. 'What did you make of this?' She indicated the spot with the crust of dried blood.

'A pimple or a boil, or maybe a flea or louse bite,' Sabin replied, 'which he'd scratched and made bleed. There are lots of them, although that's the biggest.'

Meggie said, 'Hmm,' and went on looking. 'Would you hold the light?' Sabin took it from her. With both hands free, Meggie peered at the bloody spot. Putting two fingers either side of it, she pushed the surrounding flesh this way and that.

Abruptly she stood up. She stuck the candle back in its holder and put it back at the corner of the trestle. Then, trying to keep her voice calm, she said, 'Help me turn him over. We must dress him again and cover him up.'

'What...' Sabin began.

Meggie gave a *tsk* of exasperation. 'Just *do it*, Sabin.'

Their four hands worked swiftly and efficiently, and soon the corpse appeared just as it had done when they found it. Meggie took one last, careful look at the body, the trestle table, the candles in their holders. *Have I missed anything?* she thought. Her heart was hammering in her chest. *No. I don't think so.*

She took a firm hold on Sabin's arm and said, 'Come on. We've got to get away from here.'

Up the spiral stair. Along the dark, cold corridor, their footsteps echoing. More steps, another passage ... and then they were back in the hall, and it was still empty, and there was the open door and, beyond, the courtyard and their horses waiting.

It was all Meggie could do not to break into a run.

Only when they were a good five miles from Medley, deep within a stretch of pine wood – an outlying patch of the Great Forest – and out of sight of anyone on the road going to or from Lord Benedict's house, did Meggie pull up.

She slid down from Daisy's back and, taking hold of the reins of Sabin's horse, looked up at her and said, 'Get down. I want to know *exactly* what happened.'

'But...'

Meggie ignored the interruption. 'Last night, you merely told me that you'd gone with the two canons to inspect the body, and you were very afraid you might have missed something that would be dangerously incriminating. I undertook to return with you to see if I would spot anything you'd missed.' She felt resentment rising in her, dangerously close to anger. She took a breath, then said more calmly, 'I have done what you asked of me. Now, before I reveal my conclusions – before I say another *word* – I want the whole story, from the beginning, if you please.'

With a sigh, Sabin dismounted. She took her time over looping her horse's reins round a branch, and Meggie guessed she was thinking how to begin. Finally, she squared her shoulders, looked Meggie full in the face and said, 'She sent for me. Lady Richenza, that is; she's Lord Benedict's wife. She's barely more than a child, Meggie, and yet they married her to that foul, fat old man.' She paused, her face working as if she was trying to conquer strong emotion. Then she said, 'She wanted me to give her something to stop her conceiving, and something else to render Lord Benedict impotent, and, God help me, I did.'

Meggie absorbed the information. It was not exactly what she had expected to hear.

'You're shocked and horrified,' Sabin burst out, as still Meggie did not speak. 'I *knew* you would be, I shouldn't have told you. I—'

Meggie reached out and took her hand, giving it a quick squeeze.

'I'm neither shocked nor horrified,' she said. 'I expect I'd have done the same thing myself. It's very difficult to refuse such an appeal.'

'Oh, it *is*!' Sabin agreed fervently. 'Meggie, she knew absolutely *nothing* about the mating process before she was wed to him – she told me she thought he was poking a stick into her to punish her for something!'

'Yes, many high-born girls go ignorant to marriage,' Meggie said.

'It's *wicked*!' Sabin said passionately. 'Have their mothers no compassion? No sense? Naturally, there's no hope that a girl like Lady Richenza would have had the advantage of being able to observe animals in the farmyard or fields, or even creatures in the wild, as peasant-born girls do, but if their mothers only told them a little of what awaited them, then both the girls *and* their husbands would stand a far better chance of happiness!'

'I agree,' Meggie said mildly. She wondered what had made Sabin so forcefully angry on the subject. *Ask her*, she thought. 'Were you a similarly ignorant bride?'

'Me?' Sabin gave a short laugh. 'No. You forget, Meggie, I was long a healer before Gervase and I were wed, and when finally we found ourselves in our marriage bed, I was even more impatient that he was.' A smile of reminiscence crossed her face. 'You?'

'I'm not married,' Meggie reminded her. Sabin gave her a resigned look, and she grinned. 'I was like your peasant girls, Sabin. I tended animals as soon as I could walk, and I grew up knowing full well what awaited me with the man of my choice.'

'You have made your choice?' Sabin asked. Meggie nodded. An image of Jehan swam before her eyes, his black hair loose around his dark-skinned, fine-featured face, the gold ring glinting in his ear. 'And you had lovers before?' Sabin persisted.

Suddenly another face imposed itself on Jehan's. This one wore an expression of wry amusement, and the brilliant blue eyes were so fiercely intent that it almost hurt. Out of Meggie's memory came a vignette of that day, a year ago now, when she had stood in the clearing by St Edmund's chapel above Hawkenlye Abbey, a sword in her hand, facing a short, stout stranger who promised to teach her to fight and whose charisma, even now and merely a remembrance, still had the power to make her tremble...

Enough, Meggie said silently. 'Tell me how you helped Lady Richenza,' she said firmly.

'Yes. Sorry,' Sabin muttered. 'Well, she understood nothing, as I've told you, and at first she said, "I don't want him hurting me like that," and then, "I am very afraid of pregnancy and childbirth," as if the two matters were not connected. Do you know, Meggie, she told that stinking old man that she thought kissing led to babies! Imagine those fat, slobbery lips kissing you – *euch*!'

'I'd rather not,' Meggie said soberly.

Sabin's face grew serious. 'He gave her a lesson, the night she said that to him,' she said.

'It's so deeply unpleasant that I don't want to tell you.'

'I don't want to hear.' Meggie was afraid she could imagine, all too well, what the old man had done to his child wife. 'What did you prepare for her?'

Sabin sighed deeply. 'For Lady Richenza herself, I made an emmenagogue of pennyroyal, houseleek, thyme and rue, to strengthen her menstrual flow and induce her courses. From what she told me, it seemed unlikely that she had already conceived, but, just in case, I prepared a concentrated decoction of birthwort and raspberry leaf, hoping thus to render her womb inhospitable. I also prepared a fleabane poultice for her to bind to her belly.'

'You were very thorough,' Meggie observed.

'The lady was very desperate,' Sabin replied.

'What about him?'

Sabin frowned. 'Lady Richenza said he was fat, lazy, and regularly overindulged on both rich food and fine wine, and I thought that such a man's four humours would be so gravely unbalanced that he would probably not produce healthy seed. I did, however, prepare a distillation of seaweed, which, I'm told, makes a man's seed thin and useless, added to a very few drops of tincture of fresh yew needles, to slow the heartbeat.' She glanced down, as if suddenly unable to meet Meggie's eyes. 'I added some drops of my strongest soporific, comprising woodruff, valerian and a very small amount of poppy milk, since a very sleepy man is hardly likely to want to mount his reluctant wife. I also advised her to keep him drinking plenty of wine, and, if possible, to mix in with it some *eau de vie*. Do you know what I mean by that?'

'I do,' Meggie said. 'It is a distillation, is it not, from some form of alcoholic drink? The distillation makes it very strong, I believe.'

'Yes, indeed.' Sabin gave a shrug. 'Really, Meggie, I was at a loss, for in all the years I've been practising as an apothecary, and the many years before that when I was my old grandfather's pupil, I can't remember ever before being asked for a potion to make a man impotent. The opposite, yes, all the time.'

Meggie smiled. 'I don't think I've ever encountered it, either,' she agreed. She was thinking hard. 'So, other than a large amount of alcohol, the only unusual items that your potion introduced into Lord Benedict's body were the yew tincture and the strong soporific. Is that right?'

Sabin was looking at the ground again. She muttered something.

'What was that?'

She met Meggie's eyes. 'I put a tiny amount of aconite in the mixture.'

'You – *what*? Monkshood? Why?'

Sabin looked away. 'It reduces the beat of the heart and they say it induces numbness. I thought it'd keep him flaccid.'

'But it's toxic, and you're a healer.'

'I *know*,' Sabin wailed, 'but, Meggie, the poor girl was desperate, and I had to help her.'

'Yes, of course you did, but not at the cost of risking harming somebody else!'

93

'But he was brutal to her!'

There was a short, awkward silence. Then Meggie slowly shook her head. 'Oh, Sabin.'

'What is it?' Something in Meggie's tone must have alerted her. 'Oh, God, Meggie, what's the matter?' Frantically, her eyes searched Meggie's. 'You saw something, didn't you?' Sabin's breathing was shallow and rapid now, her eyes wide with terror. 'You spotted some sign, some symptom, and now they'll notice too, that stiff-necked steward and the serving women, and they'll ask Lady Richenza, and she'll confess, and then they'll come for me and I ... I...'

Meggie grabbed her hands, briefly holding them in a tight grip. '*Stop* this, Sabin. You'll make yourself ill if you don't control your fear. I saw nothing that would have led me to suspect what you'd put in the potion that Lady Richenza gave to Lord Benedict.'

Sabin was still staring at her. 'But there *is* something wrong. Isn't there?' Slowly, Meggie nodded. 'Oh, dear God, tell me. *Tell me!*'

Meggie drew a deep breath, and slowly released it. 'I did find something, yes. Something which, were anyone else to notice it, would alert them and, in all likelihood, lead to a new and far more thorough investigation of Lord Benedict's death.' *When*, she could have added, *it is quite possible that they would cut him open and discover exactly what was in your potion.*

Sabin had gone chalk white. 'What did you find?' she said in a whisper.

'That little crust of blood, which you thought was a scratched pimple or insect bite, was noth-

94

ing of the sort.' Once more, she took hold of Sabin's hand, as if physical contact could lessen the blow. 'It was a stab wound. A very fine stab wound, made by a long, sharp object such as a meat skewer, driven, I imagine, straight into the heart. Death was instant,' she added, 'as we know by the fact that the wound did not bleed: the heart had stopped.'

'A *meat skewer*,' Sabin breathed, eyes wide with horror.

'It was done by someone who knew exactly what he or she was doing,' Meggie went on, 'because the hand that killed Lord Benedict drove the skewer between the ribs and upwards at exactly the right angle to find the heart.' Sabin did not speak. 'When they hunt for the murderer, they'll be looking for someone with detailed knowledge of the human body.'

Sabin closed her eyes. 'Someone such as a healer,' she murmured. 'Or an apothecary.'

Then her hand slid out of Meggie's as she slumped to the ground in a dead faint.

SIX

'Where's the other one?'

Helewise's quiet voice broke the silence within the sanctuary. Josse looked up, meeting her anxious eyes.

'He said, "He slew Symon right before my eyes,"' she whispered. 'We should search for this Symon, Josse.'

He held her gaze. 'The poor fellow is undoubtedly dead,' he said gently. 'As you have just reminded us, our own young man here said he saw him slain.'

'Yes, I know' – her voice was eager now – 'but presumably the killer thought that *our* man was dead, and yet he wasn't. Might he not have been similarly careless with the other one?'

'He is dead now,' Ninian pointed out gravely.

'I *know*,' Helewise said again, with the air of someone trying to keep their patience under trying circumstances. 'But he wasn't when I found him. Had it been Meggie who heard him call out, she might have stitched the wound, stemmed the bleeding and saved him.'

Josse exchanged a look with Ninian. Ninian gave a faint shrug, as if yielding to the inevitable.

Josse got to his feet. 'Very well,' he said. 'You

stay here, Helewise. Ninian and I will take a couple of lamps and have a look around.'

'Thank you,' she said.

Her eyes shone. *She believes in me*, Josse thought. In that instant, it was something to be regretted: he'd been planning to have a cursory search and then hurry back to the sanctuary, promising a more rigorous job in the morning. Now, given her touching faith in his abilities, he would have to be more thorough.

He and Ninian searched the path up to the track and the undergrowth on either side, and then they separated, he following the road towards the turning down to Tonbridge and, beyond it, Hawkenlye Abbey, while Ninian went east around the great bulge of the forest. When Josse returned to the place where the path branched off to the sanctuary, Ninian was waiting for him.

'Nothing,' Ninian said. 'Well, nothing on the road or beside it. I called and called, but, if there's a man lying gravely wounded in there under the trees, either he didn't hear me or he chose not to answer. Either way, we cannot hope to find him tonight.'

'Aye, I agree,' Josse replied. 'I did consider going on to the abbey, in case he has somehow managed to get himself there, but they'll have locked up for the night.'

'If he *is* there, they'll take care of him,' Ninian observed.

Josse grinned. 'The voice of reason,' he said.

He heard Ninian chuckle in the darkness. 'D'you think Helewise will see it that way?'

She looked up as they quietly let themselves into the sanctuary, her eyes bright with expectation. Seeing their expressions, her face fell. 'Oh.'

'We will search again once we have light to see by,' Josse said, crouching beside her and taking her hands in his.

She did not need to speak, for the look in her eyes said all too clearly: *It'll be too late by then.*

'Come on,' he said gruffly, pulling her to her feet. 'It's time we were heading home.'

But she resisted. 'You two go,' she said quietly. 'I shall stay here.'

'You'll be all alone,' he muttered. 'I don't like the thought of that.'

'I'll be quite safe,' she replied serenely. 'This place is protected, you know.'

'I wish I could be sure of that,' he said, not quite sufficiently under his breath.

'Oh, you can be.' Her tone held utter confidence.

'But—' he began.

She interrupted, putting a hand on his arm. 'Dear Josse, I am staying, and that is final,' she said firmly. 'I do not want to leave this poor young man alone. He probably has family – people who love him – and when we find out who he is and, hopefully, I meet those people, I wish to be able to tell them that he did not lie unattended the night he died.'

'Then I'll stay with you.'

'No, Josse, you won't. There is absolutely no need. I am perfectly safe here, and you should be at home, so that you can organize the search as soon as it is light.'

He held her eyes for a long moment. Then, recognizing that he was not going to win, he nodded his acceptance.

'It'll be a corpse we'll be hunting for in the morning,' Ninian said as he and Josse strode back along the well-worn track from the sanctuary to the House in the Woods.

'Aye, I fear you're right,' Josse agreed.

'He'll be somewhere close at hand,' Ninian went on, 'assuming he was attacked in the same place as the man Helewise found.'

'Because the dead man in the sanctuary couldn't have gone far in that state,' Josse added. 'I reason the same way.'

'Unless, of course, he was mounted,' Ninian went on. 'In which case he—'

'Enough,' Josse said firmly. 'It's late and I'm tired.' He was also deeply anxious about having left Helewise alone, and wishing now that he had insisted on staying with her.

Ninian touched his arm. 'She wouldn't have let you,' he murmured.

It was quite uncanny, Josse reflected, how the lad occasionally read his mind so accurately.

The House in the Woods was in darkness save for one lamp left burning, and Josse, assuming everyone had gone to bed, bade Ninian goodnight, heading for his own quarters. But as he set off along the passage, a soft voice called out, 'Father!'

Spinning round, he headed back into the hall.

Lying on the thick fur rug beside the hearth was Meggie, propping herself up on one elbow and rubbing her eyes.

He hurried to her side. 'I didn't see you there!' he exclaimed.

'I fell asleep,' she admitted. 'I didn't wake till I heard you and Ninian saying goodnight.'

He sat down on the furs beside her, not wanting to speak for a moment, content simply to be close to this beloved child. She reached out and took his hand, leaning against him, and he put his arm round her, bending to kiss the top of her head.

After a while he said, 'Why aren't you in bed?'

'I wanted to talk to you,' she replied. 'Where have you been? Why weren't you here when I got in? And where's Helewise?'

'She was still at the sanctuary when night fell, and Ninian and I went to find her,' he said. 'She'd found a young man, dying, on the path leading into the forest from the road.' He told her what little information he had, concluding with Helewise's firm decision to stay with the body overnight.

'She's sitting vigil,' Meggie said softly. 'Keeping his departing spirit company. It's a difficult time,' she added, 'the transition between life and death.'

'Er – aye,' Josse muttered.

'Never mind, Father,' Meggie said, and he heard in her voice that she was smiling. 'Nobody's forcing you to confront things you'd rather leave alone.' She twisted round so that she could look into his face. Her smile faded. 'You do look tired.'

'I am,' he admitted. 'And I have to organize a search party in the morning.' He told her about the dead young man's companion.

'I'll help,' she offered. 'I'm good at tracking. You know I am.'

'Aye, sweeting, I do. Thank you.' Slowly, painfully – he was sure he could hear his bones creaking – he got up. 'Bed. Now,' he said, heading for the door. But then, remembering, he spun round. 'You said you wanted to talk to me.' Sudden anxiety flooded through him. 'What is it? What's wrong?'

Watching her closely, he thought perhaps her smile was a little forced. 'Nothing,' she said brightly. 'It'll wait till morning.' She too was on her feet, straightening the pile of furs, checking the fire in the wide hearth. She came up to him, kissing him. 'Goodnight, Father. Sleep well.'

In the morning, Josse and his household assembled early. Gus and Will set off for the sanctuary, Will pushing a handcart with which to transport the dead body to Hawkenlye Abbey. Out in the yard, Josse prepared to set off on horseback to search further along the road, while Meggie, Geoffroi and Ninian drew on stout boots in preparation for venturing into the forest around the sanctuary. Eloise, with Inana in her arms, came out to see them off, and Tilly distributed hot bread rolls which she had cut open to insert a slab of freshly fried bacon.

Josse rode first to Hawkenlye Abbey. He nodded to the nun on duty at the gate, left his horse in the care of the sister busy in the stables, and hurried along to Abbess Caliste's room.

She looked up with a smile when she saw who was disturbing her in her work. 'Sir Josse!' she exclaimed. 'It's good to see you. How may we help?'

Swiftly he told her about the dead man, describing briefly where and how he had been found, adding, 'Will and Gus are bringing him here this morning, my lady. It seemed best.'

'Of course,' she agreed. 'I will send word to the infirmary that he is on his way.' She got up, crossing to the door and summoning one of the nuns working nearby.

When she was seated once more, Josse went on to explain how he and his household were now hunting for the companion who had been with him when he was attacked. 'It seems almost certain the other man is dead,' he added, 'for, just before he died, the man at the sanctuary said he watched as his cousin was slain.'

'His cousin,' the abbess repeated thoughtfully.

'Aye. His name was Symon. And, even if this Symon didn't die immediately, he'd have been lying out in the open all night, badly wounded. I don't hold out much for his chances, my lady.'

'No, I understand,' she said. 'We shall pray for him; for both of them.'

'I did wonder if the other one – Symon – might have made his way here, but I imagine not, or you would have told me?' He couldn't help turning the statement into a question.

'Indeed I would,' the abbess agreed. 'No, we have received no new admissions into the in-

firmary, either yesterday, overnight or this morning. And, among our existing patients, there is
none with the sort of wounds inflicted when
someone is trying to kill a man.' Her lips moved
silently, and Josse guessed she was praying.

Aye, he thought, picturing the dead man and
recalling his words: *It's a horror that's worthy of
a prayer*. He glanced around the little room,
feeling awkward about watching the abbess in
prayer.

When at length he turned back to her, he found
she was looking at him. 'We do not have your
missing man here, Sir Josse,' she said, 'but,
nevertheless, I believe I may be able to offer you
some assistance. Indeed, you are already aware
of what I'm about to tell you, for I have mentioned it to you before.'

He stared at her. His mind raced back over all
that had happened in the last day or so.
Yesterday (only yesterday!) he'd come to see
dear old Saul, and called in for a chat with the
abbess on the way, and they'd spoken about
Benedict de Vitré's death, and she'd mentioned
that there seemed to be rather a lot of important
visitors to the area, and...

Aye. Of course! Memory returned, vivid and
powerful, and he couldn't think why he had
failed to make the connection before. Eyes on
hers, he said, 'Your two bright young men. You
think one of those is our dead man, and the other,
his cousin Symon.'

'It is possible, Sir Josse.' She got up. 'Wait
here, if you will, and I shall fetch the sister who
actually saw the pair.'

He heard her hurrying footsteps as she hastened off along the cloister. Quite soon she returned, and with her was the nun who had admitted him through the abbey gates. She was in the middle years, tall and thin, and something about her suggested wiry strength. She watched him with steady hazel eyes, her face expressionless.

'This is Sister Madelin,' Abbess Caliste said, 'who has recently finished her noviciate and joined the fully professed.' *One of those*, Josse thought, *who takes the veil later in life*. 'Sister, this is Sir Josse d'Acquin, a good and long-time friend of Hawkenlye.'

Sister Madelin ventured a quick smile, there and gone in an instant. 'Sir Josse,' she murmured.

'Sister,' he replied, bowing his head.

'Please, Sister,' the abbess said, 'will you tell Sir Josse what you told me, concerning the two young men who asked you for directions?'

If Sister Madelin was surprised at the request, it did not show in her impassive face. She paused briefly, as if collecting her thoughts, then spoke. 'It was the day before yesterday,' she began, her voice low and pleasant to the ear. 'Quite late in the day.' She paused again, frowning slightly. 'Some time after nones and a little before vespers.' *Still light, then*, Josse thought, *but not long to go before it began to get dark*. 'I was watching the gate and, hearing the sound of horses approaching, I stepped outside on to the road,' Sister Madelin continued. 'There were two of them, both young men, mounted on fine animals. Bays,' she added, 'well-groomed and glossy-coated, and the saddles and bridles were of high quality. One horse had a star on its brow and a white off-front foot.'

An observant woman, Josse mused. He wondered fleetingly what roads her life had led her down before she had come to Hawkenlye.

'Both men were dressed in costly garments,' the nun went on, 'and I caught a glimpse of vividly coloured tunics beneath their heavy travelling cloaks. One man's was light crimson, and the other's was emerald green. Their cloaks were trimmed with fur and, the day being sunny, they had thrown back their hoods and wore caps with feathers in them. One man's hair was fair, stylishly cut – the lad in the emerald-green tunic – and the other's was dark, with a curl to it. I remember remarking to myself that he'd have had to cram his hat down hard on that hair, or the cap would blow away.'

'They spoke to you, I believe you said?' Abbess Caliste prompted.

'Yes, my lady,' Sister Madelin replied. 'As soon as they were near enough to speak without shouting, one of them whipped off his cap, polite as you please, and asked me if I could tell him how to find Wealdsend, adding that it was the dwelling of Lord Robert Wimarc.'

'Were you able to help?' Josse asked.

She turned to him, the calm hazel eyes on his. 'Yes, my lord.'

He was not quite satisfied. 'You know this area, then, Sister Madelin? You'd heard of Wealdsend?'

Again, her reply was brief: 'Yes, my lord.'

She did not elucidate and, much as Josse would have liked to press her, he refrained.

'What exactly did you say to them, Sister?' Abbess Caliste asked.

Sister Madelin turned back to her. 'I said, "Go on westwards along this track, and in time it'll peter out to a path, not easy to determine. Head for the higher ground that rises up to the south, and after some five or six miles, look out for a cleft between two wooded ridges that slope down towards the valley. Between them lies Wealdsend."' She paused, considering. 'They might not have been my exact words, my lady, but they're near enough to make no difference.'

'Thank you, Sister,' said the abbess. 'You may return to your duty at the gate.'

Josse added his thanks, and the tall, black-clad figure, with a swift bow to each of them, quietly let herself out of the room.

When the steady footfalls had faded, the abbess spoke. 'One of the pair was your dead young man, Sir Josse?'

'Aye, there can be little doubt, my lady. Sister Madelin's precise description accords with our man. Costly garments, emerald-green tunic, fair hair fashionably cut. He was no longer wearing his cloak or hat, and there was no sign of his bay, but I believe we have found one of the pair who asked directions two days ago.'

'Where, I wonder, is the other one?' the abbess said softly.

Josse, who had been thinking deeply, started. 'I should return to the search,' he said. 'I'll ride

106

on along the track, following the directions which Sister Madelin gave. Perhaps the attack occurred there; it's a little-used path, and quite likely the sort of place where thieves might lie in wait for unsuspecting passers-by.'

'Those two bright young men would be an attractive target,' Abbess Caliste agreed. 'But I wonder, Sir Josse, whether robbers would in fact wait under cover by a path on which so few travel?'

Her words echoed in Josse's head as he set off from the abbey. He had hoped to detect hoof prints that he might identify as those of the two young men's horses, but he quickly appreciated it was a vain hope. The main track was littered with foot, hoof and other animal prints, far too numerous to pick out those of two particular horses; and the path, when he came to it, was carpeted with the sort of deep leaf mulch on which it was hard to spot any kind of mark. Nevertheless, he followed it doggedly, searching for indications of a fight, a struggle, a fatal attack.

There was nothing. Was there any point, he wondered as he emerged into the cleft between the two ridges, in going much further towards Wealdsend? He knew that, some time in the near future, someone – probably him – would have to visit Lord Wimarc and break the sad news that his would-be visitors were not going to arrive. But it was better, surely, to wait until they had found the other young man. 'Alive or dead,' Josse muttered, trying to keep hope alive.

In his heart, he was quite sure it would be dead.

He got back to the House in the Woods as the sun was setting. Both he and Alfred were tired, filthy, hungry – or, at least, Josse guessed his horse was hungry – and decidedly out of sorts. Added to that, although Josse had ridden for miles, he had found no sign of any young man, or, indeed, of either of the bays.

He rode into the yard to find Will waiting. He slid down off Alfred's back, handing over the reins, and heard Will's quiet, reproving *tut* as he saw the state of the horse.

'I know, Will,' Josse said. His tone was sharper that he had intended, but his feet were frozen and his back ached.

'I dare say it was necessary, sir,' Will said, already running gentle hands over Alfred's muddy, sweaty coat. 'Nothing that a hard rub down and a bucket of feed won't put right.'

Josse hoped the same could be said for him.

He was heading off towards the house when Will said, 'A horse turned up. Found up on the road. Bay. Blood all over the saddle and the horse's neck.'

Josse stopped. 'Where is it?'

Will nodded towards a stall at the end of the line. Hurrying, Josse went to have a look.

The bay was indeed a beautiful horse. It was a gelding, and had a white star between the eyes. Glancing down, Josse saw a glimmer of light in the darkness of the stall: a white forefoot. Will, typically, had tended both the horse and its tack, and no trace of blood remained on either the animal's neck or its saddle.

'They found a body, too,' Will called out.

Aye, Josse thought, *I thought they would.*

'Can't say where,' Will added, vigorously rubbing at Alfred's coat. 'They'll tell you, indoors.'

Once again, Josse set out for the comforts of home.

He found his family gathered around the hearth. He allowed them to fuss round him, removing his muddy boots and cloak, escorting him into his big chair right by the fire, thrusting a mug of hot, spiced wine into his hands. He enjoyed every moment. When Tilly appeared with a pie oozing with meat, root vegetables and thick gravy, fragrant steam issuing from cracks in the pastry crust, he willingly obeyed her directive not to say a word till he'd eaten it all up.

Sometime later, warm, well-fed, and with a replenished mug in his hand, Josse looked round at the circle of faces illuminated by the firelight. Helewise, Ninian, Eloise, Geoffroi, Meggie. Meggie ... Now what did the sight of her bring to mind?

'Is Sabin no longer here?' he asked her. He ought, he realized, to have asked her last night, only he'd been so dog-tired, and so preoccupied, that he'd forgotten all about Sabin.

Meggie looked up. He had the distinct impression that, for some reason, the question was unwelcome. 'She went home yesterday, Father.'

It seemed rather a terse reply. 'Were you able to help with the matter over which she sought your help?'

'I – yes.'

Evidently his daughter did not want to discuss
the matter. Perhaps it was professional discretion? He did not know. Sabin had left, presumably satisfied with whatever aid Meggie had
been able to give, and, for the moment, Josse
was happy to leave it at that. There were, after
all, more important things to discuss.

'Will has shown me the bay gelding,' he
began, 'and he told me a body has been found.'

Geoffroi looked up at him. 'I found the dead
man,' he said quietly. 'Or, to be honest, Motley
did.'

'Ah.' *Motley*, Josse thought. Geoffroi's hound.
The brindled dog had turned up in the yard one
cold night, shivering with cold, fear and hunger.
Geoffroi had tended her, mending her hurts and
restoring her to what seemed to be her usual self:
a courageous, friendly bitch who never gave up
as long as there was a trail to follow. She repaid
Geoffroi's meticulous care (he had stayed up
with her all one long night, feeding her tiny
amounts of warmed milk and honey at regular,
brief intervals) by the sort of total devotion that
only a good dog can give.

It was illegal for ordinary households to keep a
hound unless its front paws had been mutilated;
the high lords of the land were keen to keep the
hunting for themselves. Josse sometimes woke
in the night in a cold sweat, worrying what
would happen if Motley were to be discovered.
They would just have to say she had wandered
in, presumably lost, and persuade whoever came

asking that Josse was doing everything he could to discover the identity of her owner.

'Good for Motley,' he said now to his son. 'Where did she make this discovery?'

'It was quite late in the day, and we were deep in the forest, south-west of here, south-east of the abbey,' Geoffroi replied. 'Someone had pushed him under the bracken, right inside a bramble thicket, and we'd never have found him if it hadn't been for Motley's nose. She smelt the blood, I expect,' he added, with an attempt at nonchalance. 'There was quite a lot.'

Beside him, Helewise gave a soft sound of distress. He turned to her, noticing she looked pale. *She still grieves for the young man she could not save*, he thought.

'Then what did you do?' Josse asked gently, looking down at Geoffroi. It was better, he decided, to encourage the lad to talk. He'd be thinking about that dead, bloody body constantly, in any case.

'I called Motley out of the thicket before she – er, before she was tempted, and held on to her good and tight. Then I yelled out for Ninian and Meggie, and Ninian went into the bracken to have a look.'

Aye, Josse thought. *Wise lad*. Motley had sniffed out the corpse late in the day, and she'd been running hard for hours. She'd have been hungry.

Josse turned to Ninian. 'Well?'

'He'd been dead a while,' Ninian said. 'His throat was cut. Meggie thinks–' he shot his half-sister a quick smile, as if to acknowledge the fact

111

that he was speaking for her – 'he'd have died instantly.'

'Is that right?' Josse asked Meggie.

'Yes.' She met Josse's eyes, and he saw her give a tiny shake of the head. *She'll tell me more when the lad isn't listening*, Josse thought.

'We made a litter out of lengths of dead wood and my cloak,' Ninian said, 'and brought the body back here, since the house was marginally nearer than the abbey. He's down in the under-croft.'

Where it's good and cold, Josse thought.

'Will reported that the horse was found on the road,' he said, 'but that's all he told me.'

'I found the horse,' Helewise said. 'I stayed with the dead man up at the sanctuary until Gus and Will came to take him to the abbey, and then I walked up the path to the road.' *Still looking for the other man*, Josse thought. *For Symon.* 'I walked for quite a while, first one way and then the other, and I came across the horse in a little clearing on the edge of the forest. His reins had become entangled in the branches of an oak tree, and his twisting and turning as he tried to free himself had tied him fast. He was very nervous, until he seemed to realize I was trying to help. I managed to untangle him, and I led him back to the house, where Will saw to him.'

'We reckon he must be the man at the sanctuary's horse,' Geoffroi piped up, 'because he was found nearby, and he had lots of blood on him. If the other man had a horse too, he'd have had to find his way right through the forest to have come out on the road above the sanctuary.'

112

Josse nodded. He wondered what had happened to Symon's horse. If it was of similar quality
to the gelding in the stall, then it was too good an
animal to be left to its own devices out in the
forest. *I am not going to worry about that tonight*, he thought wearily. *It is time my family
were asleep.*

He got up, stretching his back. The ache had
diminished to a dull pain. 'Go to bed,' he said to
Geoffroi. 'You too,' he added, looking first at
Meggie and then at Ninian, sitting with his arm
around Eloise, his head resting on the top of
hers. 'You've all had a long day.'

'Your father is right,' Eloise said, looking at
Josse with a smile. 'If we sleep now, we'll have
a few hours' peace before Inana wakes us all up
by informing us she's hungry.'

Meggie hung back as the others left. 'Father?'
she said softly. 'Will you come with me now to
look at the body?'

He suppressed a sigh. Glancing at Helewise –
there was sympathy and understanding in her
eyes – he nodded. 'I'll be back,' he whispered to
her as he left the hall. 'Warm some more wine.'

He followed Meggie out of the door, down the
steps and round to the little door leading to the
undercroft. Meggie had lit a torch and, once
inside the low, vaulted space, she stuck it in a
bracket on the stone wall.

The dead man lay on a trestle table, covered
with a length of linen. Meggie drew back the
linen, and Josse looked down on the evidence of
a shockingly violent death.

Someone – Meggie, no doubt, perhaps aided

by Helewise or Tilly – had cleaned up the corpse. The wide, deep slash had cut the throat so efficiently that the head was only attached by the bones of the spine and some gristly sinews. The terrible wound had been carefully cleaned, and the only blood that now remained was that which had soaked into the beautiful fabric of the pale crimson tunic. There was so much of it that Josse might have thought the tunic was blood-coloured, had he not known otherwise. A reddish-brown tunic that stank of the butcher's yard...

'Were there any other wounds?' he asked, his voice gruff.

Meggie leaned forward, picking up one of the still, white hands. She indicated the wrist, which had a bracelet of bruises. 'The other wrist is the same,' she said softly.

'He was held, then,' Josse muttered. 'Someone held his hands, behind him, perhaps, while another person cut his throat.'

'It could have been the same person,' Meggie suggested. 'This man is not particularly big. A man with large hands could have held both wrists in one hand while he wielded the blade with the other.'

'I suppose so,' Josse agreed.

But we have a witness, he thought suddenly. He tried to recall what the man in the sanctuary had said.

He – they – he came for us, and they fell on us with their terrible, sharp weapons, and he slew Symon right there before my eyes.

He – they came for us. *He* slew Symon.

114

One man or two? Josse wondered. *Two, and only one of them the killer? Or just one man working alone?* He did not know, and was not sure it mattered. If there had been two, weren't you just as culpable if you held another man's wrists while someone else slit his throat?

He stared down at the dead man. Meggie gave him a quick, questioning look and, at his nod, covered the corpse once more with the sheet.

Symon, Josse thought. *We know that about him: his given name. He is cousin to the man found at the sanctuary, and both were seeking Lord Wimarc at Wealdsend. Everything else remains to be discovered.*

He sighed. Weary as he was, just then the task ahead was more than he felt able to contemplate. 'Ninian and I will take him to Hawkenlye Abbey in the morning,' he said, putting his arm round Meggie. 'We can do no more for him tonight.'

Back inside the house, Meggie kissed him and slipped away to her bed. He wandered back to his chair by the hearth, accepting the mug of wine from Helewise with a murmur of thanks.

'Who were those poor young men?' she asked, although he knew she did not expect an answer. 'Why were they looking for Lord Wimarc?'

'I have no idea,' Josse said wearily. He forced his tired mind to think. 'I'm wondering why they ended up where they did, one at the sanctuary and this one – Symon – in the forest to the south of the abbey.' He turned to meet Helewise's anxious face. 'I spoke today to the nun who saw them at Hawkenlye, and she repeated the directions for Wealdsend that she gave them. Why, I

115

wonder, did they not follow those directions? Or, if they did, who made sure that their bodies were found elsewhere?'

'It's almost as if...' Helewise began.

'What?'

She shook her head. 'Oh – nothing.'

'Nobody visits Lord Robert Wimarc,' Josse said slowly, breaking a brief silence. 'He does not encourage it, and they say he keeps his fences high and his gates firmly barred.'

'He does not venture out, either,' Helewise added. 'I have only once encountered him outside his walls – when he came to the abbey, as I told you – and I've never heard of anyone having seen him out in the world since then. He is,' she added with a sigh, 'a veritable hermit.'

'Yet two young, handsome, wealthy young men were asking how to find him,' Josse said, frowning. 'Why?'

'There's something else.' Helewise's tone was sombre. 'Whatever their reason – whatever their business with Lord Wimarc – someone went to extreme measures to make sure they did not reach him.'

SEVEN

Meggie was awakened the next morning by Tilly, bending over her as she lay huddled beneath the bedclothes, shaking her by the shoulder and hissing, 'You've got to wake up, miss! There's someone here come to fetch you because they need your help.'

As soon as Tilly was sure that Meggie would not relapse into her warm bed and go back to sleep, she hurried away. Meggie forced herself out of her snug cocoon and, cracking a thin film of ice in the bowl of water beside the bed, splashed her face, neck, wrists and hands. It was the most effective way she knew to wake yourself up when you'd rather be asleep.

Tidily dressed, her hair arranged neatly, she made her way into the hall. It was quite common for people to seek her out and beg her help, for her reputation as a healer was spreading among those who lived on the forest borders. However, she was quite surprised to see who was waiting for her, warming hands pale with cold before the fire in the hearth.

It was a nun, clad in black with a white veil: a novice.

'I'm Meggie,' she said, striding towards the nun. 'How can I help?'

117

The nun spun round, revealing a long, plain face smooth with youth. The girl broke into a smile, the parted lips showing large teeth with a gap in the middle. The resemblance to an amiable horse was unfortunate, and Meggie drove the image from her mind.

'I'm Sister Maria,' said the novice. 'They sent me from Hawkenlye to fetch you. No!' Her face flushed, and she threw up her hands to hide the flaming cheeks. 'I mean, they sent me to *ask* you if you'd come to the abbey, my lady, as there's a patient that Sister Liese – she's the infirmarer – is worried about, and she reckons you can help.'

The nun had uttered her request without drawing breath, very fast, and now she was panting slightly. Meggie couldn't suppress a chuckle. She reached out for the novice's hand, giving it a squeeze.

'I'm not *my lady*,' she said. 'I'm just Meggie. And of course I'll come with you. First, and unless it's a matter of life or death, warm yourself a little longer.' She paused, studying the novice with a professional eye. 'Are you hungry?' she asked.

Sister Maria's eyes widened at the question, and Meggie had her answer. But, loyal to her abbey, and presumably not wanting to give the impression that she didn't get enough to eat, the novice said, 'I supped last night, thank you, my – er, Meggie.'

Meggie smiled. 'I'm sure you did, but that wasn't what I asked. Tilly – she's the one who admitted you – will be cooking, I'm sure, since there's always people to feed around here. Come on – we'll go into the kitchen and see what we can scrounge.'

A little later, leaving word with Tilly to tell Josse where she was going – nobody else seemed to be about – Meggie and the novice set out for Hawkenlye Abbey, accompanied by the sturdy young lay brother who had escorted the nun on her mission. Sister Maria had saved some of her food to give him, and he accepted it with an eager smile. The novice rode a belligerent-looking mule, and Meggie felt quite guilty saddling up Eloise's horse, which seemed particularly fine in comparison. In addition, the grey mare was full of lively energy, her dark, intelligent eyes wide with curiosity as she looked with interest at the world around her. Eloise had asked Meggie to ride her out whenever she could, since Eloise, her hands full with Inana, didn't have the time or the inclination, but Meggie had rarely found the time.

She sensed that the novice and the young lay brother felt slightly awed by her presence and, after a few not very successful attempts to engage them in conversation, she let them ride a little ahead of her, slipping in behind. After a while, she heard them talking quietly to each other. Happily, she retreated into her own thoughts.

She had very much wanted to confide in her father what she had discovered concerning Benedict de Vitré's death. Nearly two days had passed now, and still she hadn't found an opportunity. The night she had returned from Medley

119

Hall, with that alarming conversation with Sabin still echoing loud in her head, she had waited up for Josse, wanting above all else to confide in him, and ask him what she should do. But when he had finally come in, fresh from dealing with that gruesome death up at the sanctuary and clearly worried at having left Helewise there by herself with the dead man, she just couldn't bring herself to add to his anxieties. And then last night, when he'd come in dirty and exhausted after hunting all day for signs of the dead man's companion, there had been other, more urgent matters to address. She'd taken him to view the corpse in the undercroft, sensing his distress even though he tried to conceal it from her. *He is looking careworn and old*, Meggie thought with an ache in her heart, *and what I want so much to tell him would only add to his worries*.

It was, however, no reason *not* to tell him. Straightening her shoulders, she resolved to speak to him as soon as the two of them found a moment to be alone.

She left Eloise's mare in the abbey stables, bidding farewell to Sister Maria; the lay brother – who said, blushing, that his name was Watt – asked her to summon him when she was ready to leave, since the abbess did not allow women to travel unescorted.

Oh, these wretched times, Meggie thought to herself as she strode off to find Abbess Caliste. While she understood the necessity for a guard, she still resented with all her being the fact that she rarely got the chance to ride out alone any more.

Abbess Caliste answered her gentle tap on the door with a warm 'Come in!' then greeted her with a smile. 'Thank you so much for coming, Meggie,' she said, coming over to give her a hug.

'What can I do for you?' Meggie asked, settling down on the visitors' chair.

The abbess was silent for a few moments, clearly thinking. Then – and her words were not at all what Meggie had expected – she said, 'Your mother, I believe, studied with the learned men of the Brocéliande; those who study sickness of the mind?'

'Yes, she did,' Meggie replied, her mind reeling. What could this possibly be about?

'So I thought,' the abbess said. 'And you: you too have travelled in those regions. Have you also had the benefit of their teaching?'

How does she know I've been there? Meggie wondered wildly. In that first moment, it seemed all but unbelievable. Then she heard a soft, low voice speak inside her head: *Remember her ancestry.*

Of course. Caliste hadn't always been a nun. She was born to the forest people, and her twin still dwelt with them. The abbess, it seemed, had access to at least a little of the knowledge that those mysterious people usually kept to themselves.

It was not for Meggie to question the abbess's sources, however; she had far too much respect for her to do that. And, anyway, where was the

121

harm in telling her what she wanted to know? Meggie knew instinctively that whatever confidence she shared with Abbess Caliste was utterly safe.

'I have visited the place of healing where they specialize in sickness of the mind, yes,' she said softly. 'It lies deep within the forest, hidden from outside eyes, and it is very difficult, perhaps impossible, to find, unless you have a guide. It is called Folles Pensées.' She was back there, in her imagination. She saw once more the circle of simple dwellings, made out of the local rosy granite; she felt the soft grass under her bare feet as she trod the forest path up to the holy fountain; felt the clear, bubbling water urging up against her outstretched hands as she plunged them below the rippling surface.

'Did they teach you?' the abbess prompted.

'A little, yes,' Meggie answered, still half in her dream memory. 'What they tried to explain to me accorded with things I had already learned, so that it did not feel that I was starting right at the roots of it. It is, of course, a vast subject, and I was only there a short while. I ... they explained how to reach inside another's mind,' she said in a rush, instinctively dropping to a whisper. 'In order, you see, to understand what is amiss.'

The abbess nodded. 'I have heard tell of this,' she murmured. Then, her bright eyes fixed to Meggie's: 'Were you not afraid?'

Meggie grinned. 'I was terrified. But I could see, just a little, what the aim of it was. How it could help. After that, it wasn't so bad.'

Firmly she shut down the recollection of the poor young man she'd tried to help. How, tentatively extending her consciousness into his, she had seen such, horrifying things...

The abbess must have been aware of her momentary distress, for she gave her a little while to recover herself. Then she said, 'Would you, Meggie, be prepared once more to attempt this reaching-out into another's mind?'

Meggie realized that she'd known this was coming. She looked within herself. *Do I have the strength? Am I ready, perhaps, to see such abominations again?*

Then she remembered who was asking for her help. Slowly she nodded. 'I'll try.'

And Abbess Caliste leaned close and told her all she knew about a strange old woman by the name of Lilas of Hamhurst.

Tentatively, aware that the presence of yet another stranger might be disturbing to one already in distress, Meggie followed the infirmarer's pointing finger and approached the woman sitting on the bed at the end of the long ward. She had been placed in a recess, and the curtains had been parted sufficiently to enable her to look out. Or, more probably, Meggie reflected, to allow the nursing nuns to keep an eye on her.

Meggie went into the recess, drawing the curtains closed. She stopped just inside them, looking at the occupant of the bed with a smile. 'Hello,' she said. 'I'm Meggie.'

The old woman's pale blue eyes had been staring fixedly at her throughout her approach. It was unnerving; Meggie had the feeling that Lilas saw further and deeper than most people. Meggie studied her, taking in the white hair, braided and twisted in a coil under a plain white cap, and the fine bones of the thin face. Lilas was dressed in a simple gown, of old and well worn, yet clean, fabric, in an indeterminate shade between brown and grey.

She looked exhausted and anxious, and she was far too thin.

For those reasons alone, Meggie felt her heart soften. Walking up to the bed, she gently eased Lilas's legs over a little, making a space to sit down. 'Is that all right?' she asked.

'It's fine, lass,' Lilas muttered. Then, frowning, she whispered, 'Have you come to punish me?'

'No,' Meggie said. 'That's not what I'm here for. Anyway, what have you done that needs punishment?'

'I lied,' Lilas said with a whimper.

'We all lie,' Meggie said gently. 'Personally, I don't believe anyone who claims otherwise.'

The shadow of a smile stretched Lilas's thin lips.

'What was your lie about?' Meggie asked. 'Something big or something little?'

Lilas hesitated. Then, holding up her hands, she stretched a gap between them, widening it until she could reach no further.

Meggie laughed. 'That big?'

Lilas nodded.

'I'm told,' Meggie said in a whisper, leaning closer, 'that once you had a vision, and, enjoying

124

the attention, you pretended to have some more. Is that it? Is that your big lie?'

'Aye,' Lilas croaked. Her eyes held Meggie's, eloquent with appeal. 'But then, while I was pretending, the true vision intruded, and I was out of control, helpless...' She broke off, making a choking sound.

'You must have been very frightened,' Meggie said, taking one of the twisted, work-worn old hands in hers. 'I know a bit about visions,' she added confidingly. 'I have them, too, and sometimes I deliberately induce them.'

Lilas shook her head, her expression reproving. 'You don't want to go doing that, my girl. That's dangerous.'

'I know,' Meggie agreed. She hesitated, weighing her words, then said, 'The abbess told me you're scared of something beside the visions. Do you want to tell me? I really do want to help.'

Lilas was watching her closely, and Meggie saw shrewdness in her eyes. 'A girl who can have visions sounds like a useful ally,' she muttered and, briefly, she smiled. Then abject fear replaced the smile and, putting her mouth up to Meggie's ear, she said, 'They *know* about me, and what I saw. I don't know how, but somehow they found out about the visions, and they want me to repeat them and go on repeating them, and I'm scared half to death because it's not safe, not safe, not even here with all the nuns and that, because ... because...'

Abruptly she pulled away from Meggie and, burying her face in her hands, began to weep.

125

Meggie sat watching her, wondering what she should do. She knew full well what Abbess Caliste *wanted* her to do; was it right, though, for Lilas?

This poor old woman is suffering, she thought. *She is locked up with her fear, which perhaps I can alleviate if I see for myself what frightens her so.*

If she had known the nature of this mission, she reflected, she could have brought the Eye of Jerusalem with her, for it was the easiest and swiftest way of inducing trance, in herself and others, even if the after-effects were frequently painful. But she had not known, and would just have to do her best without it.

With a deliberate effort, she stilled her mind and slowed her breathing. After only a short interval, she felt the calm begin to descend. Only then did she stretch out her hands and, gently but firmly, take hold of Lilas's, removing them from her tear-stained face and grasping them so that the old woman could not draw them back. Looking into Lilas's eyes, she said softly, 'Calm yourself, Lilas. Relax with me, and breathe slowly and deeply. Yes, like that. Slow. Deep. Now, close your eyes, and I will close mine too.'

The two of them sat there for some time, and gradually Meggie's awareness of the rest of the big, busy infirmary fell away. She sensed, from the lessening of tension in Lilas's hands, that the old woman, too, was moving on to another plane.

Meggie felt the exact moment when reality

retreated and trance took over: behind her closed eyelids there was a shift in the quality of the light, and she was aware of a faint humming in her ears...

...and in the world of the vision, Meggie opened her eyes. Lilas was beside her – she knew it, but she did not know how she knew, for she could not see her. This, however, was Lilas's trance. She was quite sure of that.

The pictures began to come, busily, swiftly, one succeeding another before she had had a chance to absorb the details. The images were universally disturbing: sinister figures lurking deep in the shadows, whispering their malice, the whites of their eyes flashing; an island in a broad, swift-flowing river, and strong lords standing firm in an unyielding group around a short, stocky, defiant figure in their midst; the sea, rushing towards the land in a mighty up-surge of violent motion, turning over frail ships, drowning the men who floundered and scream-ed, while one harsh voice soared above them wailing in anguish.

A man lying in a filthy, soiled bed, twisting and thrashing, his hands clenched on his belly, crying in agony as the life ebbed out of him.

Inside Meggie's head, a deep, sonorous voice said: *Behold, the Winter King.*

Meggie moaned softly. Some quality of the vision changed subtly, and the image of the dying man was replaced by another, in which a blue-eyed stranger smiled at her and offered to teach her how to fight.

127

You swing a sword like a man, although your technique could be refined. I'll give you some lessons, if you like.

She could hear him so clearly that he might have been there beside her. And, despite all that she knew of him, everything she loathed and despised about what he had done and was still doing, yet she felt her heart ache with a sudden pain at the thought that she had just witnessed his death.

The visions were still coming, thick and fast. Weakening now, Meggie could not distinguish between those that originated with her and those which came from Lilas, for they flashed like distant lightning and there was no time to separate one from the other. Maybe they were one and the same. Now she saw fighting: the vicious clash of well-armed men, inflicting horrific wounds on each other. A dark line of alien ships, drawing ever closer to England's shore, and a young king – just a little boy – who grew to be a weak and greedy man, yet from whose loins would come a giant.

And then suddenly there are two people standing face to face in a small, simple chapel, and a memory of brilliant blue light. Someone speaks her name. *You are a vestal virgin*, he says. *Keep your fire burning ... a blue fire.*

There is a lamp on the altar, she hears herself reply. *Some trick of the light allows its flame to catch in the blue of the window.*

And the man with the stunning blue eyes says, *I would believe there was magic here, and that you, my Meggie, were a witch, only I do not believe in magic and there are no such things as witches.*

This is not trance. This is a memory, true and vivid.

I leave for London in the morning, the man says. *I wish I could take you with me.*

Then he leans forward and kisses her mouth.

He takes one long, last look at her. Then he turns and strides away.

Images reel and whirl inside Meggie's head. The forest. The chapel. Blue eyes. Blue light. Laughter. Screaming. The stink of a soiled bed, and the howls of pain quietening to a low, persistent moan.

The sea again, and those sinister ships with the alien devices on their sails.

The brilliant blue light.

Meggie is lost. She does not know where she is, or in whose vision she wanders. She is afraid. She cannot find her way back. She opens her mouth to scream...

...and strong hands gripped hers. Someone's voice said firmly, right into her ear, 'Don't cry out, or they'll come running, and you're not ready for them.'

They? Who were *they*? But the voice had spoken right, for Meggie could not even think about facing anyone yet.

But someone was right there with her; someone who understood. Her eyelids fluttered open and she looked right into the pale eyes of Lilas of Hamhurst.

Finding herself slumped across Lilas's bed,

Meggie struggled to sit up. Those same strong hands held her down. 'Stay still,' Lilas said. 'If you try to rise, your head'll spin.'

Meggie obeyed.

Lilas was stroking her hair, gently, rhythmically. 'Scared you, didn't it?' she murmured. 'Saw terrible things, eh?'

'Yes,' Meggie whispered.

Lilas leaned closer. 'You frightened me, lass,' she said in a hoarse whisper. 'One moment I sensed you there with me, next you'd gone. I didn't know where you were, or if you'd come back.'

'Was it your vision? The dark, threatening figures, the island in the river, the drowning men and the ships turned over?' Lilas nodded. 'And you saw it true, this time? You weren't pretending?'

Lilas snorted. 'You saw it too, girl. Weren't no pretence. You saw what I saw, seemingly, although I don't know how that could be.' The old eyes narrowed as Lilas scrutinized her. Lowering her voice again, she hissed, 'Got forest blood, have you?'

'Yes,' Meggie whispered.

Lilas gave her a strange look. 'Me too.'

Meggie knew she must report back to Abbess Caliste before she left, although it was the last thing she wanted to do. But the abbess had asked for her help, and she had agreed to give it.

'I believe Lilas truly did see the vision which she described,' she said, standing rigidly before Abbess Caliste in her little room. 'She is not sick

130

in her mind, my lady – or, at least, I do not believe so. She knows when the trance comes and when she's pretending, and that sounds quite sane to me.'

'I see,' said the abbess neutrally.

'She's afraid, though,' Meggie went on. 'I think, from what she said, that someone over-heard her; someone who wants to use the things she claims to have seen for their own ends.' She hesitated to be more explicit, even within the apparent safety of the abbess's own room. 'Do you understand what I mean, my lady?'

'I do,' Abbess Caliste said. 'I, too, have heard her refer to this someone, and I believe I know the use to which he – they – would put Lilas and her pronouncements.' Swiftly she rose. 'Do not fear for her, Meggie. We shall keep her here, for I have promised her safe refuge.'

'How can you?' Meggie asked. 'How will you keep her here, if they come for her?'

'Hush!' the abbess said quickly. 'Do not speak of it. We have our ways. This is still a house of God, even if the whole turbulent world seems to have forgotten it.'

Meggie shook her head, feeling suddenly dizzy. She was still dazed from the trance, and her head ached with a steady, painful throb. Little lights flashed on the edge of her vision. 'I must go,' she muttered. 'I ... I...'

The abbess came towards her, hands out-stretched, face concerned. But Meggie did not want to be caught and held; she wanted to get away. 'I'm all right,' she said, summoning a smile.

'I'll send for Brother Watt and he shall escort you home,' Abbess Caliste said, moving towards the door.

'No!' The abrupt word came out too loud, too dictatorial. 'I am sorry, my lady, but I am not going home. I'll leave the mare here in the abbey's stables, if I may. I'm going to the hut.'

My mother's hut, in the forest, Meggie could have added.

But there was no need. Caliste knew what she meant as well as she did.

Caliste was looking at her. Meeting her eyes, Meggie sensed she knew what the abbess was about to say. 'Meggie,' she began, 'now that you appear to have formed a bond with Lilas, might I ask if you will come back later, and stay here for a few days to help us look after her?' Before Meggie could reply, she hurried on, 'I'm sure Sister Liese could find a recess in the infirmary where you could sleep. You would have a little privacy, at least.'

Meggie suppressed a sigh. Lodging within the abbey was not at all what she wanted to do, but Josse would protest if she announced she was going to stay in her hut. She wouldn't have to be with Lilas all the time, and she could slip away to the hut when she wasn't needed. It was, she had to admit, closer to the abbey than to the House in the Woods.

She made herself smile. 'Very well,' she said, 'I will.'

But just now, she thought as she hurried up the

132

slope away from the abbey and towards the forest, *I have to be alone. I cannot be with people who love me, people I love; I have to think.*

She had to work out why, when she and everyone close to her loathed that man and everything he did, and when she had believed herself in love with Jehan and planning a new life with him, she should have remembered, with such rousing, stirring clarity, that moment a year ago. When, very close to the clearing she was now crossing on flying feet, a blue-eyed king had kissed her. And she had kissed him back.

EIGHT

Josse left the House in the Woods early that morning. Although he and Helewise had talked long into the night, they had come up with no sensible explanations for the deaths of the two young men, nor any obvious way to identify them. The mere name *Symon* was little enough to go on. They had concluded, feeble and unsatisfactory though it was, that the only thing to do was to ride down to Tonbridge and discuss the matter with Gervase de Gifford.

This morning, Helewise had offered to accompany Josse, but he could tell she didn't really want to. *She wants to go to the sanctuary*, he thought. *There'll be some purifying prayer she'll be eager to say, something to send the spirit of the dead man on its way and make the place wholesome for those who come next.*

She came out to the stables with him to see him off. 'You'll do what's necessary in your precious sanctuary,' he said, looking down from Alfred's broad back into her earnest face. 'Don't worry; a death or two won't keep them away.'

'Really?' Her grey eyes lit up with relief.

He'd been right, then. 'Really.' He gave her an encouraging grin, then edged his heels into Alfred's sides and trotted off.

The morning was cold, with clear skies and a wintry sun shining brightly, sparking flashes of light off frosted grass and the last of the autumn leaves. Alfred was keen to go, and Josse let him have his head. Reaching the place where the road branched off to the right to descend into the valley and the town, both man and horse were warm and exhilarated.

Josse held the big horse in for the descent, and rode into Tonbridge at a sedate trot. He turned to his left, following the lesser track along to Gervase's house, hoping the sheriff would not yet have left. It was still early.

Gervase's stable lad came out to take Alfred, nodding a greeting to Josse. 'Is your master at home?' Josse asked.

'No, sir. Gone down to the lock-up to see about a couple of drunks as tried to knife each other last night.'

'Oh. Will he be gone long?'

'Couldn't say, sir. Mistress's in, if you want to go up.'

Josse was about to decline (his business was with Gervase and, doubting that Sabin could help, he preferred to seek out the lock-up and find the sheriff) when the door at the top of the steps opened and Sabin looked out.

'Tam, I heard a horse, and then voices,' she began, addressing the lad. 'Who...?'

Josse stepped out from behind the bulk of his horse and said, 'Good day, Sabin. It's me. I'm here to—'

He did not get the chance to explain his presence. Even from where he stood, some eight or ten paces away, there was no mistaking the sudden pallor in Sabin's face, nor the look of fear in her eyes.

'Josse, you must ... I...'

She staggered and, thinking she was about to pass out and might fall all the way down the steep stone steps, Josse threw himself across the yard, bounded up the stairs and caught her in his arms. She muttered some words, but he could not make them out.

He turned to the lad, standing holding Alfred, eyes and mouth perfect 'O's of fascinated interest.

'Look after my horse,' Josse ordered. 'I'll take the lady inside.' Before the boy could reply, Josse put an arm round Sabin's waist and, half-dragging and half-carrying her, took her inside the house and firmly closed the door.

There was an oak settle drawn up beside the hearth, and a tapestry work bag lay on the stone floor beside it. The piece of embroidery on which Sabin had presumably been at work had been thrown down on the settle. Removing it, Josse sat Sabin down, crouching beside her and vigorously patting her hands. He had some vague recollection that slapping people's hands brought them out of a faint.

After a moment, Sabin, her eyes still closed, murmured, 'If you go on doing that, Josse, you're going to leave bruises.'

Instantly he dropped her hands, rising to his feet and backing away from her. 'I'm sorry,' he muttered. He waited, but she did not speak. 'Are you all right?' he ventured. When she still made no reply, he said, attempting a joke, 'I know I'm no beauty, but the sudden sight of my face doesn't usually make a woman faint!'

She opened her eyes and looked up at him. She was still deathly pale. 'She's told you, hasn't she?' she whispered. 'Oh, God, Josse, and you've come to report me to Gervase!' She bit hard at her lip, drawing a bead of blood.

Josse sat down beside her, taking her cold hand. 'Who has told me what? And what have you done, Sabin, that needs reporting?'

She was studying his face, eyes desperate in their intensity. She shook her head, apparently incapable of further speech.

'This concerns whatever it was that made you come to Meggie for help, doesn't it?' he asked. She didn't confirm it, but she didn't really need to. Josse was remembering, only too clearly. What was it Helewise said? Aye: *It was Meggie she was so keen to see. Without being actually*

*rude, Sabin managed to make it perfectly clear
that the rest of us were of no more use to her than
the flags of the floor.*

And Josse also recalled that they'd been quite
sure Gervase would have had no idea where
Sabin had gone until Josse's Gus rode down to
tell him...

'What's the matter, Sabin?' he asked, lowering
his voice, even though they were alone in the
hall and the door to the servants' quarters was
closed. 'What was it for which you needed
Meggie's help so desperately?'

She was still watching him closely, but he
thought the panic was receding. 'Don't you
know?' she whispered.

'I have no idea,' he said gruffly. 'My daughter
observes a strict, professional silence where
patients are concerned, and it appears that ap-
plies to other healers' patients, too. Such as
yours,' he added, in case the message wasn't
sufficiently clear.

Sabin wrested her thin fingers out of his grasp,
putting both hands up over her mouth, as if
trying to push back the recent flow of words.
'You're not ... you haven't...'

His anger threatening to overcome him, Josse
stood up, moving a couple of swift paces away
from her. 'I'm looking for Gervase,' he said
tetchily, 'and, as far as I can see, the business I
have with him is absolutely nothing to do with
you, with Meggie, or with the mysterious patient
you dragged her away to help you treat – if,
indeed, that's what you wanted with her, and I
don't know the truth of it because she didn't see

137

fit to tell me.'

The echoes of his loud voice rang through the sudden silence in the room. Then Sabin said meekly, 'I'm sorry, Josse.'

'Hrrmph.'

'I thought ... I mean, I had no reason to act as I did when I saw you down there in the yard.' Her tone was sweet, childlike. *She sounds*, Josse thought, *as if she's trying to get round me.* He'd played his part in the raising of three children, not to mention having lived cheek by jowl with Gus and Tilly's brood all their lives. He knew what wheedling sounded like. 'Could you – I don't suppose you could forget it happened?' She gave him a pretty, dimpled smile.

He snorted. 'Forget?' he repeated. 'Well, Sabin, I suppose I could try. But why should you—?'

She gave him no time to finish the question. Standing up and rushing to take his arm, she stood on tiptoe and kissed his cheek. 'Dear Josse, what a friend you are!' She was, he realized, gently but firmly walking him towards the door. 'Gervase is down at the lock-up. You'll find him there, or, more likely, cross paths with him on his way back here. He didn't expect to be gone long.' She opened the door, and ushered him through. 'Farewell!' she said brightly. 'Remember me to your family, won't you?'

Then the door was closed in his face.

As she predicted, he spotted Gervase riding towards him before he had gone a couple of hundred paces. In the brief interval between first seeing Gervase and being near enough to speak, Josse made up his mind not to mention Sabin's odd behaviour. It was probably some lurid woman's thing that had required her and Meggie's expertise, he told himself, and in all likelihood Sabin's rather dramatic reaction had been born of embarrassment.

In any case, Josse had a fair idea that Meggie would tell him, in her own good time. Hadn't she, after all, been waiting up for him the night after she'd returned from her mysterious outing? She'd actually said she wanted to talk to him, but then had added that it would keep till later.

It is for Sabin, not me, to raise this matter with Gervase, Josse thought. Resolutely he put it from his mind.

'Good day to you, Josse,' Gervase called out. 'You're looking for me?'

'Aye,' Josse agreed, returning the sheriff's smile. The two drew rein and, briefly and succinctly, Josse began to relate the little he knew about the two murdered young men.

Soon Gervase interrupted him. 'And they were apparently on their way to see Lord Wimarc. Yes, Josse, I already know. I'd have come to seek you out, if you hadn't found me first. Where are the bodies now?'

'The one found at the sanctuary is already in the crypt at Hawkenlye Abbey. The other one spent last night in my undercroft. Gus and Will are going to remove him to the abbey today.' Feeling that this perhaps required explanation, he added, 'It seems preferable to have both dead men in the same place, in case anyone turns up

139

looking for them.'

'Yes,' Gervase agreed. 'Is there anything to identify them?'

'One's called Symon.' Briefly Josse relayed how he knew. 'The other's his cousin.'

'Symon is not an uncommon name,' Gervase observed. 'And the descriptions, I suppose, could apply to many wealthy young men. I have no idea who they are.' He sighed. 'Wouldn't it be nice if, just once, we came across a dead body bearing a label with name, address and next of kin?'

Dismissing the question as rhetorical, Josse said, 'I had thought that someone should go up to Wealdsend to break the news of the men's deaths to Lord Robert.'

'I could send one of my men, if you're reluctant,' Gervase replied.

Josse considered the offer. It was tempting, he had to admit. He found the prospect of the reclusive lord of Wealdsend slightly alarming, and arriving to break news of the man's expected visitors' demise was hardly going to ensure a warm welcome. But experience had taught Josse that men who habitually shy away from tasks that alarm them soon become cowards. 'No, I'll go,' he said. 'After all, it was members of my household who found the bodies. The young man who Helewise tried to help, up at the sanctuary, actually died in her arms.'

'As you wish,' Gervase replied. 'Let me know how the business develops, Josse.' He frowned, his face darkening. 'I fear that perhaps...' He stopped, abruptly cutting off whatever thought he had been about to share. 'Never mind. Good-bye for now, Josse.'

With only a brief mental struggle, Josse was able to persuade himself that his mission to Lord Wimarc could wait a while. Far more urgent was the need to speak to Meggie. Although he had told himself repeatedly that this mysterious business with Sabin was a purely female affair, and nothing whatever to do with him, still it bothered him. This morning, Sabin had looked terrified, he recalled. And, he reminded himself, two nights ago Meggie had waited up specifically to talk to him...

Before I do anything else, I will go home and seek out my daughter, he thought. At the top of the long hill leading up out of Tonbridge, however, he turned first for the abbey. It was always possible that somebody had already come looking for the two young men, and his conscience compelled him to check. As he left Alfred in the stables, he noticed Eloise's mare. Barely pausing to return the greeting of the nun busy mucking out, he broke into a run and headed for Abbess Caliste's room.

'You have only just missed her, Sir Josse,' the abbess said. 'We needed her help with one of our patients, and one of my novices went out very early to ask her to come to the abbey.'

'But the mare she's riding is still in your stables,' Josse pointed out.

'Yes. Meggie asked if that would be all right. She's gone to her mother's hut.'

Josse smiled. 'Then may I ask permission to

141

leave Alfred in your care too?'

'Of course. Go and find her, Sir Josse.'

It was only as he strode up the narrow path to the clearing that it occurred to him to wonder if Meggie would welcome him. Although she was far too kind to say so, he knew full well that she often found the hectic family life at the House in the Woods wearisome, and in her heart she longed for the peaceful solitude of what had been her mother's special place. Would Meggie want him to approach? Joanna, Josse remembered painfully, had occasionally managed to disguise the hut's location when he had gone looking for her.

As he emerged into the clearing, he said a silent prayer of thanks that Meggie had never done the same.

So far.

He tapped softly on the door. 'Meggie? It's me.'

The door was flung open. 'Father, I'm so pleased to see you!' Meggie cried. She put her arms round him and hugged him. 'I've had ... I've been remembering, and...' She shook her head. 'I need to be distracted!' she said instead, with what sounded to Josse like a forced laugh. 'Come in, and I'll mix a hot drink for you.'

'Why do you need to be distracted?' he asked, going into the little room and closing the door.

Busy with packets of herbs and hot water, she did not meet his eye. 'Oh – Abbess Caliste asked me to speak to a poor old woman in the infirmary. She's been experiencing visions in which

142

she's seen dangerous things, and there's a possibility that unscrupulous men may try to use her for their own ends. It's all right, though.' She turned and flashed him a smile. 'Abbess Caliste will keep her safe.'

Now why, Josse wondered, *would that distress my daughter so?* It was not, he decided, looking at Meggie's set expression, the moment to pursue it.

He settled himself comfortably beside the hearth, and presently she put an earthenware mug into his hands, the contents of which smelt pleasantly sweet and spicy. He took a sip, then said, 'Meggie, I need to speak to you concerning Sabin. I saw her this morning – I was looking for Gervase – and something's wrong.' Meggie began to speak, but he held up a hand. 'I wasn't going to ask you about that mysterious mission you set off on with her, respecting as I do your perfectly correct professional discretion, but I'm worried, Meggie, and I really think I—'

'Father, I've been longing to tell you!' she interrupted, her expression tense. 'That's why I waited up for you the other night, when Helewise found the dying man at the sanctuary. I was going to confide in you, but you looked exhausted, and I reckoned you had enough to worry about. Then, last night, there was the body of the poor young man and, what with one thing and another, somehow there just hasn't been the opportunity to speak. Until now.' She gave him a smile. 'Here you are, the very person I could have wished for, because I can talk to you about Sabin and her patient and it'll stop me thinking about ... about something else,' she finished lamely.

Silently Josse reached out and took her hand. He held it for a moment, then said softly, 'I'm always here, Meggie.'

'I know,' she whispered. Then, with a very obvious effort, she sat up straight and said, 'Sabin took me to see the dead body of a patient. She had been treating him on behalf of his wife, who she was also treating, and her wish to help the wife led her to do something she really shouldn't have done. Then the man died, and she was very afraid that she would be blamed.'

Josse was horrified. 'So she wanted you to check to see if there was any sign of this treatment she prescribed for him? But, Meggie, that's terrible – it goes against every value that a healer ought to have!'

'I know, Father,' Meggie said calmly. 'It was very wrong of her, and also extremely unwise. But please, be assured that nothing Sabin did was in any way responsible for the man's death. She used a very small amount of something that is potentially dangerous, but, had it been in sufficient quantities to kill him, it would have done so straight away.' She paused, her brown eyes intent on his. 'He was murdered. Either through luck or uncommon skill, someone stuck a long, thin blade right into his heart.'

Josse had a dreadful feeling that he already knew the answer to his next question, but he asked it anyway. 'Who was this man?'

And his daughter said, 'Benedict de Vitré.'

He buried his face in his hands. Then, his voice

144

muffled, he said, 'You'd better tell me the whole story.'

Some time later, still digesting Meggie's dramatic revelations, Josse got up to go. He did not like leaving Meggie in the hut, but she was adamant. 'I'll come home when I'm ready,' she told him gently.

'But it's not safe to travel alone, and—'

'It won't be for a few days, though,' Meggie interrupted him. 'Abbess Caliste asked me to stay at the abbey for a while, and help them with the old woman I spoke of. Don't worry, Father.' She reached for his hand. 'I know your rule about not riding by myself.'

She didn't, he noticed, say that she would *obey* it. Trudging back to the abbey to collect Alfred, Josse wished that his daughter had a little less of her mother's independence.

He would have liked to turn for home. He wanted more than anything to tell Helewise what Meggie had just revealed. Fascinated as he was with wondering how the killer could have inflicted such a wound, and with what weapon, he hadn't even begun to consider the wider implications, and he itched to share them with his old friend. But there was something else he had to do first and, reluctantly, he turned Alfred's head to the left and, once again, set off for Wealdsend.

This time he followed the track that ran along between the two wooded ridges, and presently Lord Robert Wimarc's dwelling appeared, at the head of the shallow hanging valley opening up before him. It was quite hard to make out the details of the little settlement, for pockets of mist swirled in the valley, giving the illusion that Wealdsend was appearing and disappearing. It seemed, however, to consist of a long, low hall, beside which rose up a slender watchtower on a low rise. There might have been a curl of smoke from the roof of the hall, or it might have been a fragment of mist.

Josse remembered Helewise's description: *It is well placed, on the northern edge of the High Weald. The prudent men who originally built a dwelling place there sited it wisely, for, whilst it is itself sheltered in a fold of the hills, its tower commands a view right over the valley.*

Here was the valley, here was Wealdsend, and there was the tower. It was, Josse appreciated, a perfectly sited stronghold, and so well hidden in the landscape that, even now, it was quite difficult to make it out.

It was a lonely, haunted place. Josse felt a shiver of fear crawl up his back.

You have a job to do, he told himself firmly. *Get on with it.*

He put his heels to Alfred's sides and rode on up the track to Wealdsend.

The settlement was enclosed by a tall paling fence, and the upper ends of the supporting wooden stakes were sharpened to points. On the outer edge of the fence a ditch had been dug. Josse rode up to the gate, which was closed and, he discovered, locked. Standing up in the stirrups, he peered down into the deserted yard. He

146

called out, 'Halloa! Is anyone there? I wish to speak to Lord Robert Wimarc. Is he within?'

There was no reply. Josse gazed out at the long, low hall, at the scatter of outbuildings, at the tall tower up on its hump. No door opened; no one came on hurrying feet to enquire what the visitor wanted with the lord.

Strange, he thought. Today, Wealdsend was deserted. Yet only four days ago, two bright young men had called at Hawkenlye Abbey to ask the way to this very place. Had Lord Wimarc been expecting them? Or had they come without invitation, confident of finding the lord in residence?

Josse called out once more. 'Halloa the house! I wish to speak to Lord Wimarc, for I bring ill tidings!'

Still there was no response. The mist swirled, a solitary crow cawed as if in warning, and Wealdsend dreamed on.

The earlier shiver of fear came back again, more strongly now. Josse turned Alfred's head and, kicking the horse into sudden action, hurried away.

Wealdsend was not deserted.

Inside the great hall, an elderly man sat beside the hearth. The fire was small but hot, burning with a fierce intensity that gave off a minimum of smoke, for the old man wished to give the illusion that Wealdsend was unoccupied. He had taken the precaution of fetching blankets and a fur rug against the cold, and he was warmly wrapped as he sat on his cushions in his oak

147

chair.

He stared into the bright flames, absently turning the ring with the huge citrine.

He had suffered a great shock. Sheer mischance had almost ruined a year of meticulous planning. When he thought about how nearly the whole careful edifice had come to crashing down around his ears, it made his heart lurch painfully.

Do not dwell upon it, he commanded himself coldly.

He wondered who had come calling. He had made out a male voice, shouting something about wanting to speak to Lord Robert Wimarc.

The old man's bony face cracked into a grimace, or it might have been a smile.

Nobody could speak to Lord Wimarc now, he mused, for he was occupied, to the exclusion of everything else, with his great scheme.

Which, so far, despite what had almost happened, was proceeding just as it should.

NINE

At the close of what had seemed an endless day, at long last Josse was exactly where he wanted to be: sitting beside his own fire, mug of wine in his hand, belly comfortably full from Tilly's excellent evening meal and, with the rest of the household retired for the night, alone with Helewise.

As soon as he knew they would not be overheard, Josse leaned close to Helewise and revealed to her what Meggie had told him about Benedict de Vitré's murder.

Her eyes widened. 'Meggie is sure of this? And the death really could not have come about because of some natural cause?'

'No. Apparently not,' he replied.

There was quite a long silence. Then Helewise said softly, 'Who would have wanted Benedict de Vitré dead?'

'His wife, for one.' Quietly, Josse repeated to her what Meggie had told him regarding the potions prepared by Sabin for Lady Richenza.

'But he was not killed by any potion,' Helewise pointed out. 'Anyway,' she added, 'for a wife to wish to free herself from a fat, ugly and cruel husband's attentions is one thing. For her to resort to killing him is quite another.'

149

'She didn't mind administering a potion that would render him impotent,' Josse remarked.

'But that is hardly the same as killing him!' Helewise flashed back. 'Besides, from what we are told, Lady Richenza is small and slight in stature, and little more than a child. Can you in truth see such a girl possessing the strength and the skill to wield that slim and deadly killing blade?'

'It need not have been her own delicate hand that did the deed,' Josse replied. 'Lady Richenza was wife to a very wealthy man. Is it not possible that, in her despair, she helped herself to the means to employ another to kill him for her?'

'No, I do not think so,' Helewise said firmly. 'She had already taken measures to rid herself both of her husband's ardour and the possibility of bearing his child,' she added reasonably. 'With those ends achieved, she surely had no need to kill him.'

'Hmm.' Josse was not convinced.

'I can think of others who might have wished Lord Benedict dead,' Helewise pressed on. 'As we ourselves know from our own experience, he was ruthless and brutal in his work for the king. He took and took again, having no mind for the miseries he and his men left in their wake. His men *murdered* people, Josse – surely you have not forgotten that poor family who drowned when Lord Benedict's thugs drove them into the river?'

'I have not forgotten,' Josse grunted. 'You think, then, that someone decided to have their revenge? Some man who lost his gold and his

150

property to the king's coffers via Lord Benedict's collectors, or who was forced to watch his loved ones suffer in the wake of such theft, just happens to be skilled with the assassin's blade?'

'I don't know,' Helewise admitted. 'It is unlikely, I suppose, but I do, however, see it as *less* unlikely than Lady Richenza hiring a killer.'

'Hmm,' Josse said again.

'There is another possibility,' Helewise said after a while. 'According to what we have learned from Meggie and, via her, from Sabin, Lord Benedict was spending lavishly before his death. The manor house was being extended; apparently the lord and his lady were richly dressed, and Lady Richenza wears costly jewels.' She hesitated.

'Go on,' Josse prompted.

'It is perhaps foolish,' she said with a smile, 'but I reason like this: Lord Benedict was collecting revenues on behalf of the king, but, to judge by his own recent expenditure, it is almost certain that he was creaming off a portion of what he amassed for his own benefit.'

'It is always possible that King John knew and approved,' Josse interrupted. 'Benedict was working hard for him, and the king can be generous when the mood takes him.'

Helewise glanced at him, one eyebrow raised. Her grey eyes held a worldly expression, as if to say, *really?*

'Perhaps,' she went on after a moment, 'some truly loyal follower of the king discovered what Lord Benedict was up to and took the necessary steps to stop him.'

'Very *drastic* steps,' Josse remarked. He thought about it. 'It's possible, I grant you, for men tend to lose their heads and their hearts when they fall under King John's spell.' She opened her mouth to reply, but he forestalled her. 'Possible, but not, I think, probable. It is more likely that a true king's man, with proof of Lord Benedict's perfidy, would report the matter direct to the king.' *And John*, he thought, *would have taken his own revenge, and Benedict's death would have been far longer and more excruciating than a swift blade straight into the heart.*

It was not a thought to share with Helewise.

She was nodding slowly. 'You are right, I suppose,' she admitted, 'although I cannot shake off the thought that this death is somehow connected with what Lord Benedict was doing for the king.'

'Perhaps King John *did* come to hear what Benedict was up to,' Josse said, 'and managed to swallow back his fury and his desire to ... er, to make an example of the man. Perhaps it was John himself who sent a silent killer to make Benedict pay for what he had done.'

Helewise stared at him, wide-eyed. 'Do you really think him capable of such a deed?' she whispered.

Josse had spoken in ironic jest, frustrated by the discussion that seemed to proceed without reaching any sensible conclusion. But, the more he thought about his last suggestion, the more he thought it could just be possible. 'He'd be more likely, I suppose, to make a public accusation

152

and have Lord Benedict punished as an example to others tempted to do the same,' he acknowledged, 'but then our king must be aware that he is not popular, and such a high-handed gesture against an important lord could easily turn against him.' He fell silent, thinking.

'So?' Helewise prompted. 'Do you believe King John capable of sending a secret assassin to do away with someone?'

'Aye,' Josse said gruffly. 'Of course I do.'

'You should speak to Gervase again,' Helewise urged him the next morning as they sat beside the fire with welcome warming drinks. The weather had turned colder. 'Four people now know that Lord Benedict did not die a natural death, but was murdered by a skilled and no doubt practised hand. It is not up to you, me, Meggie or Sabin to bring the killer to justice. That's Gervase's job.'

She was right, and Josse knew it. 'But what if Sabin hasn't told him about the potions she prepared for Lady Richenza?'

'That is a matter for Sabin,' Helewise replied firmly. 'That young woman is more than capable of looking after herself,' she muttered.

'And we do have Meggie's assurance that it was nothing in Sabin's medicaments that killed him,' Josse mused. 'Very well,' he said, making up his mind and abruptly standing up. 'I shall do as you suggest, and perhaps, as far as this household is concerned, that can be the end of it.'

She looked up at him, smiling. 'Leaving you with no mysterious death to wonder about and

153

tease to a conclusion?' she murmured. 'Oh, dear Josse, I don't think you'd like that.'

'There's still the matter of the two bright young men,' he reminded her.

Her happy expression saddened, and instantly he regretted having reminded her. 'I had forgotten them for the moment,' she whispered. 'Oh, how *could* I? Josse, will you call in at the abbey on your way back from Tonbridge? Maybe someone will have come to claim them.'

Briefly he put a hand on her shoulder, giving it a squeeze. 'I will.'

Despite Helewise's remarks about Sabin, Josse still felt awkward at the prospect of telling her husband what she had done. As he set off, Josse thought it over. It was not, he had to conclude, a very responsible action for a healer, and particularly not when the healer in question was married to the sheriff of Tonbridge, and so had his reputation as well as her own to consider. But, as Helewise had said, it was a matter for Sabin...

I shall not mention it, Josse resolved as he rode down the long hill into Tonbridge. *If Gervase does, then I shall just have to tell the truth and hope for the best.*

But he found Gervase far too preoccupied with other urgent business to waste any time lamenting the behaviour of his wife.

'There's a nest of them staying up at the castle,' Gervase fumed as soon as Josse was inside his hall and seated by the hearth. There was no sign of Sabin, for which Josse was very

154

grateful. 'The de Clares are keeping their heads down, as if they don't want to be associated with Fitzwalter's lot. Some say they aren't even in residence, although I am fairly certain that the old man and his son are there.'

'A nest of what?' Josse demanded, stretching out his hands to the fire's warmth. 'Or is it who? And what is it that the de Clares are dissociating themselves from?'

Gervase leaned back in his chair, momentarily closing his eyes. 'I wish I knew, Josse. I can only surmise, however, and my conclusions make me very uneasy.'

Josse had rarely seen his old friend look so troubled. The two of them had had their dif- erences – on occasion, Josse had considered that Gervase could have stood out more firmly against some of the worst excesses perpetrated in the king's name – but, nevertheless, Gervase's fine-boned, pale face and anxious expression concerned him. 'Go on.'

Gervase opened his eyes again, turning to Josse. Leaning closer, he said very quietly, 'This must remain strictly between the two of us, Josse. Should word ever come back to me that I even *thought* about saying what I'm about to say, I shall deny it. You understand?'

Worried now, Josse muttered his assent.

His mouth close to Josse's ear, Gervase said, 'You are aware, no doubt, of what will happen next, should the king not accept the Pope's terms for ending the interdict and the excommuni- cation?' Before Josse could respond, Gervase answered his own question. 'Innocent will declare him formally deposed, which will relieve his subjects of all allegiance to him. The Pope will then grant the kingdom to Philip Augustus of France, who'll no doubt waste no time in saddling up his army, kitting them out for war, and ferrying them over the narrow seas to claim his new territory for him.'

Josse had heard the rumours. Foreknowledge, however, did not make them any less disturbing. 'You think it will come to that?'

Gervase shrugged. 'Who can say? Possibly. *Probably*, for the king is intransigent.'

'What has this to do with the men gathered at the castle?'

'Hush, Josse! Not so loud!' Gervase hissed. 'Their leader is Nicholas Fitzwalter.'

It was clear from Gervase's face that the name should mean something to Josse. Beyond a very faint memory of some mention of the man, it didn't. Josse looked enquiringly at Gervase.

'Good Lord above, Josse, you do bury yourself away out there in those woods of yours,' Gervase muttered. 'You should at least try to keep up with what's happening in the world. Nicholas Fitzwalter speaks for a large faction of discontented barons, and his eloquence in describing their grievances against the king has won him fame. Or perhaps I should say infamy.'

'You'd better tell me what these grievances are,' Josse replied, 'although even a wood-dwelling innocent such as I can probably guess most of them.'

Gervase grinned briefly. 'Yes, you probably can,' he agreed. 'It's a predictable litany of misdemeanours: they complain of the king's financial ruses, perpetually bleeding from them what remains of their wealth. They are heartily sick of the constant fines, and what our great monarch is pleased to refer to as reliefs, although the only man to gain much relief is John himself. They complain that he forces the destruction of castles said to have been built or fortified without his express approval. They moan that no castle or estate left in his wardship is safe from his ruthless depredations and, allied to that, they are furious that he marries off heiresses and wealthy widows to men who are unworthy of them, with no thought but his own profit. And – this seems to be what chiefly enrages them – there are the forest laws.'

'The forest laws,' Josse echoed dully. 'Of course.'

'Lords and their hunting,' Gervase said wryly. 'You know what they're like.'

'Indeed I do.'

Leaning close again, Gervase whispered, 'Do not think, Josse, that Fitzwalter and his faction are prompted by anything but self-preservation. They have no thought for the lot of the poor, suffering common folk; they have but one aim, and that is to limit the power of the king so that he can no longer milk them as he does.'

Josse nodded slowly. *I am not surprised*, he thought. *I have lived too long on this good earth to expect men to be altruistic.* 'How widespread is the support for this ... this faction?' he asked.

'It is by no means universal,' Gervase said swiftly. 'Many barons are still loyal to the king.'

Lowering his voice, he added, 'Fitzwalter is, I believe, organizing no more than an offensive of words: he and the other barons wish to persuade others to their cause. They will use whatever means they can drag up to persuade others to their viewpoint, and I fear it will be a dirty fight. It is to this end that they gather here, in my own town.' He gave an expression of disgust. 'Why did it have to be here?' he muttered angrily.

'You said earlier that rumours claim the de Clares are not in evidence,' Josse reminded him. 'Yet you believe they are there?'

'I do,' Gervase agreed. 'Old Richard de Clare is no supporter of the king, and his son – that's Gilbert – follows where his father leads. They may not yet have declared themselves, but, before long, they will. Of that I am convinced.'

'I'll take your word for it, since I know little about either man.' Josse leaned on one arm of his chair, going over all that he had just heard.

'They've got an influential Cistercian with them at the castle.' Gervase's quiet voice broke in on Josse's musings. 'Ralph of Odiham. Do you know of him?'

'No,' Josse admitted. 'I do know that the Cistercian order have no love for King John.' All religious houses, he reflected, had suffered greatly under the interdict, but the king's treatment of the Cistercian order had been particularly harsh and humiliating.

Gervase was nodding. 'Ralph of Odiham's a power in the Order, and it seems he's throwing his weight behind this Battle monk who's being paraded about. He's attached himself to the lad like a burr to your cloak hem, and Caleb too is here in the town.'

'Caleb. Is that his name?'

'They're using him, Josse,' Gervase said angrily, ignoring the question. 'Caleb's an innocent, and he's speaking from the heart when he says these terrible times are God's punishment for our wickedness. That's all very well in a monastery,' he went on, 'where they've got nothing else to do but pray all day, but it's a different matter for we who have to make a life of some sort out in the world. Why, we—'

It sounded, Josse reflected, as if Gervase was winding up for a long complaint. 'Why is this Caleb in Tonbridge?' he interrupted. He didn't think it was the moment to take issue with Gervase's assertion that those in the religious life did nothing but pray, but, nevertheless, he felt a moment's hot fury on behalf of Abbess Caliste and her people.

That question seemed to further anger Gervase. Leaning close again, he lowered his voice and said, 'I don't know for sure, but my men keep their ears and their eyes open, and they reckon Nicholas Fitzwalter's had spies out, searching the country for people like Caleb who are prepared to speak out loud against what the K— er, what's being done in our land.'

Even here, within his own four walls, he is afraid to utter what he would like to say, Josse thought sadly.

'A trio of wool merchants arrived here from Battle not long before Caleb was brought into the town,' Gervase went on in a practically inaudible whisper. 'At least, they said they were merchants. Rumour has it that they have now thrown off their lowly disguises and, dressed in their true and considerably more wealthy colours, are now up at the castle with Fitzwalter and his faction.' He sighed. 'Who knows how many others are out there, combing England for poor, helpless saps like Caleb who don't begin to understand the peril of mixing with ruthless and unscrupulous men?'

Unscrupulous men. Now what, Josse wondered, did that bring to mind?

He heard Meggie's voice in his head, clear as a bell. *She's been experiencing visions in which she's seen dangerous things, and there's a possibility that unscrupulous men may try to use her for their own ends.*

Aye, that was it – she'd been telling him about some old girl she'd been called to see in Hawkenlye's infirmary. *Abbess Caliste will keep her safe*, she had reassured him.

But what if some agent of Nicholas Fitzwalter already knew about this woman and her 'dangerous things'? How safe would Hawkenlye's walls prove to be, against a deputation from the barons now collecting in Tonbridge Castle?

Suddenly he was on his feet, striding across the hall towards the door. 'Josse, where are you going?' Gervase called after him, sounding half-amused, half-angry.

'Something I must do,' Josse replied.

Gervase hurried over to him, a detaining hand on his arm. 'But you haven't told me why you're here! What did you want to see me about?'

160

Josse cursed under his breath. Gervase's ranting had driven his mission right out of his head. Briefly he debated with himself: was there time to tell Gervase about Benedict de Vitré's murder, or should he hurry straight up to the abbey to check on the old woman in the infirmary?

A few moments will not hurt, he told himself.

Turning to face Gervase, he told him what Meggie had discovered on Lord Benedict's dead body.

By long custom, on arriving at Hawkenlye Abbey Josse went first to see its abbess. As she rose to greet him, he remembered Helewise's request. He returned her greeting, then said, 'Is there any news regarding the two dead young men?'

'No,' Abbess Caliste said sadly. 'I find it inconceivable that nobody has missed them, but, as yet, none have come asking about them.'

'I tried to take the news to Lord Wimarc,' Josse said, 'but Wealdsend appeared to be deserted.'

'How strange, when it was the poor young men's destination,' the abbess remarked. 'They cannot have been expected, then.'

Josse shrugged. 'Who can say?'

The abbess was studying him intently. 'Sir Josse, I sense that you are here on another matter,' she said, 'for you have an air of distraction.'

'Aye, my lady,' he agreed. 'Meggie tells me you have an old woman in your care, who you believe may be in danger because of certain visions she has experienced?'

'Lilas of Hamhurst.' The abbess nodded.

'Indeed we do, and Meggie, I believe, is with her even now. Would you like to come and meet her?'

As soon as he and the abbess stepped out into the cloister, Josse knew something was amiss. It was the noise – that great clamour of shouting male voices, interspersed with shrill female laughter, was something you never normally heard inside the abbey's walls.

Abbess Caliste, her face set in stern, angry lines, marched off towards the source of the noise, and Josse hurried to keep pace with her. 'Be careful, my lady,' he warned. 'There is violence in the air.'

She shot him a swift look. 'Violence or not, something is disturbing the peace of Hawkenlye Abbey, Sir Josse, and the maintenance of that peace is *my* responsibility.'

He had no option but to follow her.

They emerged from the shelter of the cloisters into the wide open space between the main gates and the east face of the great abbey church. It was full of a thronging, surging press of people. They represented all stations of life, from barefoot, ill-fed, gap-toothed peasants to lordly men in warm, fur-lined cloaks and fine leather boots. Among the rags and the brilliant colours, two figures stood out: one was dressed entirely in the black habit of a Benedictine monk, and the other in the plain white wool and black scapular of the Cistercians.

On the fringes of the pushing, heaving crowd, small groups of the Hawkenlye nuns, monks and lay brethren stood, mouths open in amazement at this extraordinary intrusion. Abbess Caliste, with Josse as close at her side as if he were tethered, elbowed her way to where Sister Liese and Meggie stood, outside the small rear door of the infirmary. The infirmarer was trying vainly to hush the crowd and commanding them to have some respect for the sick and the dying in her care.

Meggie smiled in relief as she caught sight of Josse, detaching herself from Sister Liese and hurrying over to him.

'They just shoved their way in, all those lords and ladies and the gaggle of hangers-on,' she said breathlessly, 'and they certainly didn't bother with asking anyone's permission, and—'

'What on earth is going on, Sister?' the abbess shouted. 'Who are all these people?'

Josse's old friend Brother Saul appeared, panting with the effort of fighting a path through the crowd. Catching Meggie's words, he shoved his way through to the abbess and cried, 'We tried to tell the men, my lady abbess, that they must speak to you first and ask your permission – me, Sister Teresa and Brother Luke, that is.' Briefly he indicated the nun on duty in the porteress's hut and the lay brother who, judging by the pitchfork in his hands, had been mucking out the stables. 'We told that lord fellow over there – the tall one in the blue cloak, him with that band of guards lurking round him – since he seems to be in charge, but he said they had a right to be heard, and the people must know the truth, and we—'

A ferocious shout cut off Saul's anxious words. *'Listen!'* a deep, authoritative male voice cried. 'Hear the words of our holy monk here, who has seen the *truth*!'

Spinning round, Josse saw that someone had dragged up trestles and boards to set up a makeshift platform, on to which the Cistercian, the Benedictine and the tall man in the blue cloak were clambering; it was the latter who had shouted. The gang of burly men, who Saul had indicated as guards, had taken up positions around the foot of the platform. At Josse's side, the abbess made to move forward, her expression thunderous, but, sensing again the threat of violence thrumming in the air, Josse grabbed her hand, holding her back. Waving his arm, he indicated the fascinated, avid faces all around. They had come here for a show, and they were not going to give it up. He said into Abbess Caliste's ear, 'My lady, if you try to stop this now, you risk a riot, in which many innocent people will undoubtedly be hurt.' Even as he spoke, someone pushed forward against the platform, and instantly one of the guards swung a heavy club and forced the man back. Instinctively, Josse put his free arm round Meggie, drawing her close.

He had always thought of Caliste as a level-headed, wise woman. Never had he been so glad to be proved right.

Still holding her hand, he felt the tension ease. Shooting him a furious look, she wrested herself out of his grasp. 'Very well, Sir Josse,' she said icily. 'Since there appears to be no choice, we will listen to what this lord would have us hear.'

The man in the blue cloak had thrust out his chest, a gesture which had set his cloak swinging, revealing a sword at his side. *He has a sword, and his men have clubs,* Josse thought. *They dare to come armed into this holy place.* Josse's apprehension grew. The man looked around the crowd ranged below him, eyes narrowed as he waited for silence. He had a thin, hawkish face, with pale and strangely unblinking eyes, and a long nose that came to a sharp point. Such was his air of command that, quite quickly, he got the silence he wanted.

'I am Nicholas Fitzwalter,' he announced, 'as many of you will already know.'

There were murmurs of assent, and someone yelled out, 'We know you all right, Lord Nick!'

Smiling, he suppressed the brief noise with his outstretched hands. 'I have not summoned you here to listen to me,' he went on, 'but to hear the words of another: one who has heard the voice of our Lord God, and who wishes to share His words with you!'

The startling announcement was greeted for an instant with dead silence. Then a soft buzz of excited comment spread through the crowd.

Watching the trio on the platform, Josse sensed all was not well. The Benedictine (young, pale and clearly frightened) was pleading with the Cistercian (older, his very stance expressive of authority) and Josse was all but certain the young monk was not at all happy ... He let his gaze roam around the crowd, studying the expressions. The mood of expectation seemed to

165

be steadily growing.

'Behold,' Fitzwalter shouted above the growing hum of excited chatter, 'I present to you Caleb of Battle! Hear, my friends, what he has to say, for he speaks for God himself!'

Even Josse, some way away, heard the agonized squeak of Caleb's reply: 'I don't! Oh, *I don't* – I never claimed that, no man has the right to speak for God! I just...' He lowered his voice to a whisper.

I need to hear exactly what passes between these men, Josse thought. He edged through the crowd until he was standing just beneath the platform, and the abbess came with him. He looked up at Caleb, taking in the extreme pallor and the shiny film of greasy sweat on the emaciated face. The black robe was threadbare, poorly darned here and there, and dotted with crusty stains.

Caleb was still stuttering his protest. But then Fitzwalter raised his arms and, as if conducting a heavenly choir, roused the great crowd. The rest of Caleb's attempt to explain himself was drowned in a tumult of clapping, stamping, whistles, yells and catcalls.

Fitzwalter waited, nodding as his eyes roamed round the crowd, then abruptly shouted for quiet. He nudged Caleb forward, and the young monk stumbled on the rickety platform. Fitzwalter, his frustration evident, said something to the Cistercian, who, grim-faced, nodded.

The Cistercian moved to the front of the platform. 'Brother Caleb is struck with shyness,' he said, one eyebrow raised ironically, 'which is

166

readily understandable, he being more used to the solitude of his cell than the company of his fellow men and women.' There were a few guffaws, and someone made a very imaginative suggestion as to how Caleb probably spent his time in the privacy of his cell, which drew a swift riposte from the other side of the crowd and a lot more laughter. The Cistercian let the ribaldry continue for a few moments, then, with a smile, said loudly, 'I am Ralph of Odiham, and I am a monk of Beaulieu Abbey.' He glanced at Caleb, standing red-faced, hanging his head. 'I have Brother Caleb's permission to speak on his behalf.'

At that Caleb's head shot up, and he looked fearfully at Ralph. He appeared to say something, but Ralph ploughed on regardless. 'Caleb has been granted a vision from God,' he said dramatically, 'and he says—'

If, by speaking for Caleb, the Cistercian had hoped to prompt him to speech, the ruse had succeeded. Hastening to stand beside Ralph of Odiham, Caleb cried, 'I didn't have a vision, not really! It's just ... I just feel...' The prominent Adam's apple bobbed in the thin throat as the young monk swallowed nervously. Then he burst out: 'It's a punishment! All this – what we're suffering – the hunger, never enough to eat, the sickness, the monstrous herd of deer, the red moon – it's God's punishment, see, because we've been bad!'

In a very obvious prompt, Brother Ralph said, 'It's a judgement on how we're being ruled, isn't it, Caleb?' He leaned and whispered in Caleb's

167

ear. 'Go on! Tell them!' he urged.

Perhaps Caleb realized that to comply was the only way to end his agony of embarrassment, and be allowed to get down off the platform. With one last, despairing look at Ralph, he muttered something inaudible.

'Louder,' commanded Brother Ralph.

Caleb looked out over the crowd. There were tears in his eyes. Then he opened his mouth wide and shouted, 'These terrible times we're having – it's all a judgement on the king!'

TEN

While the attention of every man and woman in the abbey's forecourt was fixed on the young monk on the platform, Nicholas Fitzwalter had caught the eye of an unremarkable man in a dowdy travelling cloak who stood just behind the ring of guards at the foot of the platform. Unnoticed by anyone except the man himself, Fitzwalter jerked his head infinitesimally in the direction of the infirmary.

Moving slowly and steadily, the man in the dark cloak slid through the crowds and melted away.

His name was Henri de Fougères and, only a short while ago, he had been on the other side of the Channel. In answer to the people who had demanded to know his business there (few in number, for Henri could adopt a forbidding countenance when he felt like it, and there was a sense of strength and danger about him that discouraged idle questions) he had muttered that he was a wool merchant seeking out new markets.

In fact he knew little more than the next man about the wool trade. Together with a small group of trusted companions, also in the guise of merchants, he had been sent out some weeks back to begin his clandestine work. His companions had remained in England, but Henri had been sent to France on a very different mission. With communications from some of the most discontented of England's barons tucked away inside his tunic, he had sought out those in Paris who had the ear of Philip Augustus, in the hope of thus obtaining news of the French king's current policy concerning his troublesome fellow monarch on the other side of the narrow seas. Henri of Fougères was subtle, highly intelligent and very patient, and he did not leave France until he had what he came for.

On the way back to the master who had sent him, Henri had put up for the night at a shabby inn in a small Kent village. There he had overheard the ravings of an old woman, and an idea had formed in his ever-active mind. Having proposed the scheme to his master, who had instantly seen its advantages, Henri had returned to collect her.

The suppression of his fury at discovering she was no longer there had caused him such a crippling pain in the right side of his forehead that he had been temporarily blind. But Henri de Fougères was not a man who was easily dissuaded. He had not achieved his current position – deep inside the trust of his ruthless master – by giving up at the first fence.

Now, pulling his soft, wide-brimmed hat forward to conceal his face, he opened the small rear door of the Hawkenlye infirmary just a crack, and slipped inside.

Out in the forecourt, Josse, Meggie and the abbess stood watching a scene of pandemonium. Throughout the crowd, people were turning to each other in amazement. *Did you hear what he said? Did he really say that? Surely not! He's either very brave or totally out of his head!*

Caleb was still weeping, clutching pathetically at Ralph of Odiham's white sleeve, and the older monk, slowly shaking his head, was staring at him with an exaggerated expression of horror. Then, as if responding to the crowd's astounded response, Ralph shook off Caleb's clenched fingers, stepped to the front of the platform and shouted, 'Poor Caleb is disturbed, and not himself!'

His deep voice penetrated the first few ranks of the crowd and, seeing he had more to say, people began shushing each other. Ralph waited. When the noise subsided, he said, 'We are deeply concerned for Brother Caleb. He has just expressed what I must stress is purely his own opinion; one which Lord Nicholas and I do not – indeed, cannot – share.' He turned and looked pityingly at the young monk, now visibly shaking. There were a few protests and whistles from the braver members of the throng, but Ralph was more than ready for them. 'I am a man of God!' he shouted, eyes wide as if to express his innocence. 'And Lord Nicholas Fitzwalter is a powerful figure!' It was a timely reminder, and had the effect of silencing the last of the protests. Then, in a calm, carrying voice, Brother Ralph proclaimed, 'God save and protect our beloved King!'

Josse became aware of Abbess Caliste, fuming beside him with barely controlled fury. 'They *made* the poor man say that, about ... about *him*!' she hissed. 'We only heard that Cistercian forcing him to speak out because we were right at the front. Everyone else will believe he said it entirely of his own volition!' She clenched her hands into tight fists. 'Then instantly they dissociated themselves from him, leaving him looking like the only person who thinks it! Oh, Sir Josse, how could they be so calculating? So cruel?'

'Aye, I know,' Josse said heavily. He had been disgusted by what he had just witnessed. Fitzwalter and the Cistercian were ruthless: wanting to put the dangerous words out in the open yet too clever to risk uttering them themselves, they had used the weak, unworldly and malleable Caleb.

How long, he wondered, would it take for word of this to reach the king? And what would John do? Was there any way that Hawkenlye could offer protection to the poor young monk? It would be hard, if not impossible, given that he seemed to be the protégé of Fitzwalter and the Cistercian, who, Josse was quite sure, hadn't finished with him yet. There would be other platforms, other places where people would gather to hear the powerful men's mouthpiece do their work for them, and they...

Oh, dear God.

In a flash, Josse remembered what he had come to the abbey to do. Horror swept through him. Spinning round to the abbess, he said, 'Lilas!'

'Oh, *no*!' Meggie sounded horrified; he knew she was thinking the same. Before Josse could move, she was off.

Even as Abbess Caliste's hands flew to her mouth, he was grabbing her sleeve, dragging her with him. Ruthlessly he shoved aside men, women, lords, ladies. He lunged for the small rear door of the infirmary, flinging it open. The abbess followed him inside.

'Where is she?' he demanded.

'Follow me,' she panted.

She ran down the ward, stopping at a curtained-off recess. She flung back the curtain, revealing a narrow cot covered with a couple of blankets, neatly folded. Meggie stood beside it, head bowed.

Other than Meggie, there was nobody there.

A day's ride away, King John sat in his private quarters in the Tower. He was looking out through a narrow slit of a window at the bright, late-autumn day beyond. The wide waters of the Thames slipped past, the slow, steady movement

172

stilling his ever-busy mind and body, encouraging introspection. He had eaten well, and sampled a new consignment of white Rhine wine, delicately spiced and quite delicious. He was whistling softly to himself, entirely content.

His confidence was riding high, and he was in the sort of bullish mood that made him feel invincible. He was still gloating over that summer's victory over the rebel Welsh lords. With a private smile, he turned his thoughts back to August, when he had led his army across the Conwy River, penetrated Snowdonia, burned Bangor and, in a glorious finale to his magnificent campaign, succeeded in capturing its bishop.

He wondered if his enemy Llewellyn was still smarting. It had been a sweet moment, when the man had finally accepted the inevitable and agreed to come to terms. Even sweeter was his choice of emissary: Llewellyn had sent his wife Joan, John's own daughter, to negotiate with the king.

John grinned at the memory. His daughter had clearly been embarrassed, until the ironic humour of the situation had struck her. She'd pointed out that, if John went ahead with his threat to strip Llewellyn of every last possession, then she'd have no option but to turn to her father, and she reminded him that she'd never been satisfied with anything but the best. She wasn't his daughter for nothing.

In triumphant mood, John had ignored those miserably cautious close advisers who had whispered that the surrender was not all it seemed.

That, in the light of all his long experience with Llewellyn ap Iorwerth, the king might do well to consider that, just possibly, the Welsh prince was merely playing for time. *They say he is close with Philip Augustus*, the anxious lords murmured in his ear. *Is it not possible, my Lord King, that Llewellyn plans in secret to negotiate with the French in order to strike back?*

King John ignored the doubters. Most of the time, anyway. But he was clever – too clever not to wonder, just occasionally, if there was any basis to the fears. The Welsh lords whom Llewellyn had antagonized, and forced over to John's side, were mercurial, touchy, easily offended, and basically, John had to admit, unreliable. They were quite capable of deciding they didn't want to support him after all – they were to a man notoriously unreasonable – upon which they'd all decamp and go straight back to Llewellyn.

I can do nothing for the moment, except watch and wait, John reflected.

He turned his thoughts over the narrow seas to the homeland of his great enemy. Philip Augustus's alliance with Pope Innocent was alarming, yes, but then grave problems tended to be the spur that brought about good, strong resolutions. The threat posed by the union of two such formidable enemies had forced John to form an alliance of his own. Extending his hand, he counted on his fingers those he had won over to his side: Renault of Dammartin, who controlled Boulogne; Count Ferdinand of Flanders; Raymond of Toulouse, who was married to John's sister Joan; and Otto, the Holy Roman Emperor, and son of John's sister Matilda.

Sisters and daughters, John mused. As well as being decorative, they certainly had their uses.

He stared out at the bright autumn sky. The alliance was not yet complete, for his aim was to form an iron chain that ran through all the lands bordering France, and he was considering how best to win over the princes of Boulogne, Flanders, Lorraine and the Netherlands. Good God, he was even wondering about a temporary liaison with the Duke of Brabant, a man so notoriously devious that they said he was unable to lie straight in bed...

His thoughts sped on.

Presently they turned, as they invariably did, to his struggle with the Pope.

During the previous summer he had permitted the papal legate, Pandulph, to enter England to discuss the Pope's terms for ending the interdict and excommunication. The terms were brutal and uncompromising: John must accept Pope Innocent's original candidate, Stephen Langton, as Archbishop of Canterbury, and he must also reinstate all the exiled bishops and return their confiscated property.

John had refused. For the sake of pride – and also for greed, since the latter condition would severely impoverish him – he had had no option.

Pandulph will come again, he now mused. Either him, or another just like him. In a deep recess of his mind – one he rarely visited – John nursed a secret fear. By no other will than his own, and acting entirely alone, he had slipped

175

from under the dominion of the Pope and the Church. He and he alone ruled England, and the priests had fled. His fear was that he had set the people a poor example: might it not begin to dawn on the brighter and more thoughtful of his subjects that they might similarly throw off the authority of God's anointed king?

His authority.

It was one thing to sit on the throne with the full support of mighty Mother Church. It was quite another to do it all by yourself...

Not yet, he told himself firmly. *All may yet be well.*

Suddenly he'd had enough of inactivity. Thrusting himself away from the narrow window, he jumped down from the deep embrasure and began to pace the room. The bright day outside was calling to him; he was overcome with the desire to go hunting, to chase a lively stag over miles and miles of challenging countryside, preferably with plenty of good cover. The kill was always so much more satisfying when the deer had put up a spirited fight, and, while a fast run over open ground was thrilling, it kept mind and body alert when the quarry had places to hide.

An image clarified in the king's mind. A place he had visited previously, more than once. Somewhere that held fond memories for him.

Something snagged his attention. What was it, now? A report had come in, and he had read it in a hurry, storing the contents away for action in the not-too-distant future. Turning to the wide board set against the wall, groaning under the weight of numerous rolls of parchment, scraps of vellum, and all the impedimenta of writing, he riffled through until he found what he was looking for.

Yes. He'd been right: it was the very place.

He smiled to himself. He'd been intending to go there very soon, in any case, in response to an invitation which, for various reasons, he could not refuse. If he started now, he could get in a couple of days' hunting before the official engagement. And, in truth, bearing in mind the circumstances, the sooner he got there, the better.

You just never knew where you were with dishonest men.

King John yelled for his steward, who appeared with the alacrity of a man who has been standing just outside the door. The king issued a string of instructions, then impatiently jostled the steward out of the way. Leaping down the long flights of steps, he burst into the yard far below and hurried across it to the kennels.

He was going hunting, and the first task was to make sure his favourite hound was fully fit and ready.

ELEVEN

As soon as they had checked to make sure that Lilas was not hiding somewhere else in the infirmary, Josse, Meggie and Abbess Caliste hurried outside again. Struggling with the mass of people still crowded together in the forecourt of Hawkenlye Abbey, Josse tried to hear what Abbess Caliste was saying. Something about organizing a search for the old woman.

Some hope, he thought.

Now that Nicholas Fitzwalter and his two monks had left the platform and there clearly wasn't going to be any more entertainment, people were slowly dispersing, which, if anything, made the prospect of a search even more difficult, since the crowd was steadily converged at the gates and nobody was giving way.

'I will send my nuns to check through all our buildings,' the abbess said, yelling right in his ear and making him wince.

'I'll help them,' Meggie said. She was pale, and Josse guessed she was feeling guilty about having left Lilas on her own.

'Thank you, Meggie – that would be very welcome,' the abbess said. 'If – *when* we find her, I am sure your presence will help to calm and reassure her. I suggest you join forces with Sister

178

Liese.' With a nod of acknowledgement, Meggie disappeared back inside the infirmary. 'My monks are at your disposal, Sir Josse,' the abbess added, 'for searching the surrounding countryside.'

Josse raised his arms in a gesture of helplessness. 'Nobody will be going anywhere until all these people get themselves out of the way,' he yelled back. 'I'll—'

There was a sudden commotion just outside the gates. Someone shouted, loudly and angrily, and there was a sharp cry of pain. The throng intensified as avid onlookers pushed forward to get a better view.

Over the hubbub came the single, high, clear note of a horn. Into the abrupt silence a voice cried, 'Make way for the sheriff!'

The crowd obediently bisected itself, and riding down the avenue that had opened up came Gervase de Gifford, followed by half a dozen of his men.

You have to admire the man's authority, Josse reflected, watching as Gervase let his eyes run right round the assembled masses, a frown on his face as if he was working out which were the potential troublemakers, and whether there was room in his cells for them all. But then, before he could even begin to ask questions, a small group of mounted men came clattering through from the abbey stables and, utilizing the gap that Gervase had conveniently opened up, hastened out through the gates.

At the head of the group rode Nicholas Fitzwalter. As he passed Gervase, he called out,

'Good day to you, de Gifford!'

He spurred his horse, and his retinue followed suit. Caleb, clearly unaccustomed to riding a decent, spirited horse, was almost unseated as his mare sprang forward.

The riders swiftly passed out on to the track. Very soon, the last of them had gone.

Gervase dismounted, handing his horse's reins to one of his men. Josse approached him. 'What are you doing here?' Josse asked. 'Keeping an eye on Fitzwalter and his antics?'

With a frown and a quick glance around, Gervase grabbed Josse's arm and led him out of the forecourt and into the relative peace of the cloisters. The abbess hurried after them.

Gervase stopped, spinning round to face Josse and Abbess Caliste. 'Exactly that,' he said quietly. 'Just now, Fitzwalter staged the same thing down in Tonbridge, taking advantage of market day to grab the attention of a huge crowd of locals.'

'Did he and his Cistercian get the young monk to speak out?' Josse demanded.

'Is that the skinny lad in black?'

'It is,' the abbess said coolly. 'He is a member of the Benedictine order.'

'He mumbled something about God's punishment on his wicked people,' Gervase said dismissively, 'but, according to the deputy who heard him, he didn't make much sense.'

Josse told him what had just occurred in the Hawkenlye forecourt.

'He actually said those very words?' Gervase looked horrified.

'"These terrible times we're having – it's all a judgement on the king." Aye, he did,' Josse confirmed.

'Hush, Josse! *Enough!*' Gervase hissed. 'For God's sake, don't go repeating it!' He shook his head, deep frown lines creasing his brow. 'First Tonbridge, now Hawkenlye,' he muttered. 'Anywhere Fitzwalter can be sure of a large crowd.' He met Josse's eyes. 'These speeches of his – and his tame monk – present a grave threat to peace and order, and the maintenance of those is my job,' he added gravely.

'You fear unrest?' Josse demanded.

'Of course I do!' Gervase growled. 'He...' He lowered his voice, and his next words were barely audible. 'The king grows steadily more unpopular, and I sense that we are on the very brink. I dread to think what would happen if anyone should lead the masses over the edge.'

'Is there nothing you can do?' the abbess asked, her voice cool. Josse turned to her. *You are, after all, sheriff,* her expression seemed to add.

'No, my lady, I cannot act,' Gervase replied roughly. 'Nicholas Fitzwalter is a very close friend of the de Clares, and they are the true power hereabouts.'

'Even if they appear to be undermining the authority of God's anointed king?' Her clear voice rang out.

'*Hush!*' Gervase looked wildly all around. Apart from themselves, the cloisters were empty. He turned back to the abbess. 'Forgive me, my lady,' he said swiftly. 'I have no right to com-

181

mand you in your own abbey. It's just that I fear ... I am afraid that...' He did not appear to be able to put it into words.

Looking at him with thinly disguised scorn, the abbess said, 'I believe Sir Josse and I understand full well what you fear.' For a moment Josse, observing closely, thought she would go on, but evidently she decided against it. With a quick nod to both men, she spun round and strode back towards the forecourt.

'She would have me act,' Gervase said quietly, 'although I do not know what she thinks I should do.'

Stand up to the men of power, Josse thought. *Do not let self-important barons like Nicholas Fitzwalter treat the law as if it is theirs to command.*

Looking at Gervase's stricken expression, Josse held back the words. He had a strong suspicion that, inside his head, Gervase was already hearing them.

Josse caught up with the abbess as she was emerging from the nuns' dormitory. Two novices followed her out, and Sister Liese had just hurried up to her and spoken a few brief words.

'We have now searched through the whole abbey, Sir Josse,' Abbess Caliste greeted him, 'and, as far as we can tell, Lilas is not here.'

'What about the Vale?' Josse asked. 'Could she have fled there?'

'Brother Saul has just sent word,' the abbess said. 'She is not there either.'

Josse took a deep breath, letting it out as a

long, weary sigh. Drawing the abbess aside, he said softly, 'I think you and I both know where she is, my lady.'

She nodded. 'Yes. Nicholas Fitzwalter has already taken one mouthpiece to himself. We should not be surprised, then, that he has found another.' Turning anxious eyes up to him, she added, 'Oh, Sir Josse, she was so afraid! I told her – right here in our infirmary – I told her not to worry, that we'd look after her and keep her safe, and she *wept*, she was so terrified, and she said she wasn't safe, she could never be safe, because *they* had heard her, and they'd said she must go with them and repeat what she'd been saying.' Tears welled up in the abbess's eyes. 'I have failed her, Josse, and now she has been taken away by the very people she feared.'

Josse very much wanted to put his arms round her and try to comfort her. But you did not behave like that with an abbess. Instead, he squared his shoulders, looked her straight in the eye and said, 'We won't let them get away with it. I'm going after them.'

Quite soon after arriving in the vicinity of Tonbridge Castle, Josse began to wish he hadn't rushed off so precipitously. And that he hadn't come alone.

The very edifice looked threatening. It loomed above the road that ran through the middle of the town and over the Medway, protected by a high, imposing curtain wall. Following the track that curved to the left around this wall, a steep-sided, water-filled ditch opened up before it: an effective first line of defence. Approaching the massive gatehouse, Josse was aware of the vast motte soaring up over to his right, the thick walls of the circular bailey on its summit broken only right at the top by slit-like windows. The inner defence for the castle inhabitants, he reflected, could surely withstand any sort of attack.

The outer barrier of the gatehouse was manned by half a dozen guards, one of whom detached himself from his companions to come and demand Josse's identity and his business.

Maintaining the meagre advantage of height, Josse stayed on Alfred's back and said, as calmly as he could, 'My name is Josse d'Acquin, and I wish to speak to Lord Nicholas Fitzwalter.'

'You can't,' the man said flatly. 'He's just ridden in and he's busy. Got things to see to,' he added grandly. He eyed Josse. 'Important things, see.'

Josse wondered if it was worth asking this man if he had seen an elderly woman arrive. *She is here*, he thought. *She must be.* Studying the guard, he decided on another tack. 'I just heard him address the crowd up at Hawkenlye Abbey,' he said. 'That's why I want to speak to him. Now. Straight away,' he added. The guard, he thought, seemed to be wavering.

Making up his mind, the guard yelled out to one of his companions and told them to take care of Josse's horse. Then, still eyeing Josse suspiciously, he said, 'Come with me.'

Following his guide, Josse walked the length of the long, dark passage that cut between the two halves of the vast gatehouse. They passed

184

beneath a huge portcullis, and Josse noticed two heavy, iron-studded oak doors on either side. More lines of defence – another gate, a second portcullis – and finally they emerged into the daylight on the far side.

Josse looked around, his eyes straying up to the bailey on its mound. If he had entertained hopes of being admitted to the castle's private areas, he was disappointed. Whether or not the de Clares were in residence was not obvious: the castle's living quarters were locked and barred and, apart from some activity over in the buildings in one corner of the wide expanse contained within the walls, the place might have been closed up and deserted. Men were living here – Josse knew it – but they seemed to have gone to some trouble to conceal the fact.

The guard led the way to a long, low stable building, from which Nicholas Fitzwalter emerged just as Josse and his escort approached, a stable lad at his heels.

'Sir Josse d'Acquin, my lord,' the guard said, with a nod in Josse's direction. 'Heard you speak up at the abbey. Wants to talk to you.'

Nicholas Fitzwalter turned a pair of light-blue eyes on Josse and, for an uncomfortable moment that felt to Josse like a long time, studied him intently. Wondering, in that brief time, just what was so unusual about the man, Josse realized it was his absolute stillness. He didn't, apparently, even need to blink.

'So, Sir Josse,' he said eventually, his voice, now he was no longer haranguing a crowd, soft and low-pitched. 'You heard what I and my

185

companions had to say, and you have sought me out?'

Aye, I have, but not for the reason you think, Josse thought. He did not say it aloud; if he wanted this formidable man's help, it would be better not to antagonize him. 'You say aloud what many are thinking,' he remarked instead.

'I? *I* say very little,' Fitzwalter countered swiftly. 'Because I am who I am'– idly he brushed a speck of dirt from the rich, fur-lined, fine wool cloak – 'it is possible for me to ease the way of others who wish to share their opinions.'

Such as that poor innocent fool, Caleb, Josse thought. Fitzwalter's words, however, had given him the prompt he needed. Leaning closer, as if to mutter a confidence, he said, 'There is another such as he, I'm told. An old woman from a small Kentish village, spouting prophecies and portents of doom and death.'

Fitzwalter stiffened. 'What do you know of her?' he whispered.

'I know she was at Hawkenlye Abbey and has disappeared.' Josse risked what he hoped looked like a sly, conspiratorial smile. 'Got her safely tucked away within these sturdy walls, have you, my lord?'

For an instant, or so it seemed to Josse, everything hung in the balance. He felt Fitzwalter's gaze as if it were the fine point of a blade, boring into him, trying to judge who and what he was, where his affinities truly lay.

Then Fitzwalter said coldly, 'You are mistaken, Sir Josse. There is no such woman here.'

186

Despite his determination to restrain his temper, Josse burst out, 'She must be! She disappeared from the infirmary while you were up at the abbey!'

Nicholas Fitzwalter drew himself up to his full and considerable height. He stared down at Josse as if contemplating some lower form of life. 'I say again, sir, you are mistaken.' A spasm of some strong emotion briefly crossed the patrician face. 'What on earth,' he added, sounding as if the very prospect disgusted him, 'would I want with some filthy, deranged old village crone?'

Josse's anger rose. 'You want to use her! To parade her like you did that silly young Benedictine, and make her say the things you haven't the balls to say for yourself!'

Fitzwalter went quite white. Then, in a tone of icy politeness, he said, 'I think, Sir Josse, you had better leave.' With a curt nod to the guard, lurking a few paces away, he spun round and strode off in the direction of the bailey mound.

The guard, who had evidently heard the final part of the exchange, clearly decided that the abrupt dismissal put Josse too far down the social order for the likes of him to deal with. He summoned the stable boy and said, 'Take this here knight to the outer guardhouse, where you'll find his horse.' Then, in fine imitation of his master, he too curled his lips into a sneer and strode away.

Josse was furious with himself. *I should not have let myself be affected by him*, he raged silently as he strode along behind the stable lad.

*I have antagonized him, and now he knows I am
no friend, nor a supporter of his faction's cause.*

He realized, in that instant, that he would never
put his weight behind a party that wanted to
control an anointed king. Whatever sort of a
monarch he might be. That way lay anarchy.

The stable boy led him back to the tunnel-like
passage through the gatehouse and, on the far
side of the bridge over the moat, to a lowly
building – a sort of outer guard house – where
there was stabling. There Alfred waited; the
horse, Josse noted with approval, had been provided with water.

He untied the reins and led Alfred outside. He
was about to mount when the lad caught his
sleeve and, still holding on, led Josse a short
distance down the track that wound away from
the castle. When they were out of sight of anyone in the castle or the outer guard house, the lad
said softly, 'Got any coins on you, sir knight?'

Josse's hand went to the leather purse at his
waist. 'Why?' he demanded. Was he expected to
pay for Alfred's brief stay in the stables?

The lad looked around quickly. He wetted dry
lips with his tongue. He leaned closer to Josse, a
rank stench of stables and old sweat coming off
him. 'You was asking about some old woman,'
he said, the words barely audible. 'I heard you,
see, when you was with Lord Fitzwalter.'

'What of it?' Josse asked. Excitement stirred in
him.

The lad glanced around again. 'I can help you,
if you have the coin to pay for it.'

'How do I know if what you have to say to me

188

is worth anything?' Josse countered.

The lad nodded, as if it was a fair question. 'Tell you what,' he said. 'Give me a coin for starting my tale, and if you want to hear more, give me another.'

I have no choice, Josse thought. He loosened the strings and slid a hand into his purse. He extracted a coin of modest value, and put it in the boy's outstretched palm.

Speaking softly, the lad said, 'I was in the stables when they all returned. They didn't know I was there, see – I was up in the hay loft. Lord Nick, he was angry, shouting at this fellow that was with him. He'd done something wrong, seemingly, and his lordship wasn't best pleased. "I went to the place you told me and she wasn't there," the man says, and Lord Nick replies, quick as you like, "She must have been! You made a mistake, you fool, and looked in the wrong place!" Well, the man, he didn't like being talked to like that, and he—' Abruptly he stopped. He had been watching Josse closely, and Josse realized his expression must have revealed his interest. 'Worth another coin?' the lad asked quietly.

Josse handed him a second coin. 'Go on,' he said.

The boy pocketed the coin. 'Not a lot more to tell, if I'm honest,' he admitted with a grin. 'The other fellow, he didn't like being called names, you could tell. His voice went all cold and furious, and he said to Lord Nick, "Do not call me a fool. And, before you send me off on another fruitless mission, I suggest you get your

189

facts right.'" The lad's smile widened. 'There! That was worth a modest sum, wasn't it?'

Josse couldn't help but return the smile. The boy's cheek was spectacular, but then times were hard, and you couldn't blame someone for earning a little when they spotted the opportunity. And the boy was quite right: what he had told Josse was indeed worth what he'd paid to hear it.

Back at the House in the Woods, Josse asked after Helewise. Tilly informed him she was still at the sanctuary and, hoping to find her alone, he went to seek her out.

She was tidying up, folding blankets, putting away bottles and jars containing Meggie's remedies. Swiftly he summarized his day for her, from the visit to Gervase down in Tonbridge to what had happened at the abbey, and his hurried ride back to the town to see if he could find Lilas. He told her what he had discovered. 'There's no reason to suspect the stable lad was lying,' he added. 'Why would he?'

'I'm inclined to agree,' Helewise said.

'So, if Fitzwalter's faction didn't spirit Lilas away, who did?' He had been turning it over in his mind all the way home, with no satisfactory result.

'There's one very obvious answer to that,' Helewise said.

'What? *I* can't see it,' Josse grumbled.

'We've assumed she was taken by someone who wanted to use her proclamations and her visions against the king,' Helewise replied. 'What if it's the opposite? Suppose it's some supporter of King John, who wants to *stop* her speaking out against him and winning others to the anti-John cause?'

Slowly Josse nodded. 'Aye, it's credible,' he acknowledged. He grinned. 'There's a problem, however.'

'Which is?' she demanded.

Although they were alone, he dropped his voice to a whisper. 'Is there anyone left who still supports the king?'

She shook her head, her expression rueful. 'Well, there must be *someone*, and logic suggests he must be fairly local, to be aware of Lilas at all.' Her face brightened. 'I can think of someone,' she said. 'I cannot, of course, attest to his private opinion of his king, but without doubt he's been doing very well out of the work he performs for him, which is surely reason enough not to dam the source of the spring. If you see what I mean.' She looked at Josse expectantly.

Josse thought quickly. 'You mean Lord Benedict de Vitré? Close friend and associate of King John, entrusted to amass revenue on his behalf, and therefore unlikely to want any voice to be heard that might encourage revolt against the king.'

'No other,' she agreed. He thought she sounded a little smug.

'Aye, you reason soundly, as ever,' he said. 'But you are forgetting, I think, one thing. Benedict de Vitré is dead.'

'Ah yes, *he* is,' she agreed. 'But I'm sure he didn't do all his revenue collecting on his own, Josse. Others must also have been benefiting,

191

and it is surely at least possible that it was they who decided Lilas must not be allowed to speak out again.'

'It is possible,' he said heavily. 'And, I admit, I have not been able to arrive at any better suggestion.'

She looked at him, her face concerned. 'Dear Josse, you do look tired,' she observed. 'It's no surprise, after all the miles you've covered today. Let's go home, and you can rest.'

He glanced out through the open door and up at the sky. The daylight was fading; it was too late to go anywhere other than home now. 'Very well,' he agreed.

He watched as she closed up the sanctuary for the night. Then they set off for the House in the Woods.

'Cheer up,' she said. 'Maybe Tilly will have prepared something special for supper.'

He grunted.

'What's wrong?' Helewise asked. 'You usually brighten up at the prospect of food.'

With a deep sigh, Josse said, 'I'm thinking about tomorrow, when, I suppose, I'll have to go to Medley and see if Lilas is there.'

She gave a soft sound of sympathy, tucking her arm through his. 'I can afford to be absent from the sanctuary for a while,' she said. 'I'll come with you.

192

TWELVE

Early the next morning, Josse and Helewise set out together for Medley. The morning was overcast, and a build-up of thicker, weightier clouds suggested rain was coming. In compensation, however, the temperature had risen. Will had saddled Alfred and Helewise's mare, Daisy, and he had also set out hooded capes for Josse and Helewise. 'It'll be pouring by noon,' he warned them. 'Best go prepared.'

The capes, treated with animal fat to keep out the wet, stank. Rolling them up and tying them behind his saddle, Josse thanked Will, hoping very much they wouldn't be needed.

Approaching the heavily fortified manor of Medley, they found it in a flurry of activity. The solid gates stood open, although the number of guards on duty would have deterred anyone planning an uninvited entry. Some of the guards were armed with bows, some with pikes. Josse took in the sturdy fence encircling the house and outbuildings, constructed in the usual way and positioned up on a rise, formed from the earth dug out of the ditch that ran all the way round it. The gates were set at an angle to the line of the fence, and Josse saw, as he and Helewise rode closer, that the short entry passage doubled back on the fence line and had a second, even sturdier, pair of gates at the far end.

One of the guards on duty stepped forward smartly to greet them. 'Your names, sir knight?' he asked.

He was, Josse noticed, very well turned out, with tunic and cloak made of good material, and fine leather boots polished to a shine. He was also armed, with a sword and another, shorter, blade. Benedict de Vitré's household clearly maintained high standards, and these had not been permitted to slip just because the master was dead.

Josse looked at Helewise, riding beside him. He was very glad he'd listened to her suggestion that their mission would stand a better chance of success if they honoured their hosts by dressing in their best clothes. Beneath an old but fine-quality cloak trimmed with fox fur, Josse wore a chestnut velvet tunic that he'd only had out of its storage chest twice before. He'd put a feather in his cap. Helewise – studying her, he began to smile – looked like the lady she had been born, in a beautifully cut woollen gown of deepest blue beneath a voluminous cloak with a deep border of marten fur. In her immaculate, white linen headdress under the fine wool veil, she had all the dignity that had been hers when she had been abbess of Hawkenlye.

The guard gave a polite cough, reminding Josse he was still waiting for a response to his query.

Josse turned back to him. 'This lady is Hele-

194

wise Warin, and I am Josse d'Acquin.'

'Thank you, sir. And what is your business at Medley Hall?'

'We wish to speak to whoever has charge over the household, now that Lord Benedict is dead.' He did not elaborate; it was a reasonable request, and with any luck the guard would assume they had come to pay their respects to the household in its time of loss. From the bustle of people within the circle of the fence, dozens appeared to have done the same.

'Lord Benedict's steward, Sebastian Garrique, is greeting visitors,' the guard said. 'If you would ride on within and leave your horses with one of the grooms, you'll find him in the hall.' He indicated the largest building, its wide door standing ajar at the top of a long and rather showy flight of steps.

'Thank you, we will.' Josse put his heels to Alfred's sides, and he and Helewise rode into Medley.

She came up beside him as they emerged from the inner set of gates. 'Why are there so many people here?' she asked in a low voice.

'Lord Benedict was an important man,' he murmured back. 'No doubt they've hurried here to express their regrets that he's dead, in the hope of securing the favour of whoever rises up to replace him.'

'There won't be a burial service,' she said. 'There's no priest to hold it, and anyway he wouldn't be permitted to do so.'

'No, but I don't suppose that'll stop them hav-ing a funeral feast,' he answered. 'It certainly looks as if they're preparing for something of the sort.'

'Yes,' she said, turning to look round the wide open space within the fence. He, too, ran his eyes over the bustling scene, taking in the details: a cart loaded with barrels of beer and wine; a servant struggling with a huge side of beef; a collection of sheep carcasses; fowl of all kinds from swans to chickens. To judge from the well-trodden path from the yard to what appeared to be the kitchens, considerable amounts of food and drink had already been taken inside.

Helewise's mouth fell open. 'Josse, I know we are very fortunate – and at home we eat better than most – but I haven't seen so much food in *years*,' she whispered.

Touched, he wanted to hug her.

Instead he said briskly, 'Come on, we'll leave the horses with that stable boy, and proceed with our business here.'

The stables, they noticed, had recently been extended. There was a strong smell of freshly cut timber, emanating from new partitions between the stalls. Crossing the yard to the hall, Josse stared around him, taking in the evidence of other new building work. A great deal of money had clearly been spent here.

He stood back to let Helewise precede him up the steps. As soon as they were through the wide door, a surge of warmth hit them and, moving on inside, they saw that a huge fire blazed in the central hearth. Helewise leaned close to him and said softly, 'It seems rather wasteful, even for a wealthy household, to build up that magnificent fire and leave the door open.'

He nodded. He had been thinking exactly the same.

In the group of people milling around the hearth, a man turned and stared at them. He was clad all in black, which accentuated his height and his thinness. He wore his dark hair long, brushed straight back from his lean face. The dark eyes, deeply hooded, seemed to glitter in the firelight.

Unsmiling, he advanced towards them. 'I am Sebastian Garrique,' he said, 'and I am Lord Benedict's steward.' *And*, his rigid, unsmiling demeanour seemed to add, *I am in authority here while all is in a state of flux*. 'Your names?'

He was, Josse decided, considerably less courteous than the guard on the gates. He gave his and Helewise's names, adding – for the steward's manner seemed to draw the words out of him – that they were acquainted with the late Lord Benedict. He refrained from adding what they had thought of the man.

Steadying himself (Sebastian's intense stare felt a little like an attack) he went on: 'We wish to speak to one of Lord Benedict's kinsmen, on a private matter.' Which was really a polite way of saying that it was not a conversation he was prepared to have with a steward.

But Sebastian was shaking his head. 'Lord Benedict had no blood kin. There is nobody except his widow, Lady Richenza.' He seemed to grow in stature as he said her name, Josse thought, as if to prove that anyone wanting to talk to her would have to get past him.

Josse held his ground. Beside him, he sensed Helewise move closer. 'Then please would you summon Lady Richenza,' he said politely.

For several heartbeats, nobody moved. Then, with a sort of grunt, Sebastian spun on his heel and strode smoothly away down the hall, disappearing through an arched doorway at the far end.

'Has he gone to fetch her?' Helewise whispered.

Josse smiled grimly. 'Let's hope so.'

They waited. Quite a long time passed. Then, when Josse was on the point of suggesting they gave it up, Sebastian emerged from the doorway. He threaded his way skilfully across the crowded hall like a needle through thick fabric, and very soon was beside them. 'Lady Richenza has agreed to see you,' he said. It was obvious that he thought she was bestowing a huge and unwarranted favour. 'Follow me.'

He led the way back through the doorway, along a passage and up a short flight of shallow steps, the stonework crisp-edged and obviously new. Through another arch, its heavy wooden door slightly ajar, and into a square room which, even on that overcast day, seemed to be flooded with light. Looking round in astonishment, Josse saw that the high windows were glazed. Now was not the moment to calculate just how much *that* must have cost.

In the far corner of the room, in a small recess, was a private chapel – little more than an altar bearing an elaborate, gilded cross on a richly embroidered cloth and, in front of it, a wooden *prie-dieu* at which knelt a slim, slight figure. At the sound of footsteps, she turned towards them, then gracefully rose to her feet.

She was dressed in a dark grey gown, wearing a flowing veil that entirely covered her face. Sebastian stepped forward and, leaning down to speak quietly to her, announced her visitors.

'Does she mask her grief, or the lack of it?' Helewise whispered to Josse.

'I sense we shall not be permitted to find out,' he murmured back.

Lady Richenza appeared to be staring at them, although it was hard to tell; her veil hung in generous folds, and little but the outline of her features could be seen. She made a gesture of dismissal towards Sebastian and, with a deep bow to his young mistress and a final glare at Josse, the steward left the room, closing the door with exaggerated caution behind him.

Josse, watching Lady Richenza closely, would have sworn that a great deal of the tension in her slim body left her as soon as the door closed.

'Sir Josse d'Acquin,' she said, her voice high and whispery. 'I believe I know the name...?'

Without pausing to think – he was eager to reassure her – Josse said, 'You may know of my daughter. Meggie is a healer, and came here with Mistress Gifford when ... after...' Too late, he realized his blunder. He had brought up the one topic guaranteed to terrify Lady Richenza into silence.

She was visibly trembling, the veil shaking. 'I ... I didn't...' she began.

199

With a soft sound of pity, Helewise went up to the young woman – she was, Josse saw, little more than a girl – and put an arm round her. 'We are not here to accuse you,' she said gently. She turned to glare at Josse. 'Our visit has nothing to do with the death of your husband, save that we would express our sympathy at your loss.'

'Thank you,' the girl whispered. 'He was ... he...' She gave up. Perhaps, Josse reflected, dragging up anything nice to say about Lord Benedict was beyond her. Recovering herself, she said, 'Why *have* you come?' And she went on to say, with disarming frankness, 'Most of the people crowding into my hall seem to be expecting money, for one reason or another. Either that or they've turned up early for the funeral feast. No doubt they want to make sure they're included. Medley,' she added, 'is famous for its feasts.'

'It is for neither of those purposes that we are here,' Helewise said. 'Indeed, it has nothing, really, to do with your late husband at all.'

'No?' Lady Richenza glanced over at the door, as if to make sure it was closed, then, in a gesture expressive of relief, flung back her veil.

Josse studied her. In other circumstances, he reflected, she would have been quite beautiful. Now, she was very pale; the full lips were colourless and dry, and the wide blue eyes were darkly circled. Of the swollen, pink eyelids that follow lengthy tears, however, there was no sign.

She was married to a fat, cruel and vicious old man, Josse told himself. *It is quite unreasonable to look for grief at his demise.*

'Sir Josse?' Helewise prompted. 'Lady Richenza is waiting.'

'Oh – aye, of course.' He brought his thoughts
under control. 'My lady, we come from Hawkenlye Abbey, where the nuns are concerned for
an elderly woman who has gone missing from
the infirmary. A search has been organized, and
we have come to ask if you, or any of your
household, have seen her. Perhaps she is staying
here? Perhaps you—'

'What sort of a woman is she?' the light little
voice asked.

'Er – she is old, as I said, and she has been
troubled in her mind by the signs and portents
which have been reported recently, such as—'

Lady Richenza shook her head impatiently,
setting the heavy gold earrings jingling. 'No, no,
no, I don't need the details,' she interrupted. 'Is
she quality? Is she a lady?'

Josse looked at her coolly. 'No. She's a peasant, from a little village deep in the Kent countryside.'

Lady Richenza's smooth white brow creased
in a frown. 'Then what would she be doing here,
among my guests?' she asked, sounding genuinely puzzled. 'Oh – you mean she might have
come here looking for work? We are, I suppose,
taking on extra people to help with the feast...'
She waved a vague hand in the direction of the
hall. 'Sebastian says close on a hundred will
attend.'

Josse felt his anger rising. Helewise, who had
returned to stand beside him, put a warning hand
on his arm. Swallowing his anger, he said mild-

201

ly, 'She would not have been wanting work, no. We wondered if perhaps somebody might have brought her here?'

Again, Lady Richenza seemed totally mystified. 'Why would they do that? I don't know this woman – I'm quite sure I don't. What's her name?'

'Lilas. Lilas of Hamhurst.'

The girl smiled, as if at the unlikelihood of her knowing someone with such an absurd name. 'Unless she has been smuggled in and locked in the deepest cellar, she's not here,' she said.

'Who might know, if that really had happened?' Helewise asked.

Her quiet tone seemed to make the suggestion a possibility, and, with a considered look at her, Lady Richenza said, 'Sebastian, I imagine.' She added bitterly, 'He knows *everything* that goes on at Medley.'

Josse bowed. 'Then, with your leave, my lady, we will go and ask him.' Without waiting for a reply, he strode over to the door and wrenched it open. Turning to bid her farewell, he noticed that, in that brief instant, she had already pulled down her veil. At a stroke, she had turned herself once more into the impenetrable, grieving widow.

Helewise caught him up as he hurried back down the passage. 'Well, what else did you expect?' she demanded in an angry undertone. 'She's barely more than a child, and yet some relation – some *man* – decided it was appropriate for her to be married to that fat, cruel old goat! And you act as if her failure to be driven to her knees with grief offends you!'

Stung by her fury, he stopped dead. 'I am *not* offended!' he hissed back. 'Helewise, you should know me better than that!'

She muttered something that might have been, *yes, I should.* Then, calming herself with an obvious effort, she said, 'Was it, then, her attitude to Lilas that made you so cross?'

He gave her a rueful grin. 'What do *you* think?'

She smiled back, taking his arm. 'We'd better find that supercilious steward, and ask him if he really has hidden the poor old woman away somewhere.'

Josse sighed. 'Aye, you're right, although I don't imagine he'd tell us if he had.'

They found Sebastian standing in the hall's entrance, greeting yet more visitors. Once he had ushered them inside, he turned to face Josse and Helewise. Before he had a chance to speak, Josse said, 'We are searching for an elderly woman, Lilas of Hamhurst. Lady Richenza has no knowledge of her; have you?'

'I do not know the name,' Sebastian replied. 'Why would she be here?'

Not prepared to tell him, Josse repeated what he had said to Lady Richenza.

'And you think she might have wandered away from Hawkenlye Abbey and found her way here?' Sebastian asked. 'No; as far as I am aware, she has not. Wait – I will check.'

'I think he's telling the truth,' Helewise whispered as the steward glided away. 'He was very quick in offering to ask the rest of the household,

203

and he would hardly do that if he had something to hide.'

'Aye,' Josse agreed. 'Anyway, there can surely have been no real need for him to go and check: to echo Lady Richenza, nothing happens here that he doesn't know about.'

Presently Sebastian returned. Either, Josse reflected, he was a very good actor, or the name Lilas of Hamhurst really was unknown to him. Shaking his head, he said, 'I am sorry. We cannot help you.'

'I believe him,' Helewise said as they rode away.

'So do I,' Josse agreed. 'We'll have to—'

At that moment, a rider came cantering up fast behind them, following them out of Medley's great courtyard. Josse and Helewise drew rein, moving to the side of the track to let the rider, who seemed to be in haste, go by.

The horse was a fine bay, moving with graceful, eager speed. The rider, who acknowledged Josse and Helewise making room for him with a briefly raised hand, was cloaked and hooded. Just as he passed them, an overhanging branch snagged at his hood, revealing his face. Hurriedly, he drew the heavy, concealing folds forward again.

In the brief instant in which he had been uncovered, Josse took in the features. He stared after the rider as he flew on down the track.

'What is it?' Helewise demanded. 'Do you know that man?'

'No, but I've seen him before, very recently.' Josse was thinking hard, trying to recall where

204

he'd seen the man. With its deep eyes beneath jutting brow ridges, and the sharp, prominent cheekbones, it was not a face you saw every day ... Then he had it. 'He was up at the abbey yesterday, when Fitzwalter paraded his tame monk,' he said, the words rushing out. 'He was standing towards the front, just behind the massed ranks of Fitzwalter's men. There must in truth be a link between Fitzwalter and Medley Hall, just as we thought – although I can't for the life of me think what it is – and that man, whoever he is, proves it.' Gathering the reins, he urged Alfred forward. 'We'll have to ride hard, Helewise – I will see you safely back to the turning for home, then I'm going after him.'

It was an anxious ride. Although Josse had been very glad of Helewise's company at Medley, now he felt nothing but relief when, on reaching the place where the path for the House in the Woods branched off the main track, she set off for home and left him to go on alone.

As they had hurried along, she had called out to him, suggesting that she went with him. He did not want that. He was quite prepared for possible danger – he had a strong sense that it was lurking – but would not risk her safety. Since, however, any mention of danger would instantly have glued her to his side, he said instead, 'No, go on home – I'll be faster on my own, and there's less chance of his spotting one pursuer than two.'

He knew she did not want to leave him, so, as soon as he had ridden off, he spurred Alfred on.

The sooner he was out of her sight, the better.

The rain began. He did not dare risk stopping to drag on his hooded cape, and so had to endure the downpour. It both helped and hindered: it helped because the mounted man he was trailing was now leaving a clear pattern of hoof prints in the wet mud, but it hindered because it cut visibility to perhaps twenty paces. Josse reassured himself with the thought that, if he could not see his quarry, then the man could not see him.

The horseman and Josse were now on the track that led round the northern edge of the great forest. They passed the turning down to Tonbridge on the right and, presently, the bulk of Hawkenlye Abbey. The rider went on and, to judge by the horse's imprints, he did not slow his steady pace.

Josse followed the twists and turns of his route. He thought he knew where the rider was headed, although it was a surprising destination, and at first he doubted his conclusion. This mysterious rider had a connection with both Medley Hall and the Fitzwalter faction, and surely neither could have anything to do with *this* place? After a few more miles, however, there was no more uncertainty. Careful now – he did not want to be spotted at this stage – Josse went on.

He followed the track that ran between the two ridges, emerging cautiously into the hanging valley. There, ahead, was Wealdsend – and there, even now approaching its firmly barred gates, was the hooded horseman.

You have ridden all this way for nothing, my

206

friend, Josse said silently to him. *There is nobody there.*

But the horseman had reached out and, with the pommel of his drawn sword, he was banging on the stout wooden panels of the gate. Astonished, Josse watched as a small gap appeared. It widened just enough to let horse and rider pass within, then abruptly the gates banged shut. Even from where he was, Josse heard the clang as the locking bar on the inside fell into its brackets.

He knew it was foolhardy, but he could not stop himself. He edged Alfred on, gently, cautiously, until he was near enough to make out the buildings within the paling fence. As before, all looked deserted; the rider must already have led his horse into whatever stabling was provided, for there was no sign of the bay. The man, too, was nowhere to be seen.

Then, just as Josse was about to turn and ride away, through the gloom and the ever-increasing rain there was a brief flash of brightness: as if someone had opened a door and slipped inside a lighted room.

The rider had been admitted.

Josse was all alone, out in the rain.

THIRTEEN

Josse looked down at his sodden cloak. It would be today, he reflected, when he was dressed in his best, that he would be in for a soaking. Turning Alfred, he rode back down the valley until, in the shelter of a stand of pine, he drew rein. He unrolled the rain cape that Will had given him and, removing his rain-soaked cloak, replaced it with the cape. He pulled the hood up over his head. It did not afford much warmth but it did deflect the rain, as Will had obviously known it would.

Which, Josse thought glumly, was just as well. Having uncovered a link between Medley Hill and Wealdsend, he knew what he had to do next: go back to Medley and find out the identity of the horseman, and the nature of his urgent errand with Lord Robert Wimarc of Wealdsend.

As Josse rode back along the track, vainly hoping it would take his mind off his bodily discomfort, he tried to work out what might link the inhabitants of the two manors. Benedict de Vitré had worked for the king – and, judging by the wealth evident in every aspect of Medley and those who dwelt there, had done very nicely out of his association with his monarch. Was Lord Wimarc, then, also a king's man? Had the unknown rider been hurrying to Wealdsend to take news to its master of arrangements for the funeral feast? For the redistribution of power, now that Lord Benedict was dead?

Josse shook his head. He did not know: the only thing he could do was try to find out.

He was riding past the turning to Tonbridge when, coming towards him, a horse and rider materialized out of the driving rain. Uneasy, Josse put his hand to the hilt of his sword. The rider was almost upon him.

'Who's there?' he called out. 'Show yourself!'

He did not know what he feared; he only knew that he *was* afraid. That, among the many and varied happenings of the day, something had quietly warned him: *Be careful*.

He waited.

Shapes materialized on the track. There were two of them, in single file: a young man rode in the lead, mounted on a very familiar mare, and behind him came a lad on a friendly looking brown pony.

Josse let out a yell. He hurried towards the young man who, grinning widely, said, 'It's good to see you! Helewise was worried, so, since the mare was saddled, I borrowed Daisy and came to look for you.' He glanced behind him. 'Geoffroi insisted on coming, in case I managed to lose myself in this appalling weather.' He rolled his eyes, his grin widening.

'I'm very glad to see you, too – *both* of you,' Josse said. 'As you see, I am perfectly safe. But now I must hurry on, since I need to go back to—'

His son and his adopted son, Josse realized, had taken up positions either side of him. 'She – Helewise – was worried about that, too,' Ninian said cheerfully. 'To quote her exact words: "The silly old fool will no doubt have some plan to rush off somewhere else, and you are not to allow it." So, we're not. Allowing it.'

'Father, you're soaked!' Geoffroi said anxiously. 'You must come home. The wind's getting up' – the lad was right, Josse realized – 'and you'll take chill if you stay out.'

An image of his own hearth floated before Josse's tired eyes. Food. Wine. Dry clothes. Warmth.

Medley and its inhabitants will not vanish overnight, he told himself. 'Very well,' he said aloud. And, with vast relief, Ninian and Geoffroi riding either side of him, he set off for home.

In the morning, the effects of the previous day's drenching were all too evident. Josse was shivery, his joints ached and his throat was sore, so that it hurt to swallow. His family urged him not to go out; they had all congregated round the hearth in the main house, and Helewise, Tilly and Eloise – even the usually reticent Ella – told him, with varying degrees of bluntness, that he was foolish even to contemplate it.

Helewise knew they were all wasting their breath.

'I have to go to Medley,' Josse repeated for the third time. 'I must ask that condescending steward the identity of the hooded rider. Don't you see?' he cried in frustration. 'There's a link between Medley and Wealdsend, and if I can discover what it is, it may help us find Lilas!'

'You're not the only person looking for her,' Ninian pointed out. 'The Hawkenlye nuns and monks may well have found her by now.'

But Josse shook his head. 'No. Someone's taken her. I know it.'

Silently Helewise handed him a heavy wool tunic, lined with linen and with a padded interlining, and his old travelling cloak. 'Wrap up warmly and don't stay out too long,' she said calmly. If he was set on going out, she had reasoned, she could at least try to limit the potential harm to him. 'Once you're home again, settle down beside the hearth and don't move.'

He looked up at her. His eyes were full of gratitude.

He really doesn't look very well, Helewise thought, her heart going out to him. Before her emotions could undermine her, she hurried on. 'Ninian, you and I will ride over to Hawkenlye, and ask if there are any reports of Lilas. If Eloise can spare you, that is?' She looked enquiringly at her granddaughter, sitting with Inana on her lap.

'Yes, of course,' Eloise replied. She was frowning. 'But I thought – er – you always said you'd never go back to the abbey? You said you thought your presence might remind the nuns and monks of your time in authority there, and that wouldn't help Abbess Caliste.'

And I still think exactly that, Helewise thought. *But, if I do not go, Josse will set out for the abbey the instant he returns from Medley Hall.* She met Eloise's eyes and, hoping the girl would

211

understand, said simply, 'Needs must.'

Eloise opened her mouth to speak and then, as comprehension dawned, she nodded. She gave Helewise a very sweet smile.

Helewise and Ninian took the forest path to Hawkenlye. Although the morning was dry and cold, the previous day's rain had left the main track that ran around the forest perimeter sodden and muddy. Now, in late autumn, it was possible to ride along the path through the forest, since the vegetation that clogged and narrowed it in summer had died back.

If any of the forest people were nearby and observed them, Helewise reassured herself, quelling her slight unease, it was unlikely they would be perceived as intruders. Ninian, after all, was Joanna's son.

As they emerged from beneath the trees and rode down the long slope to the abbey, Helewise drew her hood forward to shadow her face. The fewer people who recognized her, the better.

They dismounted in the forecourt, and Ninian took their horses off to the stables. Keeping to the shelter of the walls, Helewise hurried along the cloister and tapped softly on the door of the abbess's room.

A voice called, 'Enter!'

Helewise went in.

It felt so disturbingly strange to be back there that she almost turned and ran.

Don't you dare, she told herself.

She pushed back her hood, and Abbess Caliste gasped.

'Forgive me,' Helewise said quickly. 'I ought not to be here. But there is a reason.' Hastily she explained. 'So, if you can just tell me if there is news of Lilas, I'll be on my way,' she concluded.

Abbess Caliste had risen and come towards her. Now, as Helewise finished her apology, she opened her arms and took her former superior in a close hug. 'It's so good to see you,' she murmured. 'You have been away too long.' She released her. 'Now, sit down, and I will send for a hot drink to warm you after your ride.'

'Ninian is with me,' Helewise said.

'Then he shall join us. The drink, I warn you, will be watery and tasteless, but it will at least be hot.'

Before Helewise could protest, Abbess Caliste had gone to the door and issued her order. With a wry smile, Helewise accepted the inevitable and sat down in the visitors' chair.

It was some time before Ninian arrived. The abbess had informed Helewise regretfully that, despite extensive searching, Lilas had not been found. She was describing what they planned to do next when, after a cursory tap on the door, Ninian came in.

He was not alone. Behind him, holding a beautiful scarlet cap with a fox-fur trim between nervous hands, was an expensively dressed young man.

Ninian bowed to the abbess. 'Good day to you, my lady.' Obviously impatient to explain, he wasted no more time on the courtesies. 'On my way out of the stables, I witnessed the arrival of this man.' He indicated his companion, who also bowed. He shot a glance at Helewise, then turned back to the abbess. 'He wants to know how to find Wealdsend.'

Helewise shot to her feet. With an apologetic glance at the abbess, she addressed the young man.

'You want to go to Wealdsend?' she asked.

'I *have* to!' the young man said fervently. 'You can't stop me – you don't understand!' His voice had risen.

'Such a visit may not be wise,' she said. 'May we know your purpose?'

He looked at each of them in turn. Studying him, Helewise wondered if this show of passion might be disguising another emotion: fear. The youth was pale, and his forehead and upper lip were beaded with sweat. The beautiful scarlet cap was steadily being twisted out of shape by his anxious, busy hands. 'I ... there's a...' He stopped. He took a deep breath, and went on: 'I have to find two friends. I know they were going to Wealdsend, and I must follow them. We said we'd go together,' he added, 'and I could not find the courage to accompany them when they set out. Now that I've had time to think about it, I've made up my mind, and I'm going to join them.'

Helewise went to stand beside him. She said gently, 'I am very much afraid that your friends may be dead.'

He stared at her, his expression horrified. *'Dead!* No, oh, no – they can't be! Symon's strong, and he's a fine swordsman – oh, you are mistaken, my lady.'

Helewise reached out and put a hand on his. 'One was called Symon?'

'Yes – Symon de St Clair, and his cousin Guillaume was with him. He's a St Clair too – they are the sons of two brothers. It's a great family, long renowned for their prowess, with many knights among their ancestors who have earned distinction on the battlefield ... *Dead?*'

Gently, Helewise described how she had found the young man at the sanctuary, too late to save him, and how the body of his companion had subsequently been discovered. She told him how they were dressed and what they had looked like. When she had finished, the young man doubted her no longer.

He was so pale now that he seemed on the point of fainting. 'Help me, Ninian!' Helewise said, and together they led the youth to the visitors' chair and sat him down.

Abbess Caliste poured a mug of the drink for him, holding it while he sipped. 'Thank you, my lady abbess,' he said, trying to rise to his feet. Gently the abbess pushed him back.

He has been raised in courtly circles, Helewise thought. *He knows how to address an abbess, and he has good manners.* She wondered how old he was; younger than she had originally thought, she now decided. Fifteen? Fourteen? She crouched in front of him.

'May we know your name?' she asked.

He met her eyes. His, she noticed, were dark brown. They held a wounded look, giving him an air of vulnerability.

215

'Luc Jordan.'

'Luc. Thank you. I am Helewise, this is the Abbess Caliste, and the man there is Ninian.' Luc muttered a response. 'We need to ask you to do something for us,' she went on, keeping her voice calm and level. 'There can be little doubt that the dead men are indeed your friends, but it would be better to be absolutely sure, for then their names can be recorded and, in time, their kinsmen notified. Would you, Luc, be willing to view the bodies?'

He seemed to grow even paler. 'They – they are here?'

'They are in the crypt, beneath the abbey church.' Helewise wasn't sure of this, but a quick glance at the abbess earned a nod of confirmation.

'Are they...' Luc swallowed and tried again. 'Are they very damaged?'

Abbess Caliste came to crouch beside Helewise. 'My nursing nuns have prepared them for burial,' she said gently. 'They look now as if they are merely asleep.'

Luc looked up at Ninian, who was standing by the door, one shoulder leaning against the wall. 'I'm sorry to seem so weak,' Luc said. 'It's just that – well, I've never seen a dead person before.'

Helewise gave him a moment to find his courage. Then she said, 'Will you do it?'

The soft brown eyes met hers. 'Yes.'

'He bore himself well,' Helewise murmured to Abbess Caliste as the four of them returned to

216

the abbess's room. 'It cannot have been easy, viewing the friends he last saw riding off with such high hopes lying on trestles and waiting for the grave.'

'No indeed,' Abbess Caliste agreed. 'Oh, but I am so relieved we now have names for those poor young men – I will send word to Brother Saul immediately that he can now make the arrangements for interment.'

'You will put them in the abbey's burial ground?'

'I will. And,' the abbess added with some force, 'in the absence of a priest, *I* shall say the words to accompany them before their heavenly father.'

Back in the abbess's room, it seemed to Helewise that, in facing the challenge of viewing his dead friends, Luc had found some strength. And, having accepted that the worst had indeed happened, he seemed more willing to open up to them.

'How did you come to know Symon and Guillaume?' Helewise asked him.

'The three of us were squires together, in the household of Sir Eustace of Hazelgrove,' he replied. 'We began our training at the same time, and our friendship grew.'

'That is the way of it,' Ninian remarked. Helewise turned to him; she often forgot that he too had once undergone the knightly training. He smiled at her. 'It's tough,' he said. 'You quickly find life is easier with someone to watch out for you.'

217

'Yes, that's right,' Luc said eagerly. 'Although Symon and Guillaume were but cousins, and I wasn't related to them at all, the three of us were like brothers.'

'How did they hear of Wealdsend?' the abbess asked. 'What drew them there?'

Luc looked awkward. 'It's supposed to be a secret,' he muttered. 'I don't think I ought to tell you.'

Ninian made an impatient sound. Helewise looked up quickly, shaking her head. Getting angry with Luc was not, she realized, the way to make him confide in them. 'Luc, your two friends were murdered,' she said. 'They came here to the abbey to ask the way to Wealdsend – just as you did this very morning – but they never got there. Somebody made quite sure of that by killing them.'

Luc had tears in his eyes. 'They were so excited,' he muttered. 'They teased me and ragged me because I was hesitant about going with them – Symon said it would be the best adventure *ever*.' He wiped a hand across his nose.

'Who were they hoping to see at Wealdsend?' Helewise prompted. 'Its lord?'

'I'm not sure,' Luc admitted. 'We were just told the name: Wealdsend.' Again, he looked up at Ninian, then at the abbess, returning his gaze to Helewise. As if he had suddenly made up his mind to confide in them, he burst out, 'There's a group – small but very powerful – which has its own secret symbol. It's a special double-headed axe called a labrys. I've seen a drawing of it, and

218

it's depicted within a sort of maze. The group's going to do something extraordinary: something that'll change the course of England's history, so that the names of those who carry out the deed will be remembered for ever.' He sat back in his chair, looking drained. 'That's why Symon – it was his idea, really – was so keen for the three of us to find Wealdsend and join the group. He wanted to be famous.'

Helewise could have wept.

Ninian spoke up. 'If the group is so very secret, how did Symon discover where to go to find it?'

Luc risked a quick glance at him, then dropped his eyes. 'I don't know.'

Swiftly Ninian abandoned his casual pose, moving to stand in front of Luc's chair, his hands on its arms imprisoning the youth. 'I think you do,' he said softly.

Luc was no match for him. 'Symon was ... he'd gone somewhere he shouldn't have been,' he admitted. 'He overheard something.' He rallied, making himself face Ninian. 'It's no use asking me to tell you any more, because that's all I know!' he cried. 'Symon said it'd be dangerous if he told me and Guillaume. He was scared,' he added in a whisper. 'He thought whoever he spied on might have known he was there.'

'He was very brave, then, to proceed with his mission,' Ninian said. 'A lesser man might have given up.'

Luc seemed to sit up a little straighter, as if some of his late friend's courage had stiffened his own backbone. 'Symon *was* brave,' he agreed. Then, dropping his face in his hands, he whispered, 'I *wish* he hadn't gone.'

Then he began to sob.

Helewise put her arms round him, but after a few moments, he shook her off. He stood up, bowing to the three of them in turn.

'Where are you going?' Helewise asked. She felt a cold foreboding.

Luc did not reply.

'Don't go to Wealdsend,' the abbess urged. 'You don't know what you will find there, Luc. Would you risk your life, when your two friends have lost theirs?'

But Luc did not answer their questions. 'Thank you for your kindness,' he said stiffly. 'And for your care of my friends.' Then, bowing again, he let himself out of the room. They heard his footfalls striding away.

After an instant of stunned silence, Ninian flung the door open again and hurried after him.

Josse was on his way back from Medley Hall. He was cross and tired, and his sore throat was worse. Hunching deeper into his cloak, he reflected sourly that he might as well have saved himself the journey, for nobody at Medley recognized his description of the hooded rider and his bay.

Or, at least, Josse amended, *nobody's admitting to recognizing him*. Which wasn't the same thing at all.

As he rode, he tried to remember if he had actually seen the rider emerge from Medley Hall's courtyard, or if he had simply assumed

220

that was where the man had come from. He shut his eyes, the better to visualize the scene. Without a doubt, the rider had been on the spur of track that led solely to Medley, but Josse could not recall if he had seen him riding out through the gates. It was, he decided, possible, if unlikely, that the man had left his bay tethered somewhere beyond the settlement, rather than in Medley's stables. And the only reason for anyone to do that, he concluded, was if they wished to keep their visit a secret.

FOURTEEN

Late in the evening, Josse, Helewise and Ninian sat by the fire in the House in the Woods' wide hall. Eloise had retired to bed soon after her daughter, both of them worn out by Inana's fractious day. The rest of the household, too, had settled for the night, leaving the three alone.

Ninian had not managed to follow Luc Jordan. 'He evaded me,' he had announced bitterly when, cold and tired, he had finally arrived home. As he hurried out of the abbess's room on Luc's heels, Ninian had been detained: by Meggie, of all people. Still unable to find Lilas, and with her guilty conscience troubling her, she had turned to her brother in her distress, demanding if he had any news of the old woman.

221

By the time Ninian had explained that no, he hadn't, and he was in fact in a great hurry to follow and apprehend someone *else* perceived to be in danger, it was too late. Although he raced to fetch his horse and dashed straight out on to the road to try to pick up Luc's trail, it was impossible. With no real clue as to which direction Luc had taken, he was simply faced with a confusion of far too many hoof prints patterning the track. Deciding that Wealdsend was the boy's most likely destination, he had cantered off along the route to the isolated manor to see if he could catch Luc up, but without success. Although he had ridden as far as the hanging valley, there had been no sign of the lad.

Even now, some time later, Ninian was still angry with himself for his failure. 'You did your best,' Josse said, probably for the fifth or sixth time. 'We understand that you could not ignore your own sister. It was just bad luck that, unwittingly, she held you back.'

Ninian, it seemed, was not to be comforted. Filling his mug from the jug by the hearth, he lapsed into brooding silence.

It was just as well, Josse mused, that Meggie had remained at the abbey, or she might well have been the recipient of some angry words.

Helewise, evidently deciding that they needed a change of subject, said softly, 'Regrettably, the disappearance of Luc Jordan is not our only problem. There are also the three deaths – Benedict de Vitré and the St Clair cousins – as well as the whereabouts of poor Lilas. Whoever is holding her, and wherever she is,' she added hopefully, 'we can at least be fairly sure she will be looked after, since the aim of her abductors is to make her broadcast the content of her visions.'

Josse grunted. 'Not if she's been taken by supporters of the king. If that's the case, the aim will be to *stop* her talking.'

It was all too obvious, he reflected grimly, how that would be achieved. Helewise's soft 'Oh!' of distress suggested she thought the same.

'We know she's not at Tonbridge or Medley,' he said after a moment. 'We have the stable lad's evidence that Fitzwalter's man didn't find her when he went into the infirmary to look for her and, presumably, take her. At Medley, too, I am inclined to believe them when they deny knowledge of her. Can she be at Wealdsend?' he went on, half to himself.

'You suggest that there is a connection between Medley and Wealdsend,' Helewise remarked, 'since you followed your hooded man from the one to the other.'

'Aye, and the fact that I first saw him at Hawkenlye Abbey, in the forefront of Fitzwalter's gang of bodyguards, makes me conclude that he has a connection with the faction down in Tonbridge, too,' Josse said. 'Although how this three-way link works is beyond me, I confess. First, we have Benedict de Vitré, a loyal and devoted friend of the king who amassed revenue for him and, incidentally, made himself extremely rich in the process. Second, there is Nicholas Fitzwalter, whose aim, I'm led to believe, is to curtail the power of the king, thus benefiting himself and his fellow barons. Third, there is the largely unknown quantity of Lord Robert Wimarc, who may or may not be involved with some outlandish outfit known as Labrys, which – or so we're told by an impressionable lad scarcely out of boyhood – is conspiring to do something extraordinary that will change the course of England's history.' He gave a rueful laugh. 'And if *that's* not some wild tale dreamed up by a bunch of bored squires with nothing better to do, then I'm the next Pope.'

Helewise sighed. 'It does seem outlandish, I agree. And, even if there is an element of truth in it, what on earth would the conspirators want with Lilas?'

Josse shook his head. 'I have no idea.' An image of Wealdsend formed in his mind: isolated, enclosed, forbidding. 'I fear for her indeed, if they have hidden her away within those grim walls. There is an air of dark mystery there that affects even the countryside around.'

'You thought the place was deserted,' she reminded him, 'yet you observed your hooded rider being admitted.'

'Aye, I did.' He put his hand to his head, kneading his brow as if it would help him to think. 'He's a Fitzwalter man – he must be – so does that mean this Labrys business is somehow linked to what Fitzwalter's doing?'

'Josse, stop.' Her hand was on his, gently removing it from its furious massage of his head. 'Think about something else. The murders of Guillaume and Symon de St Clair, now: the

bodies were found several miles from Wealdsend, so let us speculate on why that might have
been.'

Grateful for the distraction, he said, 'Guillaume told us they – he and his cousin – were
lost. "They came for us," he said, "although I do
not know how they found us."' In a flash of
insight, he exclaimed, 'I don't think they ever
got to Wealdsend. I think someone – two men,
perhaps, maybe more – *from* Wealdsend found
them, still some way away, and, after killing
them, deliberately arranged that they were left
well away from Wealdsend.' He paused, thinking hard. 'The first one, Guillaume, we found
near the sanctuary and, according to Geoffroi,
his bitch's clever nose discovered the other
cousin, Symon, deep in the forest between here
and the abbey,' he went on slowly. 'The body
was concealed in a bramble thicket. Whoever
was responsible either dumped both of them at
the spot where Symon was found, believing
Guillaume too was dead, or else deliberately
deposited the two of them in separate places.'

'You're suggesting then, if the former is true,
that poor Guillaume crawled all the way to the
sanctuary,' she said very quietly. 'Oh, Josse! He
was looking for help, and he made such an
effort, and it was all in vain.'

'We cannot know that's how it happened,' he
said, trying to make it better but knowing he
wasn't succeeding. 'The killers may have deliberately left the two of them in different spots,
perhaps thinking that, if they weren't found
together, it would be that much harder to identify

225

them.'

She was silent for a long time. When, eventually, he looked up at her, she gave a minute shake of the head, indicating Ninian.

After a while, Ninian drained his mug and, with the briefest of goodnights, stomped out of the hall. Instantly Helewise turned to Josse. 'I didn't want to speak in front of him, as he's cross enough with himself already,' she whispered. 'But, Josse, if our postulated pair of murderers were trying to stop anyone identifying – or even finding – the dead St Clair cousins, whatever are they going to do when they find out Luc Jordan's now trying to get to Wealdsend too?'

The next day, the body of Lord Benedict de Vitré, late master of Medley Hall, was at long last going to be buried. The interment was long overdue: he had been dead for more than a week and, even in the cold cellar, time had not been kind. The delay had been unavoidable, for Lady Richenza had refused to act until some sort of ceremony could be arranged – and, with England under the interdict, that had been virtually impossible. Finally, Sebastian Garrique had managed to persuade her that they really could put it off no longer. Sitting in the solitude of the steward's room early in the morning of the burial, door firmly closed and barred against interruption, he spared a moment to congratulate himself.

He felt he understood Lady Richenza's desire to make a show of the disposal of Lord Benedict's remains. Sebastian, perhaps more than

226

anyone, knew what a truly horrible man his late master had been. The idea of being married to such a monster made him shudder with distaste. A steward was usually the first servant to enter the marital bedchamber in the morning, and, far too often in the past, Sebastian had been forced to witness the state of the young wife after a night with her husband.

Sebastian Garrique frequently found the bawdy, lewd, libidinous excesses of life revolting. Once, in his youth, he had believed he might have heard God's voice, calling him to the enclosed life of a monk. He knew he would have had little issue with obedience and chastity, especially the latter; however, his driving force was to rise out of the lowly state into which he had been born, and he knew in his heart that he would have had a problem with the vow of poverty.

He had spent several years working his way into his elevated position in Lord Benedict's household, turning a blind eye to the man's cruelty and ruthlessness and, in so doing, had managed to amass a considerable amount of money. Lord Benedict had paid Sebastian well for his loyalty and his discretion. If, in accepting the payments, Sebastian sometimes felt he had sold his soul, then that was the price one had to pay.

Sebastian was not the only one at Medley Hall to feel huge relief now that the day had finally come when they would see the last of Lord Benedict. A grave had been prepared on the far side of the manor's burial ground, a spot that was discreetly sheltered by a large yew tree. So far, so good; like everyone else in England bereft of the church's ministrations, they would simply dispose of the body as best they could. Lady Richenza, however, was not satisfied with a furtive, hurried interment. Returning once again to where his thoughts had begun, Sebastian thought he knew why: she was trying to hide the fact that she was overjoyed that he was dead.

She was planning an elaborate funeral feast, and everyone at Medley was working as hard as they knew how to make sure her wishes were obeyed. Extra hands had been called in to help; even Sebastian, nominally in charge of all the comings and goings, did not recognize some of the people bustling in and out. Everything had to be perfect; here Sebastian was entirely in accord with his young mistress. The entire household knew that many high-born, wealthy, influential and important lords and their ladies would attend. Only a very few were privy to the full guest list...

And, as if all that were not enough, Lady Richenza had refused to let the burial go ahead until some cleric could be found to mutter the right words. As if, Sebastian reflected sourly, it would make any difference. A man as evil as Lord Benedict would be lucky not to be sent straight down to the Devil.

It was Sebastian himself who had finally found the solution that would see Lord Benedict safely in the ground, and his household relieved of the torment of smelling his stinking corpse. Recalling in a flash of genius the two canons who had come to inspect the newly dead lord, he had sent word to Tonbridge, asking if, of their charity, one or other of them could spare the time to *attend the burial*, as he had tactfully phrased it, and *perhaps speak a few words to comfort the mourners*.

Word came back that Canon Stephen would be happy to oblige, and Lady Richenza at last gave her consent for arrangements to proceed. The fact that a canon was by no means a priest – and anyway, in truth, was forbidden by the interdict from so much as opening his mouth at a burial – seemed to have escaped her notice. Sebastian, for one, was not going to point it out.

The hard-working household still had a few days to finish preparations for the lavish feast. Today was for the burial. Standing up, straightening the severe black tunic and smoothing down his hair, he opened the door of his room.

The smell hit him like a punch in the face, for the steward's room was off the corridor which ran down to the cellar steps.

Sebastian took a perfumed handkerchief out of his sleeve, pressing it over his nose and mouth and inhaling the strong scent of cloves. *This will soon be over*, he told himself. He went first to the hall, where, as he had ordered, a group of six men awaited him, their faces full of apprehension. Two of them carried a hurdle between them. 'Come with me,' Sebastian said curtly.

He led the way back along the passage and down the steps into the cellar. There were one or two expressions of disgust. Someone with a weaker stomach than the rest made a retching

229

noise.

Sebastian stopped in front of the trestle, with its heavy load. Glancing round, he thought one or two more men had joined the group. *Brave, or just plain nosy?* he thought. He nodded towards the corpse. 'Get on with it,' he said.

The men with the hurdle stepped up to the trestle, resting the hurdle on the side of the planks and gently easing it under the body. Two other men went round to the other side of the trestle, and two moved to stand at the corpse's head and feet. Sebastian, intent on what was happening, was only vaguely aware of others behind him, craning forward to watch. Grunting with effort, the men stationed around the trestle lifted and shoved at the corpse, trying to insert the hurdle underneath it.

Just as they were raising the head and shoulders of the body, one of the men stumbled, falling heavily on to the chest of the corpse. There was a sudden loud squelch, and a jet of liquid squirted from beneath the body, just under the shoulder blade, the foul stuff seeping into the rich fabric of the tunic and rapidly discolouring it. The stench was appalling.

The men stopped, suddenly still as statues.

'What was that?' hissed Sebastian.

'*I* didn't do anything!' the man who had stumbled muttered nervously. He looked round at all the pairs of eyes intently watching him. 'Did I?'

Sebastian had been on the point of ordering them to get on with it. But now, unfortunately, he realized that might be difficult. People talked,

230

and there were far too many men intently watching his every move. Women, too, he noticed, glancing swiftly around the cellar; some of the female servants had come to observe their late master as he began his last journey.

Nodding at the man standing by the corpse's head, he said, 'Unfasten the tunic and the undershirt, then turn him on his side. You!' He pointed at the man who had almost fallen. 'Help him.' The men did as he commanded, their hands clumsy in their haste. Shoving the avid spectators roughly out of the way, Sebastian stared down at his late master's pale, flaccid back.

The edges of the tiny wound that had killed Lord Benedict had turned back, curling like the lips of a partly open mouth. As all those staring down at him took in the implications, there was a gasp of fascinated horror.

'Who did *that*?' someone demanded.

''E died because 'is 'eart gave out,' another voice put in. 'Them monks said as much.'

They were canons, Sebastian thought absently. His mind was racing.

'Then how come there's a stab wound in his back?' a third man asked.

'Who else saw the body other than the canons?' someone asked.

'The healer woman came with them,' a woman's voice piped up from somewhere near the steps. 'Then she came back again to lay him out, and she had that forest woman with her.'

'*I* didn't see them, Aggie!' another woman objected. 'Are you sure?'

'Sure as I'm standing here enduring that

231

stench!' said the first one crossly. 'I showed them down the passage to the cellar myself, so I should know!'

'He could have been stabbed after he died,' a voice said quietly. 'Maybe to hide what really happened.'

Sebastian spun round, trying to locate the speaker. In the shuffling, shifting crowd, now quite sizeable, it was impossible. 'Who—?' he began.

A shrill voice interrupted him. 'How else could he have died, then? It weren't any of us did for him, much as...' The words broke off in a squeak of pain as the speaker was abruptly silenced.

'He was a sick man,' the quiet voice said. Sebastian craned this way and that, trying to see who it was. 'Suppose he'd asked her for help, and she fed him some secret potion, and that was what killed him? Easy enough, when she was laying him out, to make that deep, narrow wound, in the hope that one of us would find it and think he was murdered.'

There, Sebastian thought, *that sallow man in the dark tunic...*

But then someone else came pushing down the steps, and the crowd moved again.

'That's right!' a woman cried. 'If that healer woman's gone round telling folks that the stab wound killed him, then it's only her word that says so. Nobody else saw it, did they, till *after* she'd laid him out? Not till now, this very moment!'

An excited babble broke out, everyone all at once remembering details which, Sebastian was

232

quite sure, were largely made up. He raised his hands. 'Enough!' he shouted.

Recognizing the voice of authority, the crowd instantly obeyed.

'Are you proposing–' Sebastian's eyes roamed over the crowd in the cellar as he spoke – 'that Mistress de Gifford, renowned apothecary and healer, wife to the sheriff of Tonbridge, risked her reputation and her position and gave Lord Benedict a potion that killed him? Then, to hide her blunder, inflicted a stab wound to suggest he died by other means?'

There was a dead silence, save for the fading echo of his words. Into it, a soft voice said, 'She's a fine woman, aye. But she weren't the only one as came to lay him out.'

'We shall not,' Sebastian said firmly, 'delay the burial.'

Not without difficulty, he had finally cleared the crowd out of the cellar, curtly ordering everyone but the six detailed to carry the hurdle back to their work. He had sent word asking Lady Richenza to meet him in the hall and, ushering her away from the hurdle bearers, he had told her what had been discovered. She was dressed for the interment, robed and cloaked in dark, sombre colours, her face hidden behind her heavy veil.

Which, Sebastian reflected, was a pity, since it meant he could not see her expression.

'Is ... is Canon Stephen here?' she asked in a barely audible voice.

'He is, my lady. He awaits us at the grave.'

233

'Then let us proceed.'

Without another word – with no comment whatsoever about the surprising discovery – Lady Richenza lifted her chin and strode across the hall towards the door and the steps leading down to the courtyard. Hurrying to catch her up and offer his arm – she must surely be in some distress, and must not be allowed to fall – Sebastian emerged at her side. Matching his stride to hers, they set off for the burial ground. The men raised the hurdle and its heavy load and followed.

In the feeble morning sunshine, the body of Lord Benedict de Vitré was finally laid in the ground.

In the middle of the day, Abbess Caliste heard footsteps in the cloister outside her room, and the sound of raised voices, immediately followed by a peremptory tap on her door. Even as she said, 'Enter,' the door was thrust open.

She looked up in surprise as a tall, lean man clad in black and a slight, veiled woman came in. She had the impression that there were quite a few more people out in the cloister, but the tall man quickly shut the door on them.

He turned to face her. 'My lady abbess, I apologize for interrupting you in your work,' he said courteously. She nodded an acknowledgement. 'I present Lady Richenza, widow of Lord Benedict de Vitré.' He indicated the young woman standing stiffly beside him.

Abbess Caliste studied Lady Richenza. As far as she could tell, for the veil did its job well, the

234

girl was staring straight in front of her and had not even glanced at Caliste; issuing any words of greeting did not seem to have occurred to her.

'I am sorry for your loss, Lady Richenza,' Caliste said. The only response was a curt nod. Turning back to the man, she added, 'What is your business here?'

'I am Sebastian Garrique, steward to Lord Benedict. We are searching for the healer.'

Caliste said cautiously, 'There are many gifted women among my nursing nuns. Is one of you unwell?'

'We don't want healing,' Lady Richenza said abruptly. 'We're looking for the healer woman because she ... she...'

'There is some – er – confusion over the death of Lord Benedict, my lady.' Smoothly, the steward took over. 'It has been suggested that he may have been killed by the administration of a badly prepared healing potion, and that an attempt was made to disguise this by the infliction of a stab wound, after he was dead.'

Caliste said, with a calmness she was far from feeling, 'This healer, then, must have had access to the body.'

'She did.' Lady Richenza's voice had the light, whispery tone of a girl. 'She came with Mistress Gifford, to lay him out. That's when she did it!' The sudden vindictiveness came as a shock.

With a sense of foreboding, Caliste said, 'Who do you accuse, my lady?'

'She's called Meggie,' Lady Richenza said. Her veil, it appeared, was annoying her, for suddenly she flung it back, revealing a beautiful, perfectly featured, oval face. Two spots of colour burned in her pale cheeks. 'We've heard tell she's known here, at the abbey, and we've come to apprehend her and make her answer for her crime. We—'

'We wish to question her only, at this stage,' Sebastian Garrique interrupted. He shot a glance at his mistress, which, even from where Caliste sat, it was clear meant *be quiet.* 'It is not, of course, for us to take the law into our own hands, and we intend to refer the matter to Gervase de Gifford.'

'The sheriff will act in this,' Lady Richenza said, nodding as if to emphasize the words.

'We are acquainted with de Gifford,' Sebastian put in. 'And, as we have said, with his wife, who—'

'My husband will be avenged!' Lady Richenza shouted.

The echoes of her last words rang in the little room. When they died, Sebastian looked down at the abbess and said mildly, 'Is the healer woman here, my lady?'

Caliste's mind had been working furiously. Now, with total honesty, she replied, 'Meggie has been lodging with us, yes. She has been helping with the care of one of our elderly patients. At present, however, she isn't here.'

'Where is she, then?' Lady Richenza demanded.

The truth was that Meggie was out with one of the groups searching for Lilas. To say that, however, would be to admit that the vulnerable old woman had been abducted, and Caliste felt

236

instinctively that this was not something to share with outsiders. Particularly ones who came with terrible accusations against someone she loved...

'I cannot say, my lady,' Caliste said quietly. 'Meggie is a herbalist, and much of her work involves endless and sometimes arduous searching for the plants she uses.' Little in the way of fresh ingredients was to be had in November, she reflected, but then hopefully her visitors probably would not know that.

'But she *must* be found!' Lady Richenza cried. 'We *have* to see her!'

'I cannot manufacture her for you out of thin air,' the abbess said stiffly. The young woman was both irritating her and worrying her, for there was surely something unreasoned in her wild remarks. 'When she returns, I shall tell her what you have said.'

Lady Richenza's lovely face grew taut with anger. *Was it really anger?* Caliste wondered suddenly. *Could it be fear?* 'You mustn't *warn* her,' she cried, 'or she'll run away!'

Abbess Caliste glared at her. 'In my experience, my lady, only the guilty run away.' *Or*, she added silently, *those who fear they are to be accused of a crime they did not commit, with small hope of persuading their accusers that they are wrong...*

'She *is* guilty,' Lady Richenza said firmly.

'How can you be so sure?' Caliste countered swiftly. 'I have had long experience of Meggie's healing skills, and I have never known her make a mistake.'

Lady Richenza leaned forward, her hands on

Caliste's table. Putting her face close to Caliste's, she said, 'They say she's one of the forest people – she was born there, you know, and spent her childhood out in the wilds. She hides away alone, and she is unmarried. Who knows what sort of a life she leads?' She stood up, smiling smugly, as if she had just delivered irrefutable proof of Meggie's guilt.

Caliste, to whom quite a few of those accusations equally applied, waited until she felt she could speak calmly. Then she said, 'Even if what you say is true, Lady Richenza, are any of these reasons to accuse Meggie of killing a man with a poorly prepared potion?'

Lady Richenza's mouth opened and closed a couple of times as she sought furiously for a reply. Then she hissed, *She's not like the rest of us!*'

There was dead silence in the little room. Then Caliste repeated, very softly, 'Not like the rest of us.' She glanced first at Lady Richenza, then at Sebastian. 'I see.'

The steward, at least, had the grace to look abashed.

After a moment, he said to Lady Richenza, 'We should leave, my lady, and allow the abbess to return to her work.'

Lady Richenza looked as if she was about to protest. Then, as if even she appreciated there was little point in remaining, she spun on her heel, setting her wide skirts swirling, and flounced towards the door. Sebastian slipped ahead of her just in time to open it for her.

Standing in the doorway, she turned back to

glare at Caliste. 'We will return,' she said icily. 'For now, we shall go down to Tonbridge and seek out the sheriff.' She gave a triumphant nod. 'In the meantime, I shall order my servants to search for her.' Sebastian began to protest, but she ignored him. 'She shall be brought to justice!' Then, closing the door with a bang, she was gone.

Caliste listened as the sound of footsteps faded away. She made herself wait. Too soon, and she might find Lady Richenza and her retinue still lingering on the forecourt. She must not let them see her.

Wait just a little longer...

When she could control her impatience no more, she left her room and hurried off along the cloister. First, she had to find someone fast and reliable to go and find Josse. Then she must set about finding Meggie.

Before anyone else did.

FIFTEEN

There were too many of the Hawkenlye community in the vicinity of the main gates and the forecourt for Caliste to risk leaving the abbey that way. Instead, she made for the smaller, rear gate that opened on to the path down to the vale. Slipping out, careful to ensure she was not spotted, she turned to her left, hurrying round the abbey walls until the long slope up to the forest opened up before her.

The ancient trees of the place of her birth seemed to welcome her and, as soon as she was within their embrace, the tumult of her thoughts was calmed. She stopped for a moment, her breathing steadying. Then she set about hunting for Meggie.

Still torn with guilt because she had failed to protect Lilas, Meggie had offered to go out into the outer fringes of the forest, to see if she could pick up any signs of activity. Those had been her very words, although Caliste knew what she was thinking: if the worst had happened, and Lilas was dead, then the forest was a good place to hide a body.

Caliste searched for some time. Then, emerging from one of the faint animal tracks that criss-crossed the forest, she found herself in the clear-

240

ing before St Edmund's Chapel. Emerging through its doorway was Meggie.

'Meggie!' Caliste called.

Meggie turned at her voice. 'Good morning, Abbess Caliste!' she called back.

'Wait there,' Caliste said, hurrying towards her. 'I need to speak to you, but let's go back into the chapel.' *Where we're less likely to be seen*, she added silently.

The two women entered the chapel, then embraced. 'I've been down with the Black Madonna,' Meggie said. 'I've been asking her to help us find Lilas.'

'No sign of her?'

'None. I was about to come back to the abbey and tell you so.'

Caliste paused. Then she said, 'Meggie, I have just had a visit from Lord Benedict's widow and her steward.' Succinctly, undramatically, she told Meggie what the visitors had said.

Meggie looked her straight in the eyes. 'I did not prescribe any remedy for him, and I certainly didn't kill him,' she said. 'Nor did I inflict that wound.' Her composure cracking, she burst out, 'It was I who found it; I who told Sabin and my father! Why would I draw attention to the fact if I thought I'd got away with it? Anyway, it was...' With a visible effort, she held back whatever she had been about to say. 'I am not involved in this death, I—'

'Meggie, stop.' Caliste reached out for her hand. 'I believe you.'

Meggie's wide brown eyes (*so like her father's*, Caliste thought, with an ache in her heart)

241

were fixed on hers. 'Do you?' she whispered.

'Of course.' There was nothing more to be said.

'Then ... what are we going to do?' Meggie sounded desolate.

'I've sent word to your father,' Caliste said briskly, 'and, knowing him as I do, I suspect he'll come hurrying over to help.'

'If Lady Richenza is planning on seeking out Gervase – and, presumably, bringing him back to the abbey – then I suppose she'll expect to find me there,' Meggie said slowly. 'Should I come back to Hawkenlye with you?'

Caliste gave her a smile. 'You should, my dear Meggie, but if I were you, it's the very last thing I would do.'

Meggie hugged her, very tightly. 'Please will you tell my father not to worry?'

Caliste smiled. 'I'll tell him, yes, but I'm not sure he'll take any notice.'

They stood for several moments, still hugging. Then Meggie gently detached herself. With a wry smile, she turned and slipped out of the chapel.

Helewise, standing beside the door in Abbess Caliste's room, watched as Josse furiously defended his daughter.

'Abbess Caliste, I don't believe you can know the whole story,' he thundered, 'for I doubt Meggie would have told you. It involves someone else.'

Caliste, Helewise observed, did not appear to be the least fazed by Josse's anger. *She knows as well as I do*, she thought, *that it is not directed at her*. 'I think, Sir Josse,' the abbess said mildly, 'that if I am to face Lady Richenza's accusations again when she returns, *you* had better tell me. Everything you know, please, for that way I may best be able to assist you in defending Meggie.'

'It was...' Josse began. But then he stopped. *He is protecting Sabin*, Helewise thought. *Even now, when his own precious daughter stands falsely accused, he hesitates to implicate another.* 'You must tell her, Josse,' she said quietly. 'Let us have the truth; at least here, among the three of us.'

He turned to look at her, and she was filled with pity at the pain in his eyes. Then, once more facing Abbess Caliste, he said, 'Sabin de Gifford prepared two potions, one for Lord Benedict, one for Lady Richenza.' As if having made up his mind to speak, it seemed he was going to be blunt. 'She – Lady Richenza – wanted to render him impotent and, if the worst happened and she was at risk of conceiving his child, she wanted to make sure it did not happen.'

'Were these potions dangerous?' If she was shocked, the abbess managed to disguise the fact.

'No, they were not; not really,' Josse replied. 'And certainly not fatal: I have Meggie's assurance of that. It was she who told me all this,' he added. 'She, too, revealed to me the presence of the stab wound that was the true cause of Lord Benedict's death.'

'I am very relieved,' Abbess Caliste said. 'I did not for one moment suspect Meggie, Sir Josse, but I am glad of your reassurance that Sabin's potion, too, could not have proved fatal.' As if suddenly struck by some reassuring thought, she smiled. 'Lady Richenza's steward – tall, black-clad man?'

'Sebastian Garrique. Aye, I've met him,' Josse said grimly.

'Yes. He announced his intention of involving Gervase; he said he knows him. What I am thinking, Sir Josse, is that we have no more need to worry!' Her smile widened. 'As soon as Sabin learns that Meggie is accused, she will speak up and admit it was she, not Meggie, who prepared the medication for Lord Benedict. She will be quite safe to do so, for we are certain that it was not responsible for his death.'

'Aye,' Josse said. 'I am sure you are right, my lady.'

He says the right words, Helewise thought, a shiver of fear catching at her heart. *Why, then, do I sense that he does not actually believe them?*

'I think,' she said, moving to stand beside Josse, 'that, even though we may be sure of Meggie's innocence swiftly being proved, nevertheless it might be wise for her to keep out of the way.'

There was no response from Josse. But the abbess, raising her head, met Helewise's eyes. 'I've already thought of that,' she murmured.

When the summons came, Helewise thought Josse was going to refuse it. 'Why should I have to hurry down to Tonbridge to answer for my daughter?' he raged. 'Especially when she's

244

innocent!'

Gervase's messenger stood in the doorway of the abbess's room, looking as if he wished he was anywhere but there.

'Perhaps it would be as well to do as Gervase asks, Sir Josse,' the abbess said. 'The summons is, after all, for Meggie, and we are unable to comply since she is not here. If you go immediately, your assurances on her behalf, as well as any new evidence that may be presented, may carry sufficient weight that the charge against her is dropped.'

She is right, Helewise thought. She realized – as Josse apparently had not – what the abbess did not want to say in front of the messenger: that, as soon as Sabin spoke up, the case against Meggie would dissolve.

'I will come with you, Josse,' she said. 'The day draws on, but we should go straight away. The sooner this is resolved, the better.'

They did not speak on the ride down to Tonbridge. Riding side by side behind the messenger, Helewise knew Josse would not want to discuss what was foremost on their minds when the man might overhear. To talk of anything else just then was, Helewise thought, out of the question.

The messenger led the way to Gervase's house. She followed Josse up the steps, and, as if someone within had been looking out for them, the door opened to admit them. Helewise, looking at the tableau before her, drew in her breath sharply. Seated in a semicircle beside the hearth

245

were Lady Richenza, Sebastian Garrique and Sabin de Gifford. All three stared at Helewise and Josse as if they had just been tried and found guilty.

Gervase, perhaps deliberately distancing himself, stood apart. Then, as the frozen moment broke up, he stepped forward, greeted them and drew up two more chairs.

'You have not brought the healer woman,' Lady Richenza said.

Helewise sensed Josse's furious response. Hastily she put out a hand, taking hold of his arm. 'Gently,' she whispered.

He took a very deep breath, then said, 'The healer woman is my daughter, and she has a name. Meggie has not yet returned to the abbey, and so we have come in her stead.' He turned to look straight at Sabin. 'I would have thought,' he added, 'that this misunderstanding ought to have been resolved by now.'

Sabin held his eyes for a moment. Then, flushing slightly, she lowered her head.

Lady Richenza's light, glassy voice rang out again. 'My husband was given a potion which, in all likelihood, caused his death. During the laying-out of his body – a task performed by your daughter, Sir Josse – an attempt was made to disguise the manner of his death by the inflicting of a deep, narrow stab wound. Thus, by trying to confuse the cause of death, did this healer seek to cover up her own culpability.'

'But that wasn't...' Josse began. Then, as the truth dawned, he gasped.

Helewise, who had reached the same conclusion an instant before, leapt to her feet. Before Josse could say anything (she feared that an explosion of furious indignation would only make matters worse) she said, 'There is no reason to suspect that the potion prepared for Lord Benedict caused him harm. We have been assured by Meggie that none of the ingredients could possibly have been fatal.' She turned, very deliberately, and stared very hard at Sabin.

Again, Sabin dropped her head.

'Who but she knows what went into the potion?' Sebastian Garrique said. 'Did anyone else verify the contents?'

There was a tense silence.

Then Josse, too, stood up. 'Meggie did not prepare it,' he said. He walked over to Sabin, standing right over her. 'It was prepared by Mistress Gifford here, and it was you, Sabin, who hastened in fear to consult Meggie when Lord Benedict died, desperate for her reassurance that your potion was not to blame.'

For a heartbeat, Sabin looked up and met his eyes. Then, very coldly, she said, 'I didn't.'

Amid the shocked tumult of reaction whirling in her head, Helewise had one single, clear thought: *I knew this was going to happen.*

She said, trying to sound calm and reasonable, 'But, Sabin, we know that is not true. You came to seek out Meggie and, although at first she respected your confidences, once she had found the stab wound, she felt she had no choice but to tell her father. Sir Josse and I are privy to the whole story, my dear,' she went on, trying to put some warmth and compassion into her voice, 'and we know that you first visited Medley Hall because Lady Richenza summoned you, and you subsequently prescribed remedies for both her and Lord Benedict. Then, as Sir Josse has just said, when you feared that you had inadvertently harmed Lord Benedict, you asked Meggie to go with you and reassure you that you had done nothing of the sort. Meggie,' she added meaningfully, 'was happy to oblige, and readily gave you the comfort you so badly needed.'

Even as Helewise addressed her, Sabin was shaking her head, muttering, 'No, *no*.' Looking up at Helewise, she said, 'The first time I went to Medley Hall was in the company of the two Tonbridge canons, Stephen and Mark, who asked me to go with them to view Lord Benedict's body, and try to ascertain the cause of death.' She turned to stare first, very intently, at Lady Richenza, and then at Gervase. 'It's a lie, to say I had been before!'

Stepping forward, Gervase said, 'What did you and the canons decide, Sabin?'

'Lord Benedict died from a spasm of the heart,' she said firmly. 'Canon Stephen – he's the infirmarian – said Lord Benedict had recently been to consult him, and Stephen told him to eat less and take more exercise, which would improve his health and help his heart.'

'Lady Richenza?' Gervase turned to her. 'Did you know of this?'

'I ... no.' The lovely face creased in a frown.

There was a moment of stillness. Helewise found she was holding her breath. Then, just as she had known he would, Gervase said quietly to

248

Lady Richenza, 'And did you summon my wife and ask her to prepare remedies for yourself and Lord Benedict?'

There was a long pause. Then, her face very white but her voice firm, Lady Richenza said, 'No. My late husband must have met her in private, for I knew nothing of it.'

'It could equally well have been Sabin whom he summoned,' Helewise said firmly.

Gervase looked at Josse. 'It is, I fear, a case of Lady Richenza's and Sabin's word against Meggie's,' he said, frowning.

'Others at Medley will bear witness that Meggie came with Mistress Gifford to lay out the body,' Sebastian said. 'A woman servant who has long been with the household remembers seeing them, and sending them on to the cellar where the body lay. I am sure others, too, will remember.'

'But that in itself is not in dispute!' Josse fumed. 'It's—'

Sabin's voice, sharp with anxiety, interrupted him. 'I *swear* to you that my visit with the canons was the first, and it was after Lord Benedict was dead!' Jumping up, she ran to Gervase and took both his hands. 'Send for them, Gervase! Oh, *please*, do as I ask! They'll confirm that I had no prior knowledge of the house or its inhabitants, and that will prove to you all that I could not possibly have consulted Lady Richenza and prepared any potion for Lord Benedict!' She paused, breathing raggedly, and then added coldly, 'If, that is, you all require more proof than Lady Richenza's word.'

There was an awkward silence. Gervase, after a puzzled look at his wife, lowered his eyes. After a moment he said, 'I will send word to the priory, and ask the two canons to join us.'

The wait – not, in the end, a very long one – seemed interminable. Unable to go on watching Josse look as if he'd like to pounce on Sabin and shake the truth out of her, Helewise suggested they go outside.

The two canons arrived, and Helewise and Josse followed them up the steps. Gervase took the canons to the far side of the hall, and, in low tones, muttered to them for some time. Helewise tried to persuade herself that he would balance both sides of the argument, and give no more weight to Sabin's version than to Meggie's. Once, she would have trusted him. Now, she found she wasn't so confident...

She heard movement. Looking up, she saw that Gervase was ushering the two canons towards the seated figures. 'Canon Mark and Canon Stephen,' he began, 'you asked Sabin de Gifford, here present, to go with you to view the dead body of Lord Benedict de Vitré. Sabin has a question she would like to put to you.' He turned to his wife. 'Sabin?'

What does this mean? Helewise wondered. *Does Gervase doubt her? Is he leaving it up to her to tell her lies?*

She listened closely as Sabin started to speak. 'Brothers, you led the way to Medley that day when you asked me to accompany you, didn't you?'

Canon Mark glanced at his companion, looking slightly perplexed. 'Yes, Mistress Gifford, I suppose so. I can't, in truth, recall who rode ahead, but it seems likely.'

As if anxious to move on from his slightly ambiguous answer, Sabin said quickly, 'Yes, quite. And, once at the hall, you showed me where to go.'

'It was the steward who escorted us down to the cellar, as far as I recall,' Canon Mark replied. 'We had not been there before, my lady. Canon Stephen had consulted Lord Benedict previously, it's true, but Lord Benedict came to see him at the priory.'

There was a pause. Sabin appeared to be floundering. 'I am trying to persuade these people that I had not previously visited Medley Hall,' she said eventually. 'Since that is undoubtedly the truth, I require you, Canon Stephen, Canon Mark–' she bestowed on the latter a ravishing smile – 'to confirm that I displayed no knowledge of the place.'

Mark, looking slightly dazzled, returned Sabin's smile. 'No, I don't believe you did, Mistress Gifford.'

'Thank you,' Sabin murmured. 'Canon Stephen?'

Just for a moment, he hesitated. Had Helewise not been watching so closely, she might have missed the quick, slightly apprehensive look he shot at his fellow canon. Then he said, 'No.'

Into the sudden hush, Lady Richenza said, 'There! Now you have it. Mistress de Gifford did not prepare any potions. It is the forest healer

251

woman who is culpable.'

Josse's rage broke. Turning on Gervase, he said, 'A word. Now.' And, giving Gervase no chance to refuse, he strode out of the hall and headed down the steps into the courtyard, Gervase following him.

The two canons hurriedly did the same. Helewise was on the point of going over to try to reason with Sabin, but found that she could not bear to let Josse face Gervase alone. She went to stand at the top of the steps. Josse, she realized, was trying to persuade the sheriff of Meggie's innocence. Unfortunately, he was desperate and, unwittingly, going about it in entirely the wrong way...

'Josse, what you ask of me is impossible!' Gervase shouted eventually. 'I cannot support you just because you tell me to! You believe your daughter; I believe my wife.'

'But she's lying!' Josse cried.

This is making matters worse, Helewise thought frantically. Should she intervene? She did not know.

Hesitantly, she started to descend the steps. Then something occurred to her. She stopped, thinking hard.

Hoping neither Josse nor Gervase would notice, she stealthily jumped down the steps and, crossing the courtyard, hurried off up the road that led into the town.

She knew Canon Stephen was the infirmarian, and so looked for him in his place of work. He had clearly gone straight back to whatever task

252

he had been doing before the interruption, and was in a small side room, pouring some thick, greenish liquid from a large jar into smaller bottles. He looked up as she was shown in, the frown replaced by a smile of welcome.

'I am sorry to disturb you in your labours,' she said.

He bowed courteously. 'It is a pleasure to be sought out by the abbess of Hawkenlye.'

'Not any more,' she said swiftly.

He smiled again. 'Perhaps not, my lady. Yet we hear that your good works continue. What can I do for you?'

It might have been wishful thinking, but she had an idea that he was eager for her to speak. She paused. Now that the moment had come, she did not know how best to say what she had come to say. *Just tell him what you thought you observed*, a calm voice said in her head. 'When Mistress Gifford asked you just now to verify that the visit she made to Medley with you was the first time she'd been there – when you went to view Lord Benedict's dead body – I was watching you. I may be wrong but I thought you hesitated.'

He studied her for a long moment, not speaking.

'*Please*,' she whispered. 'A young woman stands accused of something that I know she did not do.'

Slowly Stephen nodded. 'I did hesitate, yes, although I'm surprised you noticed. Oh, I've tried to tell myself it's nothing, but nevertheless, it's bothering me, and I can't seem to get it out

253

of my mind.' He smiled quickly. 'In fact, I was relieved to see you, when you arrived just now. I suppose there's no harm in telling you...'

She waited.

In a rush, he said, 'It was just that, when Mistress Gifford, Brother Mark and I entered the house, she – Mistress Gifford – made a remark that seemed to suggest she'd been there before.'

Helewise's heart gave a thump. 'What did she say?' she asked urgently. 'Can you remember?'

He frowned. Then he said, 'She remarked that we must be in the original part of the house, and I thought she was about to say it was different from the newer sections, only she suddenly seemed to realize what she was saying, and she stopped. I prompted her to continue, and she said something about it being dark and cold.'

'Dark and cold,' Helewise echoed absently.

'Oh, and she said it was frightening, too. But...' He stopped.

'Go on,' she urged.

He shook his head. 'I *could* be mistaken, but, just for an instant, I had the clear impression that she was familiar with the house.'

She had been there before, Helewise thought. *Of course she had, for she went to see Lady Richenza, to prescribe the potions for her and for Lord Benedict, just as Meggie says. That earlier meeting with Lady Richenza can't have been witnessed by anyone – and, if both women deny it, what on earth is to be done?*

If Sabin had admitted to that earlier visit, her thoughts ran on, *then people might have started*

254

to suspect that one of her potions had killed Lord Benedict.

As it is ... Helewise was torn between anguish for Meggie and fury at Sabin's treachery. *As it is, she's trying to put the blame on Meggie.*

Oh, dear Lord, how could she!

Canon Stephen, she noticed belatedly, was anxiously hovering. 'My lady? Are you unwell? You look rather pale.'

'I am quite well, thank you,' she managed to say.

Then – although she could see that he longed to ask her to explain – she wished him a firm good day and hastened back to the sheriff's house.

Lady Richenza and her steward had gone, and Gervase was nowhere to be seen. Josse, waiting for her with obvious impatience, was standing in the courtyard, holding their horses' reins. 'A moment,' she said, giving him an apologetic smile.

Inside the hall, Sabin was alone. Approaching her, Helewise said, 'Sabin, you must tell the truth. It *was* you who made the potion.'

'It wasn't!' Sabin cried.

'In any case–' Helewise pressed on as if Sabin hadn't spoken – 'it was a blade, not any potion, that killed Lord Benedict, so, in the end, you have nothing to fear. Can you not admit to having prepared the medicament? You are protected by your reputation as an apothecary, and your status as Gervase's wife. But, Sabin, Meggie has no such armour. The fact that the stab wound

255

actually killed him is being overlooked as people rush to put the blame on her, purely because she isn't like everyone else.'

Sabin looked at her, just once, then swiftly turned her eyes away. 'I didn't do it,' she muttered. 'Lady Richenza supports me. We never met, and I am blameless.'

It was, Helewise reflected wearily, turning into a mindlessly repeated incantation.

Sick at heart, disgusted with Sabin and worried to the depths of her being about Meggie – and about Josse – Helewise turned away.

SIXTEEN

There was, Meggie reflected as she hurried away from St Edmund's Chapel and plunged into the welcoming shelter of the forest, only one place to go. She knew she could look after herself in the hut; she'd lived there through much colder winter weather than this when she was a child, and her mother had taught her how to make sure of the things human life had to have to sustain it: warmth, shelter, water, food. She always kept some supplies in the hut, and a good reserve of firewood stood neatly stacked against its side wall, sheltered by the overhang of the roof.

Nobody outside her immediate circle knew how to find the hut, or was even aware that it existed. Moreover – and this really should have come first – Josse would not worry about her quite so much if he knew that was where she was. *I can't go and tell him*, Meggie thought as she paced along, *because they may already be hunting for me*. She did not pause to define *they*. It was too frightening. *But it's all right, because he'll know*.

She hoped very much she was right.

The anxious fear would not leave her. *As soon as Gervase becomes involved and Sabin finds out what's happening*, she told herself, *the truth will emerge, because Sabin will speak up in my defence*. The injustice of it hit her suddenly. *She came for my help! I gave it willingly, because she was desperate!*

Desperate. The word echoed in her head.

She seemed to hear a wise voice say, *Sabin is desperate, yes. Do not rely on her, for she fights to save herself*.

And then Meggie knew why she was so afraid.

She made herself go on. Forcing her mind away from the worst of her dread, she tried to summon facts that might work in her favour. She was a healer, and the number of people she had helped and advised over the years was uncountable. She had a good reputation at the abbey, and Helewise often said that she would not be able to do her work at the sanctuary without Meggie, her knowledge and her remedies.

All that, she realized with a sinking of the heart, *is nothing when set against the fact that I am an outsider. Born out of wedlock to a forest woman* (Joanna's pedigree had in fact been far

257

more elevated than anyone else's for miles around, but hardly anyone knew that, and those who did kept it to themselves) *and raised, wild and barefoot, in its secret fastnesses.*

No. If they were determined to find someone to blame for poisoning Lord Benedict de Vitré with a potion, and then attempting to cover it up with a wound inflicted after death, then they wouldn't settle for Sabin de Gifford, Tonbridge apothecary, healer and wife to the sheriff. Not when the other option was the strange, unknown, outsider: Meggie.

The hut seemed to reach out to her, offering its secure roof and walls, and its wonderfully secret location, as the one place she wanted to be.

She quickened her pace. Just in case anyone should come after her – it was not unknown for hounds to be used to track a fugitive – she took a twisting, turning route, doubling back on herself several times. She even removed her boots and hose and, for far too many very cold paces, waded along in the little stream that wound its way through the forest.

At last, she came out into the clearing where the hut stood waiting for her. The familiar scene opened up before her, every inch of the terrain and the surrounding trees known and loved. She hurried up to the hut...

...and saw, as soon as she was close enough to make it out, that the intricately knotted rope which she used to secure the door hung in a loose loop from the door latch.

Instantly she stepped back, leaping into the shelter of the trees and crouching down behind a thicket of brambles. Who was inside? Was it – hope flared swiftly – was it Jehan?

Just as quickly, disappointment followed: if it was Jehan, where was his horse? Where was Auban, that patient, comfortable, chestnut horse? And Jehan, she knew in an instinctive flash, would have been looking out for her. Would have sensed, in all likelihood, that she was near, and come out to greet her. Open his arms to her. Hold her tight and kiss her, with all the passion built up by absence.

Stop thinking about Jehan, she ordered herself.

Cautiously she emerged once more into the clearing. She looked round for a weapon; it was foolhardy, surely, to approach an unidentified stranger unarmed. She had a light, beautifully crafted sword that Jehan had made for her, and she knew exactly where it was. She pictured it, hidden beneath the straw-filled mattress on her sleeping platform. Inside the hut.

It was no use lamenting the fact. She bent down and picked up a length of wood, checking it was sound. Weighing it in her hands, she felt her confidence creep back.

She walked stealthily back to the door of the hut.

She raised the latch, carefully, making no sound.

She edged the door open, just a tiny amount, and peered through the gap.

She suppressed a gasp. Then, a wide grin spreading across her face, she flung the door wide and hurried inside.

The old woman crouched by the fire that glow-ed in the hearth, rosy-cheeked from the warmth, well wrapped-up in one of the woolly blankets from Meggie's bed. She returned the grin, eyes crinkling.

She said, with an edge of laughter in her voice, 'Knew you'd be along, sooner or later.'

Meggie knelt down on the floor and took Lilas in her arms.

'How did you find it?'

The first swift spate of questions – *Are you all right? Are you eating? Have you been keeping warm enough?* – were out of the way, and Lilas had reassured Meggie on every one. Now the next, equally important, queries could begin, first of which was how Lilas had managed to discover the hut.

'I was drawn here,' Lilas said, lowering her voice to a dramatic whisper. 'There's some power hereabouts, and it led me to your little hideaway.'

'A power,' Meggie breathed. Imagining some great, glowing light drawing Lilas on through the hidden ways of the forest, she said, 'This power must have felt your need, and—'

Lilas leaned over and dug her in the ribs. 'I'm teasing you, girl. I just stumbled on it, and recognized it as a good place.'

'Oh.'

Lilas said, 'Magic doesn't really work that way – leastways, not in my experience.' She must have noticed Meggie's disappointment. 'That's not to say there isn't power here,' she added gently. 'There is.' Fixing her eyes on Meggie's,

260

she murmured, 'Not yours, I sense, although you're well on your way.'

'My mother lived here,' Meggie said. 'And, before her, my grandmother. They say she was one of the Great Ones.' She wondered if Lilas knew what that meant.

She need not have worried. Lilas was nodding, accepting the statement as readily as if Meggie had just commented on the weather. 'What was her name? Your grandmother, I mean.'

'The Outworlders knew her as Mag Hobson. To the forest people, she was Meggie.'

'Your mother named you after her,' Lilas observed. 'Wise of her.' She nodded again, making a strange little gesture of reverence towards the hearth. 'She was indeed a Great One, and no mistake.'

'You've heard of her?'

Lilas grinned. 'Course I have. Didn't I tell you I have forest blood?'

'Yes, you did,' Meggie muttered. Discovering the old woman in her hut was proving not to be so strange, after all. People like Lilas – like Meggie – would readily feel its benign power and be drawn to it.

Meggie pulled her thoughts back to the moment. 'Why did you flee from the Hawkenlye infirmary?' she asked, although she felt she already knew. 'Did something – or some*one* – scare you?'

'Scare doesn't begin to describe it,' Lilas said with a shudder. 'I heard the commotion outside, in that big, open space inside the gates, and that puffed-up lord shouting his mouth off, and then

261

he made that poor, feeble, lily-livered sap of a monk speak up like that, and I guessed it wouldn't be long afore they came looking for me. I'd escaped the buggers once!' she exclaimed. 'Apparently, some grim-looking feller came to Hamhurst to fetch me away to that hawk-faced, bolt-eyed lord—'

'Nicholas Fitzwalter, do you mean?'

'Aye, him. Anyway, when his man came to fetch me, I wasn't there, see, because the village elders had got in a flap about me and my visions, and they'd decided, in their wisdom, to pack me off to Hawkenlye and get me out of the way.' Her indignation threatened to choke her.

'I'm sure they were thinking of your welfare,' Meggie said. 'The abbey nuns are very good at looking after people.'

'That's as maybe,' Lilas said with a sniff. 'But you can't tell me the villagers weren't also concerned for their own safety. It was dangerous, see, for all of them, to have an old crone spouting bad things about the king. Outsiders might have thought they all agreed with me.'

'They probably did,' Meggie murmured.

'Didn't have the guts to say so, though, did they?' Lilas countered.

There did not seem much point in pursuing it. 'So, when you were in the infirmary, you realized you had to get away?' she prompted. 'Before Fitzwalter's man came to find you?'

'Aye, I did,' Lilas said grimly. 'There's that little door at the far end of the ward, which opens on to the forecourt, and I'd been peeping out to see what was going on. I guessed he'd come in

262

that way since it was nearest. So I crept out through the main door, at the opposite end, and made my way out through the little gate that opens on to the valley behind the abbey. That looked a bit open for my needs, and besides, I could see lots of monks and other folk milling around. Besides, in the other direction was the forest. Knew I'd be safe there.'

'And you found my hut,' Meggie said. She took Lilas's thin old hand, squeezing it. 'I'm so glad you did.'

It was all very well to be warm and, with any luck, safe, Meggie reflected the next morning. With the stream running past close by, she and Lilas would not go thirsty. Food, however, threatened to be more of a challenge and, for the first time since her early childhood, Meggie was thrown back on her own ingenuity. There were root vegetables out in the plot in front of the hut, and late autumn in the forest provided berries and a few last fungi, in addition to the stores of chestnuts and hazelnuts that Meggie had already set aside. For the solid base without which a meal did not keep hunger away for long, however, she was going to have to remember all that her mother had taught her, and go foraging.

Leaving Lilas pulling and preparing roots, Meggie set off on to the hidden network of animal tracks deep within the forest. She had spent the previous evening fashioning a couple of traps out of withies, and, from the hook in the corner of the hut where it had hung since Joanna

263

had last put it there, she took down her mother's catapult. The leather sling had been stiff and dry, and Lilas had sat patiently rubbing animal fat into it until it had regained its flexibility. Whether Meggie would be any good with it remained to be seen. Geoffroi had, on rare occasions, allowed her to have a go with his, but the smallest target she had ever managed to hit was a tree.

After a long time of quietly wandering the tracks, studying the pattern of animal prints, eventually she set her traps. If they failed, she would resort to snares, although it would be with reluctance. It was one thing to imprison a creature in a cage supplied with bait and then dispatch it swiftly by wringing its neck; quite another to send it wild with panic and pain because it could not free itself from the ever-tightening loop of the snare.

Her first attempts with the catapult were risible. Then, with the images of both her mother and her brother in mind, she made herself relax and tried to copy the way they did it. She began to improve.

Back at the hut, Lilas greeted her with the cheerful news that the food was ready. The vegetable and chestnut stew was good, except there wasn't enough of it.

It was too soon to go and check the traps, so Meggie made herself relax. It was warm by the fire and, leaning back on a straw-filled sack covered with a sheepskin, she was very comfortable. She had started out early that morning, and walked many miles in the course of her foraging. Presently her eyelids began to droop, and soon she was asleep.

In the dream, she is walking with Lilas in a remote part of the forest that she does not recognize. Lilas is humming softly: a repetitive, hypnotic series of notes that seems to penetrate Meggie's mind, weaving its way deep inside and twining itself with her thoughts and her memories. She is aware – although she does not know how she knows – that this trance is like nothing she has experienced before.

She sees her mother, long dark hair streaked widely with grey. Her mother gives her a smile so full of love that Meggie hears herself sob. Joanna wears a bear's claw mounted in silver on a thong around her neck. Oh, Meggie remembers that claw! Her mother is speaking, very quietly: *There are portals in the world that you have not even dreamt of, my daughter.* Meggie stretches out a hand, as if to take hold of her mother, and Joanna melts away.

Now the vision is changing. There is a man, and there is danger. A long and very thin blade is held up to the light of a candle: it has a wicked point and both edges have been honed to razor sharpness. It is a killing weapon.

Horrified, Meggie watches as a hand raises the knife. It plunges up in a tight arc, energy concentrated in its point. There is a terrible sound as it finds its target.

Meggie cries aloud. From somewhere very close, Lilas hushes her.

'Go on,' a voice murmurs. Lilas's?

A funeral procession, and a coffin draped in brilliantly coloured cloth is borne aloft. Then, in a swift succession of images, violence, fighting, bloody death. And a fleet of ships sailing with deadly intent coming towards the shore, an army poised to disembark...

'No!' Meggie cries. She feels hot, then very cold, so that she begins to shiver. She is lost, lost, deep within an imaginary forest in her own mind, and she cries out in fear.

Meggie opened her eyes. Lilas was bending over her, holding both her hands between her own, chafing them. 'Are you back, child?' she demanded anxiously. 'Have you returned?'

Meggie looked up at her. 'I think so,' she said cautiously. But the trance images were still far too vivid, and she was not really sure which world she was in.

'I'm sorry,' Lilas said. 'I took you too deep. I was curious, see, because I knew you had the ability to come with me.' She made a grimace. 'Should have asked you first, though, shouldn't I?'

'Yes,' Meggie said shortly. Reality was hardening around her, and the fear was slowly ebbing away. 'Did you put something in the stew?' she demanded, staring hard at Lilas.

'Didn't need to,' she replied. 'You were sleepy already, so I took the opportunity and sent you off.'

Meggie remembered the soft humming. 'Remind me,' she said neutrally, 'never again to let

266

myself fall asleep while you're still awake.'

Lilas chuckled. Then, anxiety returning, she said, 'Sure you're all right?'

'Quite sure.' Meggie risked getting to her feet. So far, so good.

'Did you ... er, did you see anything?' Lilas asked, with an attempt at nonchalance that didn't fool Meggie for a moment.

But Meggie was not ready to talk about it. She grabbed her grey cloak, swinging it round her shoulders and drawing up the hood. She picked up the sword that Jehan had made for her. She sensed – although it could have been an after-effect of the visions – that danger was near. The blade was light, and not very long, but it was extremely sharp. 'I'm going to check the traps,' she said. Then she hurried outside and, before Lilas could say a word, firmly closed the door.

One of her traps held a plump partridge. Bending down, she murmured softly to the bird, then, taking hold of it in firm hands, swiftly wrung its neck. She stowed it in the leather bag she carried over her shoulder.

She was in the forest to the south of the abbey, heading back towards the hut, when she heard it: close at hand, although out of sight, someone was whistling.

Meggie slipped into the shadow of a bramble thicket. The day was drawing to its close, and she was pretty sure she could not be seen. She breathed a prayer of thankfulness that she had not come across this intruder, whoever he – or she – was, any nearer to the hut: she was still some miles away. The hut's location would remain secret.

She edged forward, parting two strands of entangled bramble so that she could look out.

He was sitting in a small glade, formed where a tree had come crashing down to create an almost perfect circle of light amid the dense forest. He was half turned away from her, leaning back against the trunk of a winter-bare birch tree, and he looked utterly contented.

Even from where she stood, Meggie could make out enough details of his appearance to see that he was no peasant or forest dweller. He wore tunic and hose in shades of greenish-brown, but the sombre colours, she guessed, had been carefully chosen not for cheapness but so as not to advertise the huntsman's presence, for the quality of the garments was sumptuous. He wore a pair of boots in soft, supple leather, and a heavy cloak warmly lined with fur. Stealthily she removed the bag from her shoulder and pushed it deep into the undergrowth: lords out hunting did not take kindly to people helping themselves to game.

She watched him. He wore heavy leather gauntlets, on which she thought she saw the dull gleam of blood: yes, he was indeed a hunter, and he had clearly done well. She wondered what had happened to the kill – no doubt, she thought, the deer, or perhaps the boar, had been carted away by the minions dancing attendance. Men of high status didn't have to drag their own meat home.

She moved nearer, drawn forward by some sort of force she did not understand. Still keeping under cover, automatically moving with the soft-footed quietness she had long ago been taught, she approached the glade.

He turned, looking straight at where she stood in a half-crouch in the undergrowth. She was sure he couldn't see her, for she was peering out at him through a dense tangle of dead wood and brittle branches. After a moment, his eyes moved on. Nothing in his demeanour suggested she had been spotted.

But that brief glance had been enough. She had sensed, the instant she set eyes on him, that he was familiar. Now, she knew for sure. Slowly she stood up straight. Stepping out from the concealing undergrowth, she walked up the narrow track and emerged into the clearing.

He had turned to see the source of the sound: no longer feeling the need to keep silent, she had pushed aside the dry and brittle stems of the thicket, snapping them. Now, as she approached, his eyes were intent on her.

She stopped before him. She bowed her head, then, raising her eyes again, saw that he was smiling. 'I knew you were there,' he murmured. 'Or, to be honest, I knew something was there, although you might have been a hind or a she-boar.'

'Either creature would have taken alarm at the scent of blood on your gauntlets,' she pointed out. 'The hind would have bounded away and the she-boar would probably have charged.'

He nodded. 'And you: you emerge from your

hiding place and calmly walk into my glade.'

Yes, she thought, *it is indeed his glade.*

He was watching her closely, the heavy brows descending into a frown. 'Last time we met,' he said, 'there was something blue...' Impatiently, he shook his head. 'I cannot bring it clearly to mind.'

He sounded, she realized, as if that failure angered him. She thought it was probably a rare occurrence, for him not to be able to summon instantly anything he wanted to recall. She waited a moment in case he remembered – it would not do to antagonize him – and then said, 'We were in the chapel. St Edmund's Chapel, by Hawkenlye Abbey.' She hesitated. 'We are very near the chapel now.' *It will do no harm*, a self-preserving part of her mind warned her, *to remind him that sacred ground is close by.*

He smiled grimly. 'Oh, I know all about St Edmund's Chapel. Go on.'

'The sun was shining and it sent its rays through the blue of the stained glass, where it forms the sky behind St Edmund's head,' she said, choosing her words with care. 'It has the effect of bathing the whole chapel in a blue light.'

'Yes,' he said. 'That was what you said at the time.'

I didn't believe you then, hung in the air, *and I don't now.*

She made herself go on looking down into the brilliant blue eyes. She could have sworn she felt heat emanating from him, such was his physical presence. Shifting her gaze a fraction, she took in the heavy frame running to fat, well-disguised by the beautifully cut garments but nevertheless discernible, if you studied him closely.

Which she did not seem to be able to stop herself doing...

He stood up, moving towards her so that they stood face to face. They were almost of a height; she was very slightly taller. 'You smell clean,' he said. 'I told you that before, and you said it was a residue of the herbs with which you work.'

'Yes,' she said. She was trembling.

He leaned towards her, and, taking her hand, very gently put his lips to it. A jolt of pure sexual excitement raced through her. She made herself stand perfectly still.

He drew off the bloody gauntlets, flinging them away from him. Then he put his hands either side of her face. His touch was soft, but she felt the power that was concealed not far below the surface.

He was staring right into her eyes. 'I...' He shook his head, an ironic smile twisting the well-shaped mouth. 'I know what I *want* to do,' he murmured, 'but it is as if something holds me back. Now what, my Meggie, could that possibly be?'

He remembers my name.

She was thinking, so fast that it threatened to make her faint. She knew she was in peril for, in that instant, she wanted him too. But she would not – *must not* – let that wild, unreasoning element of her nature get to the fore. For one thing, there was Jehan. For another, there was the voice of her mother, echoing in her head as it had done on that day a year ago: *Have no truck with men like him, for they take what they want and do not give anything in return.*

Meggie knew exactly why he felt as if he were held back. Last year, inside the spiritually charged atmosphere of the chapel, she had entranced him and, while he was in thrall, firmly told him that she was not for him: *My fate is connected with the secret of this place*, she had said, *and I would not have you risk its vengeance by taking from me what I do not freely give you.*

As she fought with the part of herself that was trying to shout, *I do give myself! I do!* she was, at the same time, struck anew with the power of the object with which she had enchanted him. She wished she had the Eye of Jerusalem with her now, but it was stowed away safely back at the House in the Woods. Nobody in their right minds carried a sapphire the size of a big man's thumbnail with them when they went to live in the wilds.

She breathed deeply a couple of times, each time exhaling tension and excitement, inhaling calm. She took a step back, away from him, and his hands fell to his sides. Another step. And another.

When she stood perhaps five paces away, at last she felt she was safe. She met his eyes, and saw that he was smiling.

'I still think you have magic in you,' he said quietly. 'Except that I don't believe there is any such thing.'

They stood, immobile and silent, for several moments. She was still wrestling within herself, but now it was to a different question that she sought an answer. She knew what she ought to do: there were countless reasons why it was the right thing. But those reasons appeared to have lost their powers of persuasion.

His intense gaze had not left hers. She wondered what she was going to do.

The hooded rider settled the corpse more securely in front of his saddle. He had not yet gone sufficiently far and, despite the fact that it was getting dark and the weather was worsening, he knew he must go on for many more miles yet. His horse was nervous: perhaps aware of the dead body it was being forced to carry. The hooded man shortened his reins, tightening his control. The horse gave a shudder.

Killing this one had been even more like child's play than the previous two; one of them, indeed, had managed to put up quite a fight. The man's face twisted in a sneer. Boys dressed up as knights should not, he thought grimly, come out to play in a world they did not begin to understand. Those others – the cousins called St Clair – had been behind it, filling each other's heads with grand notions of great and noble deeds which would be remembered for ever, and no doubt they had persuaded this other simpleton (the man glanced down at the corpse, face-down across his saddle bow) to join them. The three had, after all, been squires together, and the hardships of the training made tight bonds of friendship.

It was as well, the man mused, that he had

273

taken such great pains to forge a ring of watchers to guard the secret. The network spread its threads widely, and, although none of the people had any idea of what their information was used for, they did their job well. News of the young cousins' approach had reached the isolated valley long before they had got anywhere near it. Knowing the third youth would follow, it had only been a matter of time before he too met the same fate.

The mystery was, of course, how they had come to hear of the conspiracy in the first place, for the very few people in the know had been sworn – on pain of death – to secrecy. The hooded man was already planning to find out who had spoken where he shouldn't. Once this present situation had been dealt with, he would devote himself single-mindedly to rooting out the weak link and eliminating it.

It was the sort of work he did best, and he was very, very good at it.

SEVENTEEN

Sebastian Garrique stood beside the dais in Medley's great hall, rigid with tension. The long-awaited moment had almost arrived; the culmination of what seemed endless days of intense and painstaking preparations, every last fine detail dictated and overseen by Sebastian himself. It had to be right, he reminded himself for the hundredth time. Benedict de Vitré was dead, but the hospitality of his house was nevertheless about to be judged: by the most eagle-eyed, rigorous and intolerant judge in the entire land.

It was no wonder that, for the past three days and nights, Sebastian had barely slept.

Lord Benedict might have been put in the ground in a private and somewhat hasty fashion, but the funeral feast that was about to begin could not have been more of a contrast. The guest list approached a hundred, and that was without the guest of honour's own retinue. Far from reflecting the fact that the feast was to recognize a death, the hall was decorated as if for a wedding, or perhaps a birth. Although the day had been sunny and bright, now, in mid-afternoon, already the light was fading, and dozens of flares were spaced at intervals around the walls. On the long trestles, there were beeswax candles for the important guests and rush lamps for the more insignificant. There were going to be so many courses that Sebastian had to consult the cooks before he could remember every one.

The kitchens were like a scene from hell. Extra hands had been brought in and, now that the frenzy of baking, roasting, basting, broiling and stewing was at last almost done, the cooks and their minions could finally afford a moment to slip outside and cool their hot, red, sweaty faces. Soon the first service of dishes would be set out, and the feast could begin.

Sebastian was very aware of Lady Richenza, standing just in front of him. The fast rise and fall of her chest gave away her nervousness; otherwise, she appeared calm. She was dressed in a gown which Sebastian had not seen before: deep-blue velvet, with wide sleeves lined with embroidered silk in lighter shades of blue. He noted with interest – and not a little regret – that since the demise of her lord husband, she now wore her necklines considerably higher. To augment the impression of a demure and modest widow cast into gloom at her loss, the severity of her headdress was worthy of a nun. The starched white wimple revealed not so much as a wisp of her hair, and the close-fitting gorget covered her throat and chin. Her veil was made of very fine wool, and she had styled it so that its scalloped folds fell around her face, moving as she turned her head so that sometimes her features were hidden, sometimes revealed.

The effect, Sebastian reflected, was tantalizing.

The hum of excited chatter out in the courtyard suddenly ceased. A horn sounded: a single, pure note. It was the signal that announced the approach of their guest, and Sebastian saw Lady Richenza straighten her back. Then, without so much as a quick glance to see if he was following, she set off down the hall to take up her post in the great arched doorway. He moved silently to support her, glancing quickly around the hall to check one last time that all was ready.

Then he raised his head and stared out through the door down into the courtyard. The king was coming to visit Medley, honouring the house with his presence, and Sebastian Garrique did not intend to miss a moment.

The feast was going well. The king's famous blue eyes had lit up at the sight of his hostess waiting at the top of the steps and, as she dropped into a deep and very graceful curtsy, he had reached out a hand to gently cup her chin, raising her to her feet. Then he had taken her hand in his and permitted her to lead him the length of the hall to his place of honour on the dais. Waving away the local lords who tried to declaim their lengthily rehearsed speeches of welcome (he had given the impression of a man who had heard it all before, which, Sebastian reflected, undoubtedly he had) the king turned to Lady Richenza and said, with a smile, 'My lady, I am both hungry and thirsty, but chiefly thirsty. Is this prettily set board just for looking at, or are we going to be fed and watered?'

Lady Richenza had smiled coyly up at him, her

cheeks dimpling, then, turning, she gave the nod to her great gaggle of servants. The feast began.

Now Sebastian was on his fourth or fifth tour of the hall. Moving slowly, not drawing attention to himself and careful to keep out of the way of the hurrying serving men and women, his self-imposed task was, ostensibly, to make sure everyone was being served with all that they wanted – especially the lords and ladies at the tables nearest to the dais. The king's own steward served the king.

In truth, Sebastian had another motive: as tongues were loosened by ale, mead and wine, he was listening, as well as he could amid the hubbub, to what the guests were saying.

He knew exactly why the king had come to Medley Hall. While it was true that he and the late Lord Benedict had been close, Sebastian did not fool himself that King John's presence at the funeral feast was motivated by the respect owed to a long friendship, or affection for a dead companion. No: the king was here purely to make sure he received every last coin of the revenues which Lord Benedict had amassed on his behalf. Even now, while the king and his personal circle tucked into goose, jellies, pike, tartlets, honey cakes and wine, five of his officials were in Lord Benedict's private sanctum, counting money and going through the records like a dog snuffling for fleas. Sebastian knew they were, for, at the king's peremptory order, he himself had shown the officers where to go.

He came to the end of another circuit and, positioning himself in the shadow of the dais, looked up at the king flirting with Lady Richenza. The girl was handling it well, he had to admit, responsive enough so that King John did not take offence, yet from time to time allowing a small sigh to escape her full lips, accompanied by downcast eyes, as if she was momentarily overcome by her grief. It was, Sebastian reflected, a brilliant performance.

He studied the king. It was the first time he had ever seen him, and that, he thought, probably applied to everyone there, other than John's own retinue. Only the great lords like the late Benedict de Vitré actually got to meet their King. Sebastian had overheard some of the local men of power make the sort of boastful, bragging comments that suggested they were on intimate terms with the monarch, but Sebastian thought they were probably exaggerating. At most, they might have seen him in the distance at some court function. Much, indeed, as they were seeing him now.

Sebastian brought himself out of his brief reverie. It was time to start another circuit.

At a trestle down at the far end of the hall – where, lit only by cheap lamps, it was dark and shadowy and a very long way below the salt – a sallow-faced man sat mechanically chewing his way through whatever appeared before him. He was quite calm, for, as invariably happened, his meticulous planning had paid off, and everything had gone as smoothly as silk. He had reconnoitred extensively, finding the safest place to hide his horse, the least overlooked way into the fenced enclosure of Medley, and a handy and little-used passage that gave direct access to the hall. He had insinuated himself over the course of several visits, so that, although nobody knew exactly who he was or what role he performed, his presence was accepted. The man on his left had greeted him with a friendly slap on the back as he took his place on the bench, and said, 'Come on, Hugh, hand me that mug and I'll soon fill it up for you!'

The sallow-faced man's name wasn't Hugh. He was called something else by his present paymaster, and that wasn't his real name either. Not that it mattered; with a quick grin that did not reach anywhere near his eyes, he complied.

His mug had just been filled for the third time. Not a drop had passed his lips: he had to maintain a state of high alert. It had been easy, as his companions surrendered their wits to drink, to empty his mug on to the rushes that covered the floor. By the time this feast was over, he mused, ale would not be the only liquid soaking into the rushes.

The sallow-faced man watched, and waited. Had anyone taken the trouble to study him, he or she would have been hard put to describe him: short, dark hair, lean face, clean-shaven, mid-coloured eyes, medium height, simply dressed in dull shades; cloak with a deep hood, thrown back. It could have applied to scores of men.

He was good at being nondescript. Long experience had taught him it made him safe.

The short autumn day had faded to evening.

280

More candles were lit, and the fires in the central hearth were stoked up, sending a blaze of orange sparks up into the high roof of the hall. Lady Richenza, who had long ago stopped even pretending to eat, sat back in her high-backed chair, watching the king picking at the last stubborn piece of flesh on a chicken drumstick, occasionally dipping it in the pool of gooseberry sauce on his silver platter and sucking at it.

Lady Richenza had a headache, and wished they would all go away so that she could retire to her bed. Her wonderfully soft, wide, warm bed, which now – thank the dear, good, merciful Lord above – was blessedly empty of her late and entirely unmourned husband.

The entertainments had begun, and the dancers, musicians, jugglers, tumblers and jesters were every bit as gaudy, as ribald and as noisy as Sebastian had feared. His expression of shocked amazement when she had first told him that there were to be entertainers at her late husband's funeral feast had been wonderful; she had found it hard to bite back her laughter. Now, as the rowdiness swiftly accelerated, she thought in bitter triumph, *There, Benedict, you evil old sod! See how I choose to celebrate your death! And look at how ready everyone is to be happy! Nobody else mourns you any more than I do.*

Lady Richenza watched as a line of ten acrobats came flying up the hall, five each side of the central hearth, twisting, flipping, cartwheeling, until they were just beneath the dais, whereupon they gave the king a deep bow, turned and tumbled back again. They were very good, Lady

Richenza had to admit. To a man – to a woman, too, she noticed – they were lithe and slim; so supple that they appeared to have no bones. They were dressed in close-fitting black, and each wore a short, brightly coloured tunic sewn with some sort of glittering shapes – made of metal, she thought – which caught the light of the flames so that, as the troupe twisted and turned, they seemed to be on fire.

Like everyone else in the hall, she couldn't take her eyes off them.

Like *almost* everyone else...

Deep in the shadows at the far side of the hall, a figure sidled slowly and stealthily along the tapestry-hung wall. The tapestry's colours were sombre and, dark-clad as he was, he hoped he would not be visible. Little light fell out there beyond the circle of fire, lamp and candlelight and, whenever he reached a place where a torch blazed in its bracket overhead, he crouched down while he passed through its pool of illumination. He did not think there was much danger of being noticed. The tumblers were well into their performance now, and the crowd was shouting out loud cries of appreciation and encouragement. As if in response, the musicians were playing full blast. Nobody was concerned with a figure creeping in the shadows.

He stepped over a comatose body, its head in a puddle of vomit. The body emitted a groan.

The man moved on. Now he was at the far end of the hall. He moved carefully out of the depths of the darkness, crossing the floor on feet as light

282

as a cat's. Then, in one smooth, continuous movement, he drew the narrow blade out of its sheath inside his boot and leapt up on to the dais. He had positioned himself perfectly, crouching directly behind the king. In a brutal version of a lover's embrace, he wrapped one arm around the barrel chest, drawing the king close and holding him steady. With the other hand, he thrust in the long, thin blade. His precision was perfect: the blade was aimed between the ribs, its angle inclined upwards so that, as it plunged in, right to the hilt, its tip would penetrate the heart.

And King John would be dead.

Aaagh!

The man's steady heartbeat suddenly raced.

Making the sort of instant decision that had kept him alive in a highly dangerous profession, the man turned, jumped lightly off the dais and sprinted away.

Side by side, shoulders touching and affording a little comfort, Josse and Helewise stood in one of the curtained recesses of the Hawkenlye infirmary, staring down at the dead body of Luc Jordan. He had been found that morning, lying in a tangle of dead and rotting vegetation in the shallows at the far end of the lake below the abbey. A small family party of pilgrims had made the discovery and, shocked at finding such a violation so close to holy ground, had hurried along to the monks in the vale. Four of the lay brothers had accompanied them back to their gruesome find, and the body was borne up to the abbey.

283

The boy's throat had been cut, and although the compassionate hands of Sister Liese and her nurses had removed the blood-sodden clothing and washed the body, still the ghastly wound gaped wide and red.

Above it, his deathly pale face looked oddly peaceful, for one who had died so violently.

'So now all three are dead,' Helewise said softly. 'Those fond young men, who went searching for a grand adventure that would ensure their names resonated through history, have each been dispatched by a skilled and ruthless hand, as if they were no more than an unwanted and inconvenient litter of puppies.'

'Aye,' Josse said with a deep sigh. 'It's cruel, to see the last of them come to this.'

They stood in silence, although Josse could hear her thoughts as if she spoke them aloud. Eventually he said, 'We must inform Lord Robert Wimarc of their fate.' He turned to her with a brief grin. 'Just as you were about to say, I believe.'

She returned his smile. 'Indeed I was.' Then, her features twisting with pity, she added, 'He must by now suspect something is amiss, if he was indeed expecting his young visitors. It is strange, if he was, that he has not sent out to ask if there is news of them. Hawkenlye is the nearest establishment of any size to Wealdsend, and it seems likely any such messengers would have enquired here; yet none have come.'

Josse said, 'I cannot say why, but I am all but certain Lord Wimarc does not know anything of the three young men's proposed visit. Or, perhaps I should say, he certainly did not invite them.'

'I don't think Luc said they had been *invited*,' she replied. 'It was more that he and the cousins St Clair picked up word that some thrilling scheme was being planned in the secret depths of Wealdsend and, being young and desperate to test their courage and their hardihood, they resolved to seek out the place and offer their services.' She paused, and Josse saw tears well up in her eyes. 'They probably thought they'd be welcomed with open arms,' she whispered.

He reached for her hand. 'Aye, I know,' he said heavily. 'It's hard.'

She squeezed his hand quickly, then gently disengaged hers. He suppressed a grin: they were, after all, in the Hawkenlye infirmary. For so much of their shared past, her former position here had placed such gestures firmly out of bounds. Memory, it seemed, died hard.

'We can be there and back while the light lasts if we set out now,' she said. She was looking at him with what, over the long years, he had learned to recognize as her determined expression.

'You're surely not proposing to come with me?' he demanded, although he knew it was hopeless.

'Of course I am,' she replied briskly. 'We shall be breaking the sad news of three deaths, and even if Lord Wimarc does not know our young men, none but the hardest heart could fail to be moved. It needs,' she said, with the air of someone adding the final, irrefutable argument, 'a woman's touch.'

He followed her out of the infirmary. Still uneasy in his mind – although he was not entirely sure why – he paused, and beckoned to Sister Liese, who, with an enquiring glance, hurried over.

'Sister, would you please make sure that a message is sent to the abbess?' he said quietly. She nodded. He leaned down and spoke in her ear. Her eyes widened briefly, then, wiping the reaction from her face, she whispered, 'I will go and give her the message myself, Sir Josse.'

There is a connection between Medley Hall and Wealdsend, Josse thought as he rode ahead of Helewise down the track that led westwards away from the abbey. *I saw the hooded man emerge from the Medley courtyard, and I followed him and witnessed the fastness of Wealdsend open briefly to admit him.*

What was that connection? It could have nothing to do with their current mission, and the deaths of Luc Jordan and the St Clair cousins, for Luc had made no mention of Lord Benedict de Vitré or his manor. Perhaps it was no more than the desire of a recluse to keep at least half an eye on what was going on around him. It was possible that news of Lord Benedict's death had permeated to the inhabitant of Wealdsend, and maybe he wished to be kept informed.

And how did these events connect to the presence of the various discontented factions in the vicinity at the moment? To the grumbling barons flocking to Nicholas Fitzwalter, and that poor puppet, Caleb of Battle, who had been

286

forced into expressing what none of the great lords dared say? And where, on the good God's earth, was Lilas?

Josse's whirling thoughts threatened to rise up and engulf him. 'One thing at a time,' he muttered to himself. 'We'll pass on our sad news to Lord Wimarc – if he lets us – and then we'll address everything else.'

'What did you say?' Helewise had drawn level with him, and overheard his mumbling.

'Just thinking out loud,' he replied. 'Not that my thoughts have achieved anything.' Impatient suddenly, he spurred Alfred, who broke into a canter. After a moment, he heard Daisy's lighter hoof falls hurrying behind him.

Wealdsend presented its usual forbidding face.

'It looks quite deserted,' Helewise observed as they drew rein before its gates. 'You are sure there is someone within?'

'There was when I came here before,' Josse said. He nudged Alfred, moving the big horse closer to the heavy gates. Drawing his sword, he banged the hilt hard against the wooden panels, several times. 'Halloa Wealdsend!' he shouted, his sudden loud voice making the horses start nervously. 'We wish to speak to Lord Robert Wimarc!'

There was no response. Josse tried again, this time adding, 'We have grave news to import, and I have no wish to relay it at the top of my voice!'

'Hush!' Helewise held up her hand. 'I thought I heard something.'

They sat in silence. Quite clearly on the still air came the thud of footsteps on the far side of the fence, sounding very close. Then there was a deep rattle, as if a chain had been moved, and the long drawn-out sound of wooden bars being pulled back. Finally, the gates parted fractionally, revealing a man in plain, dark livery. The fabric – of fine quality – was all of the same sable shade, and was unadorned with motif or device. The man's face was expressionless, and he exuded a slight sense of menace.

He studied Josse and Helewise for a while, then said, 'Who are you?'

'I am Josse d'Acquin, and this is Helewise Warin. We come from Hawkenlye Abbey, with grave news for Lord Wimarc.'

The man inspected them for a little longer, and then Josse caught his swift glance behind them, back down the valley. *He checks to see if we are accompanied*, Josse thought.

The man looked straight at Josse. 'You had better come in,' he said. 'Follow me.'

He opened the gates just enough for Josse and Helewise to ride through. Once they were within, he closed and barred the entrance once more. He led them across a wide, grassy space, at the far side of which the main hall and the outbuildings which constituted Wealdsend crouched beneath the rising land beyond.

With a sense of deepening unease, Josse fought to keep at bay the thought that this just might have been a mistake.

EIGHTEEN

Their horses were led away by a scared-looking boy who scuttled out from a reed-thatched, wattle-and-daub building on the far side of the yard, which appeared to be the stable block. Like the rest of the structures on that side of the wide, grassy space, it seemed almost to merge with its surroundings, for moss grew on the sloping roof and the earth-coloured daub was virtually indistinguishable from the muddy, churned-up ground.

The man who had admitted Josse and Helewise led them across the open space to the manor house. It, too, looked as if its builder's intention had been to make it blend in with the natural world; to limit to a minimum the signs of man's hand at work. The contrast to the brash new extensions which Benedict de Vitré had commanded at Medley could not have been more marked. *But this place, Wealdsend, is old*, Josse thought. Someone – Helewise, probably – had told him that it had been here in its secret, hidden valley for generations before the coming of the Normans.

Their guide ushered them up a short flight of steps and into the main hall – and again Wealdsend's ancient origins proclaimed themselves.

289

Lord Wimarc, Josse observed, must approve of the style of living chosen by those long-ago people, for he kept to the old ways. The low, dark building was made entirely of wood, and a fire pit ran the length of it. The roof was supported by two rows of heavy pillars, marching either side of the long, narrow hearth; it was steeply pitched, rising to perhaps three men's height at the apex, where there was a line of smoke holes, and descending so low at the sides, where it met the walls, that an adult would have had to crouch. The light was dim out there, away from the hearth, but Josse thought he could make out bundles of rolled-up bedding. Like a chieftain of old, it appeared that Lord Wimarc's retainers slept in their master's hall, perpetually on guard.

Josse's unease deepened. With what he hoped was an unobtrusive movement, he took a couple of steps round behind Helewise, so that now she was on his left side rather than his right. If he should need to draw a weapon, better to make sure she would not be able to grasp his sword arm and impede his swing...

At the far end of the hall, so close to the fire that his outstretched feet all but overhung it, an old man sat on a huge chair, the wood elaborately carved, its hardness softened by cushions. He was wrapped in a fur-lined cloak, its folds tightly wrapped around him but leaving his hands free. The huge, yellowish stone of a heavy gold ring on the right hand caught the light. On a board beside him there was a spread of pieces of vellum, each covered in blocks of dense script. One piece appeared to have been used to draw a rough map.

Noticing Josse's eyes on the work, the man stretched out his arm and swept every last scrap to the floor.

The servant who had ushered Josse and Helewise into the hall went up to the man in the chair, bending to speak quietly to him. The old man nodded, and the manservant stepped away, back into the shadows around the room's perimeter.

Then, staring at Josse with an intent glare, the old man said, 'I am told you and the lady bring tidings from Hawkenlye Abbey.' His deep voice was hoarse; perhaps, Josse wondered, from disuse. The pale eyes moved to Helewise. 'I cannot imagine,' he went on, his tone disinterested, 'what sort of news from that place could possibly be of interest or relevance to me, but since you have made the journey here, I am prepared to listen to what you have come to say.'

He spoke, Josse realized crossly, as if he were conferring a huge favour merely by being prepared to listen to them. Beside him, as if she felt his rising anger, he heard Helewise give a quiet cough. 'Let me,' she whispered, so softly that the words could surely not have been overheard. He nodded.

He heard her take a breath. Then she said, 'You are, I presume, Lord Robert Wimarc?'

'I am.'

'Then it is to you that we must speak. Sir Josse and I have had the sad task of being involved in the deaths of three young men: Guillaume

291

and Symon de St Clair, who were cousins, and their friend Luc Jordan. All were found in the vicinity of Hawkenlye Abbey, where their bodies have been taken to await burial. We understand that they had set themselves upon a mission, and to this end they were making their way to—'

'What has this to do with me?' Lord Wimarc's voice cut across hers.

'They asked at the abbey for directions to Wealdsend,' Helewise replied. 'They were coming to you, Lord Robert, for they believed you were embarking on some great plan which would resonate down through history, and they wished to be a part of it.'

Lord Wimarc sat, silent and immobile. Then he said, 'They were mistaken. I make no plan, and have no wish to be immortalized. I live the quiet life of a recluse, and I do not welcome strangers.'

His last words, accompanied by the icy look he shot from his pale eyes, first at Josse, then at Helewise, could not have been more blunt. *And that includes you*, hung unspoken on the air.

Josse's fury rose anew. 'Yet not one but three young men believed otherwise, and all now are dead,' he said coldly. 'Have you any comment to offer? Any explanation, as to why all three came to be so mistaken?'

Lord Wimarc shrugged indifferently. 'None.'

'But you can't simply—'

Suddenly Lord Wimarc stood up, the heavy cloak swirling around him. He was tall, his long body curving over in the hunched posture of a

292

great bird of prey. *'Can't*, Sir Josse?' The husky voice was strong now, the tone aggressive. 'Do not presume, in my own hall, to tell me what I can and can't do.'

Josse stepped forward, anger driving him on. 'You have spies out there,' he cried, waving an arm behind him in the direction of the valley and the land beyond. 'I know this, for I followed a hooded rider from Medley Hall to your own gates, where, for all that the place appeared deserted, I saw him admitted. What was he up to, Lord Robert? What information was he bringing to you? Did it form another vital element in your secret plot?'

Lord Wimarc appeared to shudder – perhaps with the effort, Josse speculated, of suppressing the desire to jump down and strike him. But when the old man finally spoke, his voice was as chilly and detached as before. 'I cannot be expected to recall the details of every man who rides through my gates,' he said dismissively. 'If you believe, Sir Josse, that I have the time and the inclination to concern myself with such trivialities, then you are mistaken.'

'This was no triviality!' Josse shouted. 'This – this hooded rider who came here brought you, did he not, news of the outside world? News from—' He had been on the point of saying, *news from Lord Benedict de Vitré's manor of Medley*, but even as he spoke, he thought he finally understood the true import of that hurrying, secretive figure. 'He'd found out about your would-be visitors, hadn't he?' His eyes were on Lord Wimarc's impassive face, searching desperately for some sign; some tiny indication that the furious words were hitting home. There was nothing. 'Your spy had somehow discovered that three naive and foolish young men were looking for you, coming to disturb your precious seclusion,' he plunged on, 'and yet, although you must have suspected they could be in danger – youth and foolish naivety are poor companions out in the wilds – you did nothing to help them. Did you order your gates barred to them, too, when they came here to offer you their swords? Did you watch from the shadows as they rode dejectedly away?' He took another step towards the old lord. 'Do you even care that they now lie dead?'

His furious words echoed up into the rafters. He raised his arms in a gesture of frustration, but in that atmosphere of high tension, Lord Wimarc misread it. Spinning round, eyes searching the shadows at the edges of the hall, he shouted out one single word: *'Manticore!'*

And, from the corner where he had been standing, silently and motionlessly observing, a slim, spare figure moved out into the light. Although he was not wearing his heavy, deep-hooded cloak, there was no mistaking his identity: it was the man who had stood with the Fitzwalter faction at Hawkenlye Abbey while Caleb of Battle had been tricked into speaking treason; the man who, later, had ridden at speed past Josse and Helewise on the road leading from Medley. In the poor and inconstant light of the dimly lit hall, it now struck Josse that the sparsely fleshed, pale face, with its prominent

294

brows and sharp cheekbones, resembled a skull...

The man sprang forward, as light on his feet as a cat, and even as he advanced, he had slid his sword out of its scabbard. Moving to stand before his lord, face to face with Josse, he said with quiet intensity, 'Get back.'

It was not the moment to argue; his eyes fixed on the sword point only inches from his face, Josse did as he was commanded. Resuming his place beside Helewise, he felt her grope for his hand and clutch it tightly.

'I had no intention of harming your lord,' he said, staring right into the swordsman's eyes. 'You have my word.'

'Your word,' the man echoed neutrally. 'I see.'

He was still standing in front of Lord Wimarc, who now, with a quiet groan, returned to his chair and sat down. The slim man took up his position at his side, still holding his sword with its point towards Josse. From his belt, Josse noticed with concern, hung a long knife in a leather scabbard. Next to the belt buckle was stuck a short, stabbing blade.

Seeing him clearly now, Josse took in the details of his face. The man's skin was sallow, almost olive in colour, and his close-cropped hair was so dark that it appeared black. His lean face was close-shaven, the lips of his wide mouth narrow and pale. His high cheekbones stood out like blades, casting shadows on the lower part of his face, so deep that they looked like wounds. His eyes seemed to change colour, now appearing mid-brown, now shadowed to profoundest black. They were, Josse noticed with a shudder of unease, quite dead.

He thought back to that single word, spoken by Lord Wimarc in the instant that he thought he was about to be attacked. *Manticore*. It was vaguely familiar ... A legendary beast, Josse thought, dragging up the memory from the depths of his mind, which combined the most ferocious aspects of all the killer creatures, and was crueller than any of them.

Was the word a command? Or was it, God help them, this dead-eyed man's name?

The man nodded, as if he had been aware of Josse's thoughts and waited only for him to finish. 'You came to ask if Lord Wimarc knew these three young men who have unfortunately died,' he said, 'and, now that you have been given his answer, there is no more reason for you to remain. I will—'

'I know you,' Josse interrupted. 'You were at Medley Hall, and I followed you here. You were also at the abbey when Nicholas Fitzwalter spoke, and I believe that you abducted an old woman who was being cared for in the infirmary. You probably brought her here, although you will of course deny it.' He raised his hand, gestured wildly in his frustration. 'What are you up to?' he shouted. 'What's going on, and why were those three young men killed? I *know* you are involved, so don't try to—'

The man shot towards him, sword swinging above his head in preparation for the down stroke – the killing stroke – and in that instant of greatest peril, the stillness of his face and the violence in his movements formed such an extreme contrast that it was in itself an affront.

Hastily Josse shook off Helewise's hand, and he was drawing his own weapon to defend himself – to defend them both – when Lord Wimarc barked an order: 'Manticore, *no.*'

The old man's voice spoke out with clear authority, and the swordsman stopped dead. *So Manticore* is *his name*, Josse thought, feeling the tremor in his tight muscles as his whole body responded to the threat. It served only to increase the horror of the man.

Lord Wimarc was beckoning, and his swordsman lowered his weapon and went to his side. Lord Wimarc muttered a few words, too soft for Josse to make out. Then Manticore looked around the hall, paused for a moment as if considering, and made a brief gesture. There were sounds of movement all around the hall, and into the light from the fire pit stepped perhaps ten or twelve men. All wore the plain, unmarked, sombre-coloured livery of the house.

All were armed.

Josse pushed his sword back into its scabbard – he knew he must not give any man the excuse to attack – and put his left arm around Helewise's waist, drawing her close. His heart aching, he thought, *I let her have her way and come with me, when my instincts told me not to. And now my impulsiveness – my weakness; my desire for her company – means we are both in grave danger.*

He did not even dare admit the thought that the

297

danger might well prove fatal.

There was a long pause. Then Lord Wimarc said, as if initiating a courteous mealtime conversation, 'Do you know what has happened this day?'

Josse met the old man's steady gaze. Watching him closely, fear putting every sense on the alert, he noticed that, while a quick glance suggested that Lord Wimarc sat there totally composed, as still and majestic as a standing stone, yet there was tension running below the calm surface. A tic jumped in his eyelid. The long fingers of his left hand played constantly with the huge citrine ring on the middle finger of his right.

'No,' Josse replied shortly. 'I don't know. Something of import, I imagine, to judge by your tone.'

Lord Robert's eyes seemed to bore into him. Now there was jubilation in his expression, tinged with another, more dangerous emotion, which Josse feared was the sort of fanaticism that is almost madness. Not looking away, forcing Josse to go on staring right at him, Lord Robert said, 'The king is dead. He has been killed. The land is free of him, and a great evil has left the world.'

Josse heard Helewise's gasp of horrified dismay. He tightened his grip on her hand. In that moment of deepest peril, he feared very much that a wrong word from either of them would invite the same fate as the king had just suffered.

Then he stopped thinking of Helewise and himself, and the import of what he had just been told sank in.

King John was *dead*? Oh no, no – it was impossible. Lord Wimarc was lying. He had been misinformed; misled. He was misleading *them* – Josse and Helewise – for some deep purpose of his own. He was deranged.

It could not be true!

John was dead.

King John; son of the great Henry II and his magnificent wife; brother of Richard, who had been the hero of his age. In a series of images that flashed across his mind like summer lightning, Josse saw the life of the man who he had known, on and off, since John was a furiously angry little boy, hurling platters and lying on the ground stuffing rushes in his mouth because he could not get his own way.

He was a cunning, self-serving, ruthless devil of a man, Josse thought as he felt the pain of loss begin. *But, dear God, I liked him.*

He wondered if he could speak without giving away what he was thinking. Lord Robert was clearly waiting for a response; sitting there in his vast, ostentatious throne, he was gloating like a man who had just won a great and unexpected victory against overwhelming odds.

Which, in a way, Josse reflected, he had.

'From your demeanour,' he began, gratified to discover that his voice did not shake, 'I would surmise that you had a hand in this death.'

'You surmise correctly,' Lord Robert said grimly.

But Josse could not absorb it. 'You cannot have done this deed!' he cried. 'The king is better-guarded than any man in England.'

Lord Wimarc inspected the citrine stone on his right hand, turning it this way and that. 'Nevertheless, he is dead,' he said softly.

Slowly, Josse shook his head. 'Why?' he asked simply.

Lord Robert eyed him suspiciously. 'Do you need to be given reasons, sir knight? The people of England long to be rid of this monster. Is that not sufficient?'

'Some – aye, if not most – probably agree with you,' Josse acknowledged. 'But to wish for the death of God's anointed monarch in a moment of anger and frustration is a very different matter from perpetrating the deed.'

Lord Wimarc made no reply.

'In any case, why should you, in particular, wish so fervently for the end of this rule?' Josse pressed on. 'What has King John done to you that you find so much more unbearable than the hardships the rest of us are forced to suffer in these tumultuous times?'

Still Lord Wimarc sat silent.

'Do you intend,' Josse asked, 'to join the self-serving barons who flock to Nicholas Fitzwalter? Do you too wish to clip the wings of whoever sits on the throne, so that the high lords of England can keep more of their wealth and their power for themselves?' Warming to his theme, words seemed to flood up, and he did not try to hold them back. He and Helewise stood, alone, amid a circle of well-armed and, presumably, well-drilled men. There was no hope for them, unless Lord Robert Wimarc was going to be merciful. *We have nothing to lose,* Josse thought savagely. *And, dear God above, I will know the truth of this.*

He pressed on. 'Perhaps it is that you shudder at the thought of what would happen if King John didn't yield to the Pope?' he suggested. 'For they say, do they not, that Pope Innocent plans to invite Philip of France to invade? You reason, I might guess, that it is better to see John die now, before Philip can have a chance to strike?'

Another thought occurred to him. Watching Lord Wimarc closely, very aware of the silent presence of Manticore, standing just behind his lord, Josse said, 'Or, possibly, you think to see the crown pass to John's young son Henry? You would prefer a four-year-old child on the throne as Henry III, and perhaps you aspire to have a say in how the land is governed while he remains too young to do it himself? If this were to happen, then there would indeed have to be a council of regents, and might the lure of a place on that council be sufficient to entice you out of your isolation?'

Josse stopped, panting slightly. He realized he had barely drawn breath in the course of his passionate outburst. He sensed Helewise edge closer. 'Are you all right?' she whispered.

'Aye,' he muttered.

There was utter quiet in the long hall. *You would never believe,* Josse thought with strange detachment, *that twelve men stood around the walls, for they make no more noise than a dozen statues.*

301

He glanced at Manticore, whose dark eyes were narrowed into slits as he watched and waited. Then he turned back to Lord Robert.

'Is it worth it?' he asked softly. 'You have killed your king, or your man here has done so on your orders.' He shot a glance at Manticore. It was a guess, but Josse was all but certain he was right. 'Which, be in no doubt, will be judged to be the same thing.' He edged a little closer. 'Do you imagine you will not be brought to justice? Do you think to live in peace under whatever new regime evolves? Think again! Oh, Lord Robert, new rulers do not allow the murderers of their predecessors to go on living in happy isolation, for there is always the fear that, having once committed regicide, it may become a habit. At best, you will be closely watched till the end of your days. At worse, you may be deemed too much of a worry, and they will quietly dispose of you. Your—'

Lord Robert broke his long silence, and his voice was cold with fury. 'I care not a jot for those puffed-up lords who only wish the king curtailed because he is too powerful, and who bleat because that power damages their own position and bleeds their wealth!' Emotion twisted his face; it was clear he despised the Nicholas Fitzwalters of the world. 'In addition, I am quite indifferent to which royal backside sits on the throne of England.' He leaned forward, craning his stringy neck towards Josse. 'What has King John done to me, you ask?' The mocking echo of Josse's words was eloquent with pain. 'Listen, sir knight–' he turned briefly to Helewise and, strange amid the powerful tensions in the hall, gave her a quaintly old-fashioned bow – 'listen, my lady, and you shall hear.'

He leaned back in his chair, wrapped the fur-trimmed cloak more closely around his thin old body and, after a short pause, resumed.

'I have always shunned human company,' he began, 'perhaps because of a harsh upbringing, which made loneliness preferable to the cruel jibes, the days spent in solitary confinement and the regular beatings. For, you see, my family name was deemed one to live up to, and those men given the task of raising me were harsh in the administration of the necessary lessons. When I came of age, I thought to spend my adulthood alone; indeed, by the time I became a man, I had become unfit for company. Especially, you will appreciate, the precious, delicate company of a lady.' He shot an almost apologetic glance at Helewise, as if, as the sole representative of her sex who was present, it was for her, on behalf of all women, to hear his account of himself.

Then, lowering his head, he stared down into his lap. There was a pause, and then he said, 'Once free of my tormentors and able to make my own decisions, I spent many years shut away with my books, my manuscripts, my writings, my thoughts, and the world left me alone. I reached the advanced age of thirty-five, and then the miracle happened: by pure chance, I met a young woman barely out of girlhood, and she saw through all my deep and carefully raised defences and fell for me.'

His voice had changed, Josse noted; suddenly the grim tone had lightened, as if the sun had come out after a week of cloud.

'Of course, I reciprocated,' Lord Wimarc continued, a smile stretching the tight lips, 'for she was utterly lovely. Despite my lifelong resolve to be alone, I let down every last guard, and declared my love for her. Her name was Agnes; she had hair like ripe corn, which she loved me to brush for her, and her eyes were like the summer sky at twilight.' He paused, and Josse saw his throat working as he sought to control himself. 'Agnes and I were wed,' he went on softly, 'and she conceived a child.'

There was a long pause. Josse sensed grief creep out of the old man, emanating out of him to spread like darkness covering the ground. 'She died,' Lord Robert whispered at last. 'My Agnes died, giving birth to our child.' He covered his face with his hands, and the huge citrine glittered in the firelight. 'I had to bear my heartache and go on living without her,' he went on, dropping his hands back into his lap, 'even when I longed with all my soul to follow her into the grave, for I was not alone: in Agnes's stead, I had a little daughter to look after, and I could not abandon her. In time – in not very much time – I grew to love Tiercel, my own child, just as profoundly as I had loved her mother. I made up my mind not to lose her as I had lost my beloved Agnes and, accordingly, I shut us away here at Wealdsend and vowed to devote what remained of my life to her care, her protection and her happiness.'

304

He paused again, seeming to be all but choked by whatever strong emotion coursed through him.

When he resumed, there was a new note – of cold detachment, Josse thought – in his voice; perhaps it was the only way he could steel himself to go on. 'When my sweet Tiercel was fifteen years old, we had a visitor. Oh, but she was so excited!' Briefly the pale eyes shone. 'Although she loved me devotedly, she had suffered from my determination to keep her enclosed and apart from the world, and I knew full well that she longed for company other than mine. Now, she believed, the world was coming to knock on her door, and her life was about to begin. Indeed it was, for our visitor was the most elevated man in the land, and he had announced he wished to stay at Wealdsend while he hunted in the forest.'

Oh, dear Lord, Josse thought. Apprehension flooded through him.

'This high-born visitor who was honouring us with a visit was drawn to my beautiful, innocent daughter from the instant he saw her.' Now, Lord Robert's tone was coolly neutral. 'Not recognizing – no, not *wanting* to recognize that the life she had led had kept her a child far beyond childhood, he pursued her, right here under my own roof. He seduced her, and he bedded her. When he had gone – never, I might add, to return; never more to contact me or my daughter with even one single word – she confessed her terrible sin to the priest, and then she took her own life.'

305

Josse heard Helewise sob: a tiny sound, barely audible, quickly suppressed.

'I have never been able to forgive myself.' Lord Robert spoke with infinite weariness, staring down at his hands folded in his lap. 'I kept her enclosed here with me for my own sake, because I could not bear the thought of any threat to her. Because of my selfishness, she was quite unprepared for the world; for the debauched depredations of a man so much older and more experienced than her; who, smitten with her smile, her demeanour that was ever willing to please, her talent, her skill at singing and playing the lute, her lovely young face, her affectionate nature, did not hesitate. He took what he wanted from a girl who had not the least idea how to defend herself – who did not know, even, if defending herself was the right thing to do.'

Now, at long last, he raised his head and Josse saw his face. Ravaged by long grief and unending guilt, he looked as if he was already in the grave.

'The man who came to visit and who is responsible for my beloved Tiercel's death was, as I am sure you have both guessed, King John,' he said quietly. 'It is for that reason, and no more nor less, that I decided he must die.'

Not knowing how to reply, Josse did not speak.

'I have been working out my plan these many years.' Now a little life returned to Lord Robert's voice, as if he were animated by describing his own cunning. 'I took as my talisman the labrys: that ancient symbol that, deep in its maze, represents intrigue on the profoundest level. I shared my aim with barely a soul, save my faithful Manticore here, known to me all his life and my true man through and through.' He looked up at the man who stood by his side, and Manticore gave a grunt of acknowledgement. 'I made my preparations. I knew I had to draw the king out of his fastnesses, for within them he is inviolate, even to one such as Manticore. You see, I had to devise a means by which he would come willingly to a less secure place.

'I contemplated the long list of those who declare themselves close companions, friends, supporters of the king, and then I narrowed it down to those who the king believed he had the greatest cause to watch. I lighted upon one who, while he boasted to all and sundry of the vast amounts he amassed on the king's behalf, yet cheated his sovereign every single day, setting aside the greater portion for the realm while keeping back a share for himself. Naturally, King John knew of this treachery.' Lord Robert paused, gazing intently at Josse and Helewise as if ensuring they understood. 'There is a saying, is there not,' he said quietly, 'that you set a thief to catch a thief? In a similar vein, a man as acquisitive and as venal as our lord king – a man who does not hesitate to lie and cheat to obtain what he wants – is the very person to perceive instantly when someone else is cheating *him*. King John knew what his dear friend Lord Benedict de Vitré was up to, I would guess, almost before de Vitré pocketed his first silver coin.'

Lord Robert paused, breathing deeply as if to

restore his strength. Then he continued. 'If anything was to happen to Lord Benedict – if, for example, he were to die – then it seemed all but certain that John would arrive hotfoot at Medley to collect all that was his. I resolved, therefore, to slip my own man inside Lord Benedict's household, where, once he was familiar with the daily habits and routine of Medley, he would be able to kill its lord while ensuring he got away.' He turned briefly to the silent Manticore. 'For I had not finished with him yet.'

'So the day that I saw you leaving Medley wasn't the first time you'd been there,' Josse said to Manticore, who did not deign to acknowledge the remark. 'You'd been there some time, learning the ways of the place and, no doubt, blending in with all the rest of the staff.'

'Having baited the trap by despatching Lord Benedict,' Lord Robert went on, 'Manticore was to keep his eyes open and his ears ever alert for news of the king. I *knew* he would come,' he said, his voice becoming animated, 'and the announcement that he would grace the funeral feast with his presence was perfect, for it is easier to carry out a secret act when there are many people about.' He smiled at Josse and Helewise, as if inviting them to congratulate him. 'Manticore's final order was a simple one: merge with the guests at the feast and, when the opportunity arises, kill the guest of honour.' He turned to look up at his man, on whose impassive face not a flicker of emotion showed. 'Which, this very day, he has done.'

Then, suddenly, Manticore made a movement;

it was almost imperceptible, and had Josse not been watching him so closely he would have missed it. But before either Josse or Manticore could speak, Lord Robert rose to his feet.

Sweeping his cloak aside, he took two steps towards Josse, who swiftly altered his position so that he stood immediately in front of Helewise. The move was instinctive; prompted, perhaps, by the experiences of a fighting life.

For he felt the threat, like a fist flying through the air towards him.

Lord Robert Wimarc spread his arms wide, like a good host offering the best his household could provide. Smiling benignly, first at Josse, then at Helewise, he said pleasantly, 'And now, my lady, sir knight, it remains only to decide what we shall do with you.'

NINETEEN

'Be *careful*!' the man cried. 'That hurts!' Then, suddenly noticing the broad-shouldered, deep-chested, black-clad figure who had approached and stood silently watching, he muttered, 'I'm sorry, my lord. It's – it's rather painful.'

The wounded man was seated on a stool, his chest bare, and Lady Richenza's personal maid-servant was applying a cloth wrung out in cold water to the huge bruise swiftly spreading across his back. The man in the costly black velvet robe leaned down to get a closer look. 'Yes, I imagine it is,' he agreed.

He bent down and picked up the mail shirt which the wounded man had been wearing beneath his outer garments, now lying discarded at his feet and half-hidden by the gorgeous scarlet tunic and the fur-trimmed cloak. The black-clad man weighed the mail shirt in his hands, inspecting the fine, linked steel rings. On the area which would have covered the left side of the wounded man's back, some of the rings were slightly distorted, although that was the only visible damage. 'The mail lived up to its reputation,' the black-clad man observed. 'It ought to be good: it cost me enough.' He laughed softly, and the man with the bruise made a brave attempt to join in.

The man in black velvet suddenly crouched down, his hand on the wounded man's arm. 'You have just done me a great service, Matthias,' he said gravely. 'I selected you for your resemblance to your king, and you agreed to help in this deception. It was bravely done, and it shall not be forgotten.' He held out a leather bag which, as it fell into Matthias's hand, gave out the chink of coins.

Matthias attempted to rise, dropping his head in a bow. 'Thank you, my lord.'

The black-clad man turned to leave, his mind already moving on to other matters. Then, as if struck by an afterthought, he turned back to Matthias. 'Oh, and you can keep my scarlet tunic, too.' He laughed again. 'Something to remind you of the night you impersonated a king, and took a blade intended for him.'

Then, whistling quietly under his breath, King John walked away.

In the master guest suite at Medley, the king lay on the soft feather bed, thinking hard. He had dismissed his bodyguard – they had fussed round him once too often that night, and he had kicked the most insistent in the backside – and now, at last, he was alone. His men were not far away – he could hear them, moving about and muttering quietly just outside the door – but at least the room, empty but for himself, gave the illusion of solitude.

She'd been right. That fascinating, elusive woman – softly he said her name aloud: 'Meggie' – had warned him what was going to happen and, thank the good Lord, he had believed her. Entirely because of her, he was alive and un-harmed, instead of lying dead on the stone-flagged floor of Medley Hall. There could be no doubt that the deadly blade would have inflicted a fatal wound: John had seen that vicious bruise on Matthias's back. Had it not been for the mail shirt, the blade would have gone in between the ribs and, driven up at the right angle by a skilled hand, would have penetrated the heart.

They had told the king how his old friend Benedict de Vitré had died. If tonight's would-be assassin was the same man (dear God, surely there could not be two!) then, but for Meggie's warning, his victim would now be as dead as Benedict.

John did not often pray, unless by so doing there was some worldly advantage for him, such as being observed in his obedient piety by someone likely to be impressed into doing whatever he wanted of them. Had anyone dared to ask him, he might have confessed to doubting whether God in fact existed; the god of the ubiquitous, carping, nagging men of the church, anyway. But now, all alone in the luxuriously furnished room, the brazier in the corner warming it to a pleasantly balmy temperature, he sent up a word of thanks, to whoever or whatever might be listening, for the accident of fate that had brought him and Meggie together in the forest glade. He closed his eyes, and instantly her face formed in his mind. Smiling, he relaxed into the self-indulgence of memory.

When word had been brought to him that Benedict de Vitré was dead, he had resolved straight away to go down to Medley Hall. Attending his old friend's funeral feast was a good enough excuse: the reasons behind it were rather more complex. Of course, John was aware how efficiently Benedict had been collecting taxes on his monarch's behalf, an efficiency which, according to John's spies, was closer to extortion. The man had been ruthless, and his brutality had spread down to infect the men who worked for him. Not that the king had objected. Money was money, and he always needed more.

He was also aware that Benedict had been robbing him. Now, briefly coming out of his reverie, he opened his eyes and glanced around

312

the sumptuous room. Fabrics and furniture like these had not come from some local workshop. Added to that the brash new extensions that had been added to the mellow old house, the brilliant jewellery and the glorious gowns worn by Lady Richenza, the smart livery of the household servants, the crude extravagance of that evening's food and drink, and the glass and silverware with which it had been served, and the obvious conclusion had to be that Benedict's theft had been on a grand scale. John was still making up his mind how to retrieve what was rightfully his – an image of publicly stripping the young widow in the midst of her full household was quite tempting – but the one certainty in his mind was that he would regain every last penny. In addition, the officers he had ordered to go through Benedict's accounts would report faithfully and accurately concerning the amassed revenues currently locked away in Medley's cellar, and the king would take the lot away with him when he left.

His sudden decision to travel down a day or two before the funeral feast had been because he wanted to go hunting. The great forest perpetually beckoned, and the opportunity to answer its potent summons did not crop up nearly often enough. On the edge of the forest, too, was St Edmund's Chapel, and somewhere nearby lived the mysterious woman who, even after a year, still danced in and out of his dreams.

They'd had a fine day's hunting, he and the close band of companions he'd chosen to go with him. The forest had lived up to its reputation, and he had been more than satisfied with the chase. Augmenting the thrill of the hunt – and something known only to himself – was the secret awareness that deer and boar were not the only quarry he intended to pursue.

As the day drew towards its end, he had remarked to his party – in tones of well-simulated but false surprise – that they appeared to find themselves in the vicinity of St Edmund's Chapel. Affecting nonchalance, he told his companions to go on to the hunting lodge where they were all putting up. 'Don't wait for me,' he said, 'it's a chore and a bore, but, since we are close by, my conscience compels me to pay my respects at the chapel which my late and esteemed lady mother ordered built to commemorate the life and the amazingly heroic deeds of my beloved elder brother.'

One or two of those closest to him had suppressed smiles. They knew what he had thought of his mother and his brother. He had detailed his bodyguards to stand watch, looking down on to the abbey and the roads leading in and out. Then, his heart beating hard, he had gone to the chapel and waited. Nobody was there; nobody came to join him. Impatient, stricken with the first doubts (*what if she doesn't come?*) he hurried out into the clearing, stopping on its perimeter and standing behind the concealing bulk of a mighty oak. Still nothing. Then an idea occurred to him: she was a creature of mystery, wasn't she? Then surely the most likely place to find her was deep inside the forest. Suddenly confident, a smile spreading across his face, he turned his back on

314

the glade and the daylight and plunged off into its dark depths. And, a little later, sitting propped against a particularly graceful birch tree, suddenly he knew without a doubt that she was near.

He could almost make himself believe that she had been on the lookout for him...

Lying on Benedict de Vitré's luxuriously appointed guest bed, he gave himself up to the memory of those first few moments.

Presently, he turned his mind to what else had occurred between them.

'You're here because Lord Benedict is dead,' she said. 'I thought you would come.'

'To pay my respects to my old friend?' he suggested.

She smiled. 'If you say so, my lord.'

She knew, though; there was no need to ask. Looking into her clear brown eyes – the setting sun had set sparkling lights dancing in them, he recalled – he wondered fleetingly if she thought the less of him, for using the excuse of honouring a loyal servant to cover up his urgent and rapacious desire to get his hands on every last penny that de Vitré owed him. *It does not matter what she thinks*, a cold voice said inside his head.

Attuned to her as he was, he sensed there was something she wanted to tell him. Then – and it had astounded him – she revealed that she stood accused of causing Benedict de Vitré's death with a dangerously powerful potion.

He wondered why he had not been told of this. A cold, hard anger began to simmer deep inside him; when he returned to Medley, the fury would emerge. For now, there was her.

'I did not kill him,' she said. 'It was I who discovered the wound that penetrated his heart and brought about his death. If my hand had indeed wielded the blade, why, in God's name, would I have proclaimed its discovery?'

He nodded thoughtfully. 'Why indeed.'

'Besides,' she ploughed on, 'I had no reason to kill him.' He kept his eyes fixed to hers, willing her to continue. 'Well, other than the fact that he was a savage bully,' she added after a brief pause. 'Quite ruthless and totally without compassion, in addition to which he was robbing you blind, keeping back a portion of everything he collected in your name to spend on himself, that pretty wife of his and that spectacularly garish new wing on the side of his house.' She stopped. *'Oh!'*

He felt almost sorry for her. Never having experienced the method with which he extracted the truth from those tempted to hold it from him, she was, he realized, quite defenceless. Deliberately he softened his expression, and smiled at her.

'Benedict de Vitré was a dishonest rogue,' he murmured. 'Yes, so I have reliably been informed.'

She was still staring at him. Now, he almost felt that it was *she* who was determined that *he* should say more... 'I believe you,' he said. Then, wanting to laugh with the pure joy of the moment, he added, 'I can well believe you might want to kill a man, Meggie. But you would not do it by means of a poisoned potion. You would

316

do it face to face, no doubt with that slender but extremely elegant blade that you carry by your side.'

With a quiet gasp (of dismay? But why should she have been dismayed?) she glanced down at the sword. He held out his hand, and she drew it, presenting it for his inspection.

It was a beautiful weapon, made by an outstanding craftsman. The hilt was bound with fine leather, stained with some subtle dye that gave it a purple hue. The colour, it was clear, had been chosen deliberately, for, running through the dull, grey steel of the slim blade with its very slight curve, was a sheen of violet.

'Where did you get this?' he asked, genuinely intrigued. He turned the sword over in his hands, watching the play of the light on the metal.

'It was made in a forge in a Breton forest,' she said. He detected a change in her voice. 'On a bright day, when the sun on the peaty water made it dance with gold.'

'Hm.' *Very poetic*, he thought. Then, in almost the same instant: *Made for her by someone she loves*.

Practised as he was in the art of love, he knew he was right.

He raised the sword and, stepping away from her, made a few sweeps through the air. The sword seemed to sing.

He glanced at her, and saw she had not taken her eyes off him. 'My ... it's said all good swords should have a name,' she said. 'My blade is called Limestra.'

'Limestra,' he repeated, looking at her and

317

raising one eyebrow.

She grinned. 'No, I'd never heard it either. Apparently it means *purple* in Breton.'

Turning the hilt towards her, he handed back the sword. 'I recall that, once, I offered to teach you swordplay,' he remarked. He heard her quick intake of breath: she, too, remembered. He studied her very closely. 'I imagine that, now you have your own instructor, there is no need.'

She met his eyes and did not look away.

'I would not raise a sword to you, my lord,' she whispered.

'Your lord?'

She bowed; a graceful movement, her body supple as a willow whip.

She still held her sword in her hand. He drew the long hunting knife from its scabbard on his belt. It was only a hand's breadth or two shorter than her blade. Slowly, deliberately, he drew it this way, then that, in a series of movements that were more like some formal, stately court dance. She responded, mirroring his actions, her blade meeting his, parrying, then, when she saw a gap, swiftly sweeping into it, yet always stopping short.

They moved closer and closer. Then, dropping his knife, he took her in his arms. As he had longed to do when first she came into the glade, he drew her close to touch his lips to hers.

Before, just now, there had been resistance; he had seen – or perhaps recalled – that sudden flash of blue, and in his memory the warning had rung out, clear as a sweet, high bell, that she was forbidden.

318

This time, he – she – ignored it.

Suddenly she wrestled herself out of his embrace, and a great sob broke out of her. She put her hands to her head, as if to contain some terrible thought or image. Briefly she closed her eyes, then opened them again. Violently she shook her head, as if in pain or terrible despair.

'What is it?' he asked.

She began to speak, stopped, then took a deep breath and started again. 'You are in danger,' she said, her tone strangely detached. And, fluently, clearly, without a single hesitation, she described a hall, a high dais, gloriously clad lords and ladies, wildly extravagant amounts of food and wine.

And a silent assassin, who crept out of the shadows with a deadly blade in his hand.

Now King John lay on his soft bed, hands behind his head, letting the images – and the thrill of excitement and pleasure they had set off – fade and die.

She had warned him, and he had believed her. It had been fairly easy to find a man who looked sufficiently like him in colouring and stature to fool those who did not know him personally – the vast majority of those attending the feast – especially once Matthias had been decked in the king's garments and jewels. Those who knew what he looked like were, of course, aware of the subterfuge. And, beneath the rich silks and velvets, Matthias had worn the mail which had turned the knife; the huge, purple bruise would fade, in time.

He had also worn, between the mail and the outer garments, a strange device: over the ribs that guarded the heart was a shoulder of pork, wrapped in a length of muslin wound tightly around his chest. It had been John's idea: if indeed someone was out to kill him, he reasoned, then if they realized the first stab into the heart had been unsuccessful, they would be more than likely to go for the throat instead. Of course, it wouldn't have mattered all that much if Matthias had died, but John liked a challenge, and the idea of outwitting his would-be killer appealed to him. Let the man believe he had succeeded; now *that* would be a triumph indeed.

The ruse had worked. In every single detail, the elaborate scheme had gone off without a hitch. And, because of Meggie, John was unharmed.

Eyes still closed, he brought to mind an image of her face. His hard, cruel features softened into a smile. He was going to have to decide how to thank her...

He allowed his imagination free rein for a while. Then, returning with an effort to reality, two thoughts occurred to him. The first was that, now that the assassin had acted again, only the obtuse or the biased could possibly go on doubting who had killed Benedict de Vitré: it was beyond reason that more than one man would operate in so exactly the same way. And it followed, of course, that this foolish idea of Benedict having been poisoned by a fatal potion was no longer credible.

The other thought – and now John was getting

320

to his feet, drawing on his beautiful boots – was that it was time to find out if there was any news on the hunt for the man who had just tried to kill his sovereign lord. There damned well should be, he reflected, for he had dispatched orders to every sheriff within a ten-mile radius to organize search parties. John was still furious that the assassin had managed to escape. It wasn't as if his guards had not been warned: they had been fully briefed to expect an attempt on the man sitting up on the dais, dressed in the king's fine garments. Yet the would-be murderer had managed to creep round behind the dais, leap up, make what should have been his deadly stroke, and then melt away like a patch of shadow under the midday sun.

It had been skilfully done, John had to admit. Those blasted acrobats and tumblers had drawn every eye in the hall – he felt the hot rush of blood as he remembered one particular young woman, with a body as supple as a snake and a strangely beautiful face as seductive as a siren – and he wondered now if that had been the intention all along. He had thought it odd, to have entertainers at a funeral feast. Did it mean that whoever had commanded them to appear had needed the distraction they would obviously provide?

He thought about it. If that were so, then either the lovely young widow or that sinister steward of hers – perhaps both – were behind tonight's plot. Which meant they had also been responsible for putting old Benedict in the ground.

The king paced the room. While he waited for

his men to bring in the assassin, perhaps he should summon Lady Richenza. When the killer was eventually dragged before his king, the lady would be summoned to watch.

The sport promised to be better than hunting the wiliest, fiercest, biggest boar ever born.

In the hall at Wealdsend, Josse held tight to Helewise's hand and waited to see what death would look like. He had inched his right hand down until it hovered close to his sword hilt, and already he was planning the move that he would make – practised over a lifetime – as soon as the assault began.

It probably wouldn't help much, for he and Helewise were but two, and Lord Wimarc had a dozen hard, well-drilled men at his command, not to mention a killer with dead eyes who had just slain the king. But Josse was a fighter, and it would not feel right to die without his sword in his hand; without getting in at least one blow in return.

Lord Wimarc was out of his vast chair, moving across the floor towards them. 'I have consider-ed the options,' he said, as calmly as if he were choosing what to offer them for dinner, 'and I am tempted to have you taken well away from Wealdsend, whereupon I would shut and bar my gates and return to my isolation.' He sighed deeply. 'But I very much fear that would not be the end of it, for you know I'm *here* now, don't you?' He looked at Helewise, then at Josse; long, searching looks, as if this were a reasonable point and he was keen for them to agree with him. 'Oh, I know how it would be,' he muttered, half to himself, returning his gaze to Helewise. 'It would begin with a mission from those good nuns and healers at Hawkenlye Abbey, disguising their intrusion as loving kindness and concern for my loneliness and my grief, but that would not be the truth of it, would it, sir knight?' In an instant, he had spun round to Josse, his eyes burning in his tense, pale face. 'A little while ago, you were kind enough to point out what my future would be. However, you left out one important fact: those would be the likely outcomes only were it to become known whose hand was behind the assassination, whose will guided the killer.' He looked briefly at Manticore, standing impassively beside him. His voice dropping to a whisper, he said, *'You* know, Sir Josse, and so does the lady here.'

He stepped back, and a terrible smile stretched the thin mouth. 'Do you see? You do, don't you? I'm very afraid that you leave me no choice.'

As he turned to give to Manticore whatever brief command would end Josse and Helewise's lives, Josse drew his sword, the sound almost deafening in the silence. Throwing his free arm round Helewise's waist, he dragged her roughly to him, holding her hard against his side. In the same instant, he took two steps back, then spun round and, praying with all his heart that Helewise was still as strong and agile as he remembered, he started to run towards the long fire pit. Selecting a spot where the flames were no more than a glow, he increased his pace – she did too – and together they leapt over the pit.

Lord Wimarc shouted something, and feet pounded on the stone flags of the floor. But Josse barely heard, for the blood was pounding in his ears, deafening him, and all his attention was focused on what lay ahead.

Only three of the guard were on this side of the long hearth and, too far away to have overheard the conversation between Josse and their lord, they seemed unaware of what had happened. Two stepped forward, one with drawn sword, and Josse yelled, 'See to your master! He is in dire need!'

The great doors to the outside world – to safety, to remaining alive – were ahead. But now someone was hard on their heels: someone who ran with the swift, sure steps of a man who had just been given an order, and who would let nothing obstruct its completion.

As Josse reached out a desperate hand to pull apart the doors, they were thrust open from the other side. Helewise gave a cry of alarm.

Gervase de Gifford, sheriff of Tonbridge, stood at the top of the steps leading up from the court-yard. Behind him, in neat, disciplined order and armed with sword, knife and cudgel, stood more than twenty men.

In a heartbeat of stillness, Josse met Gervase's eyes.

'I understand from Abbess Caliste that you might need some help,' Gervase said. Then, with the grin of the fight-hungry boy he must once have been, he turned to his men, raised his sword arm and cried, *'Go!'*

From behind him, someone shoved Josse

aside; a hard push that felt like a vicious punch. He stumbled and, but for Helewise's strong arms, would have fallen. A dark-clad figure leapt off the top of the steps, flew through the air and, more than a tall man's height below, landed lightly on his feet.

'*After him!*' Josse roared. Gervase spun round to him. 'He's the killer! *Don't let him get away!*'

Four of Gervase's men scrambled back down the steps and ran off after the fleeing figure. Peering into the darkness, Josse realized, with a sinking heart, that Manticore was already out of sight. *He knows this place*, he thought, sick. *He is a survivor, and he will long have worked out any number of escape routes. Gervase's men don't stand a chance.*

He turned and, clutching Helewise to him, limped back into the hall, to instantly find themselves in the midst of a battle. Tired, hurt and, more than anything, concerned for Helewise, Josse admitted to himself that it wasn't his fight. He led her aside, away from the violence, and together they watched as Gervase and his men gradually overcame Lord Wimarc's guards.

'He's the man responsible,' Josse said to Gervase as, from the top of the steps, they watched Lord Wimarc being led away to captivity, his eight surviving guards following behind, and all under the tight control of Gervase's toughest deputies. 'It was Lord Robert Wimarc who ordered the murders of both Benedict de Vitré and King John.'

'He's not dead, Josse,' Gervase said quietly.

325

'The king, I mean.'

'He is!' Josse insisted wildly. 'He was killed this night, at Medley Hall, as he attended the funeral feast of Lord Benedict! Haven't you been informed? He was slain by the hand of the same assassin who—'

'Josse, it seems he was forewarned,' Gervase said, speaking loudly against Josse's ranting. 'They found another man with a passing resemblance to the king, and dressed him up in the royal garments. They took the precaution of providing a mail shirt, which is just as well because otherwise the poor sod would be as dead as Lord Benedict.'

Helewise touched Gervase's arm, attracting his attention. 'You must understand that Lord Robert Wimarc is a man lost in a dark world of grief,' she said softly. 'Please, Gervase, listen to him before he is condemned.'

Gervase looked at her. 'He ordered the death of one man, and wished also to kill his king,' he said coolly. 'Do you really think, my lady, that there will be mercy for him?'

'At least let him have the comfort of a priest,' she persisted, 'for he has suffered for half a lifetime; perhaps more.'

Gervase went on staring at her, not speaking. 'You owe us this, Gervase,' Helewise said very quietly.

With a curt sound of impatience, Gervase turned on his heel and strode away.

In the sudden silence of the rapidly emptying hall, Josse turned to her. 'Are you all right?'

'Yes,' she said. 'I'm fine.' She smiled. 'It's not

326

every day you come close to losing your life. I must say, it tends to enhance the joy of still being alive.'

He chuckled. 'It does that. Aye, I too thought our time had come.' He hesitated. Then, taking her hand, he said quietly, 'There's nobody I'd rather die beside than you.'

She gave a soft sound, perhaps a sob. Then she said, 'But not just yet, hmm?'

TWENTY

In the hut in the forest, Lilas said suddenly, 'Something's happened.'

Meggie struggled up out of her first, deep sleep; they went to bed early out there, usually tired from a long day out of doors, and she knew from the quality of the darkness that the night was not yet far advanced.

She wriggled to the edge of the sleeping platform and looked down at Lilas, huddled in her blankets. Lilas, offered the choice of where to sleep, had opted for the floor beside the hearth. *Old'uns like me need to get up and pass water in the night*, she'd said, *and I don't want to break my neck trying to clamber up and down that tiddly ladder when I'm half asleep.* Meggie had been hugely relieved. She liked her sleeping platform to herself.

'What's the matter?' she murmured, yawning hugely. 'Are you unwell?'

But she knew, even as she asked, that it was nothing within the little hut that had disturbed Lilas's sleep. She felt cold suddenly. She demanded urgently, *'What's wrong?'*

Lilas did not at first reply. Meggie jumped down from the platform and poked up the embers in the hearth, sending small flames along a smouldering log. By the soft light, she studied the old woman's face.

'There's been peril this night,' Lilas intoned quietly, eyes staring out unfocused into the gloom. 'Blood; woundings; death. And a man running, running ... they pursue him, but he will never be caught. He'll vanish, like the mist before the sunrise...'

Meggie felt her heart thumping in her chest. What did this mean? Had the warning failed? Was he...?

She found she could not bear to even think it.

Lilas would say no more. In the face of Meggie's increasingly desperate questions, she simply pressed her lips firmly together and refused to be drawn.

Sleep was a very long way away. Meggie fetched a blanket from the sleeping platform and, settling down next to Lilas, she stoked up the fire and prepared for a night of vigil.

Someone was tapping gently on the door. 'Meggie?' a voice called softly. 'Meggie, are you awake in there?'

Meggie leapt up and flung open the door. The

moon had set, she noticed absently: dawn must be close. Outside, warmly wrapped and with excitement flashing in her dark eyes, stood her friend Tiphaine, the herbalist.

'What's happened?' Meggie demanded, dragging her inside and shutting the door. *'Who is dead?'*

The last words emerged as a suppressed shriek. Tiphaine took her hand, speaking soothing words. 'Hush, child. Nobody you love has been hurt – or, at least, nothing that won't soon mend.'

'Tell me!' Meggie thought she would burst.

'I've just come from the abbey,' Tiphaine said. 'An attempt's been made on the king's life, while he was at that Lord Benedict's funeral celebrations. He's unharmed, because somehow he knew what was going to happen–' she shot a very knowing look at Meggie, although *surely*, Meggie thought wildly, she could have no idea – 'and a substitute sat in his place, protected by mail. Your father and the abbess–' in moments of tension, Meggie had remarked, Tiphaine often referred to Helewise by her previous title – 'were seemingly at the home of the man behind the attempt, and Josse had left word with Abbess Caliste to send for that Gervase, and he took a band of men and there was a fight, and men were killed, so they say, but, like I told you, your father and the lady are all right.' She paused, frowning. 'Oh, and it seems the killer got clean away.' She gave a snort of disapproval. 'De Gifford should have gone better prepared.'

'Wouldn't have helped,' Lilas murmured.

'They won't find him.'

Meggie looked at her. 'Did you see it, too?' she whispered. 'The attempt on the king's life?'

Lilas shook her head. 'No, lass, reckon that vision was saved just for you. I saw him in danger, aye, although I wasn't permitted to see the source of the threat, and then I saw him unharmed. Won't do him any good, not in the long run,' she added briskly. 'He has a few more years, but what I *have* seen is how it ends. It's not pretty.' Briefly there was sympathy in her eyes, as if she saw into Meggie's thoughts and understood her tangled emotions.

'I don't know...' Meggie began. But she found she couldn't speak.

'They're down there at the abbey,' Tiphaine said into the silence. 'Your father and Helewise. He'd like to see you, child.'

Oh, and I'd like to see him! Meggie thought, a sudden longing for Josse flooding through her. She touched Lilas's hand. 'Will you be all right here, or do you want to come with me?'

Lilas smiled. 'I'll do very well here. In fact...' She shifted her position, plumping up the straw-filled sacking palliasse. 'I reckon I'll go back to sleep.'

Mounted on Eloise's mare, Meggie was on her way down to Tonbridge. Ninian rode ahead, detailed by Josse to escort her on her journey. She had tried to accept the necessity for her brother's presence with good grace – she knew Josse only acted out of concern for her safety – but, as always, it chafed. Ninian, too, she reflected, probably had several places he would rather be: back at home with his wife and his enchanting infant girl, for one. Inana, her aunt thought fondly, was becoming prettier by the day.

Life at the House in the Woods had settled down again over the past few days and, as ever, the ordinary daily routine became more valuable immediately after events had conspired to threaten it. It was clear to Meggie that her father and Helewise had not told the entire truth about what had happened up at Wealdsend: they had merely said that they had been talking to Lord Robert Wimarc about the three dead young men – asking him if he had known they were coming to see him – when Gervase and his men burst in to arrest him and his killer for the attempted murder of the king. She knew, in her heart, that it had been considerably more dramatic than Josse would admit. For one thing, there were all sorts of unanswered questions and, in addition, she was quite sure, in her own mind, that her father and Helewise had been in grave danger. She had noticed that the pair of them repeatedly caught one another's eye, exchanging a secret look which she could not interpret but which she guessed meant something like *we nearly lost each other; thank God we didn't*.

Lord Robert Wimarc was awaiting trial. Everybody believed he would hang, for King John would not tolerate a man to live when that man had sent a skilled assassin to kill him.

Of the assassin there was no sign. Gervase de Gifford had delved into his own purse to hire parties of extra deputies, selecting skilled huntsmen, subtle trackers, upright citizens and even reformed poachers, and the countryside around Wealdsend had been scoured over and over again. Meggie could have told Gervase not to bother. Undoubtedly, the killer was far away by now.

Meggie wondered how he would have felt when he heard – *if* he heard – that the man he had been commanded to kill was alive and thriving; when he discovered that he had stuck his lethal blade not into living flesh, but into a shoulder of pork.

With a shudder, she turned her mind away from the subject. She almost wished she had not been told the details, but Gervase appeared to be under the impression that, after having treated her so unfairly over the matter of Sabin's potion, he owed her the full story.

In front of her, Ninian turned in the saddle. 'All right?' he asked.

'Yes.'

He nodded and turned round again. She smiled; knowing him as well as she did, she guessed that this chance to think his own thoughts was as welcome to him as it was to her. *People with whom you can be happily silent*, she thought, *are both rare and to be treasured.*

Her thoughts roamed on. Her innocence in the matter of the death of Lord Benedict was now beyond dispute, the true story having been broadcast by the highest in the land. 'The man known as Manticore is responsible for both the death of Lord Benedict de Vitré and for the attempt on the king's life,' said the proclamation,

332

widely believed to have been worded by King John himself, 'and the forces of law and order throughout the land will hunt him down and bring him to justice.'

That, thought Meggie, recalling Lilas's prediction, *remains to be seen*.

Ninian, she noticed, had got some way ahead of her and, as she urged the mare after him, down the long hill towards the town, her mind stayed with Lilas.

The old woman had gone when Meggie finally went back to the hut. Initially Meggie had been very concerned: surely it wasn't safe to leave, because the Fitzwalter faction might very well still be hunting for the old woman. But then, on further reflection, she came to understand that perhaps there was no need to worry...

News had spread like fire about the assassination attempt on the king, and now people were doing their best to make out they were fervent John supporters and had been all along – and wasn't it a terrible state of affairs, when a man plots to murder God's anointed sovereign lord? In this climate of self-righteous loyalty to King John, Nicholas Fitzwalter had gone rather quiet. Ralph of Odiham had apparently decided he was suddenly needed back at his monastery, and it was rumoured that Caleb of Battle had fled; taking advantage of the flurry of activity in and around Tonbridge Castle, he had quietly slipped away, presumably back to the safe, strong walls of his abbey. Word was that he had learned a hard lesson: *keep your opinions to yourself*.

Maybe, she reflected hopefully now, Fitz-walter no longer wanted to get his hands on Lilas? She smiled. In the light of what she had recently learned, it seemed unlikely that he would find her, even if he wanted to...

It had been a day or two before Meggie learned what had become of Lilas: she had gone off with Tiphaine. Lilas had no desire to return to Hamhurst, Tiphaine reported when she came to explain the old woman's disappearance. She had no kin there, and her outspokenness – seen as a threat by many villagers to their anonymity and their safety – had made her unpopular, and she knew full well that nobody in Hamhurst was going to welcome her back with open arms.

Tiphaine was going to take Lilas to meet the Domina. Putting village life behind her forever, the old woman was about to embark on a very different life and, according to Tiphaine, she was embracing the prospect joyfully. The forest people were far away now – Meggie knew this without being told, sensing it as a sort of sad absence deep in her heart – and from now on Lilas would be out of the reach of anyone who wanted to use her or harm her.

With a soft smile, Meggie remembered their exchange: *Got forest blood, have you*? Lilas had asked. When Meggie had said yes, she'd replied, *Me too*.

Perhaps, after all, Lilas was going home.

Sabin de Gifford was in the cool little room where she made her preparations. When Meggie was shown in, she greeted her unenthusiastically. 'Oh. It's you.'

Meggie, fully prepared to be forgiving, was taken aback. 'Yes, it is,' she agreed. After briefly looking up, Sabin was once more intent on her pestle and mortar, her head down. 'I believe,' Meggie went on, 'you owe me an apology.'

Sabin did not reply. The hand wielding the pestle stepped up its efforts.

'Sabin, look at me,' Meggie commanded. Reluctantly, Sabin raised her eyes. 'You came to me for help,' Meggie went on, 'quite desperate, because you thought one of your potions was responsible for the death of Lord Benedict. It certainly was potentially harmful, I might add, since it contained ingredients that must be treated with the greatest care, although I haven't said too much about that to anyone else.' She paused, watching Sabin intently. 'In your panic, you demanded that I go to Medley Hall with you, to make sure, as I later realized, that his death could not possibly be attributed to your potion.'

'You...' Sabin began.

But Meggie hadn't finished. 'Then, when suspicion fell on me and they said *I* had made and administered a harmful potion, I thought – I remember it vividly – I thought, *Sabin will speak up, and tell them it was she who made the remedy.*' She paused, waiting until she had controlled the flare of anger. 'But you didn't,' she said neutrally. 'You kept your mouth tightly shut, and you let me take the blame.'

'I have a husband, children and a reputation as the town apothecary!' Sabin cried. 'I could not

335

risk losing all of that!'

'But it was all right for me to risk *my* reputation?' Meggie flashed back. 'Which surely you must see would have been wrong and totally unfair, when I hadn't had anything to do with the accursed potion?'

'You're different.' Sabin spoke the two words with cold detachment. 'It doesn't matter what people think of you, because you're a...' As if she was suddenly aware of what she was saying – who she was saying it to – she stopped. A faint flush crept into her cheeks.

'Because I'm a bastard child born to a forest woman,' Meggie finished softly. 'Yes, Sabin, I know what I am. But, unlike you, I know what constitutes honourable, decent behaviour, and allowing a friend to take the blame for my own mistakes is not something I would ever contemplate.'

It was a relief to emerge out into the courtyard, where Ninian waited for her with the horses. He took one look at her face, then handed her the mare's reins and said, 'Let's go.'

Riding home, Meggie fought to overcome her disgust and, she had to admit, her deep disappointment. Sabin, she realized, had put self-interest – and the advancement of her husband, herself and their children – far above anything and everything else. So far above, indeed, that Meggie's possible fate, if she had been arrested and put on trial for murder by potion, had not affected her at all – or, if it had, not enough to make her confess and take the blame on herself.

336

Where it belongs! Meggie thought, fury racing up again.

Sabin really was not to be trusted.

They had reached the summit of the hill, where the road out of Tonbridge met the track that ran round the forest, turning right for the abbey and left for the House in the Woods. Ninian had gone on ahead, towards home, but she hesitated, not sure which way to go; not sure, in truth, whether she was yet ready to follow him. Turning in the saddle, she gazed down at the town in the valley below.

I thought better of Sabin, she reflected sadly. *I believed we were friends.*

She found that her confidence in her own judgement had been badly shaken. To have had faith in someone, and then been let down, was, she discovered, a hard lesson.

From somewhere within herself, she seemed to hear a very familiar voice: *Meggie, you're grown up now*, it said. Its tone was calm, and very, very loving. *It's time to realize that not everyone's nice.*

Ninian, noticing she had stopped, had turned his horse and was riding back towards her. 'Are you coming?' he asked.

She looked at him, her eyes suddenly full of tears. 'I just ... I heard our mother's voice,' she said quietly. 'She ... I was a bit upset about something, and she was giving me a piece of wise advice.'

He was watching her, understanding and love in his bright blue eyes. 'She does tend to do that from time to time,' he replied. He grinned and

337

then, seeing her tears, reached out for her hand. 'Don't be sad,' he said. 'She's with us, you know, all the time.'

She sniffed, wiping a hand across her face. 'Yes, I know.' She managed a smile. 'I'm so glad you sense her, too.'

'I,' he said with dignity, 'am her oldest child. Of course I do.'

Her smile broadened. 'Pompous ass,' she muttered.

'Forest child,' he flung back.

It was normally funny, but it wasn't today. Jerking her head towards the town, down in its valley, she said, 'She just said as much to me. *You're different*, she said. *It doesn't matter what people think of you*. I knew exactly what she meant.'

Ninian gave a sound that eloquently expressed his disgust. 'Meggie, you and I didn't have the conventional family arrangement to bless our birth, any more than Geoffroi did, but, personally, I've always thought that to be an advantage.' He hesitated, then said, 'I never met my real father, and once I'd outgrown some childish notions concerning him, I didn't want to. We share our mother, and both of us know how special she was. I wish that, like you and Geoffroi, I was Josse's blood son, but he is my father in every other respect.' Again he paused, watching her with an expression so kind that it brought more tears to her eyes. 'We couldn't do any better, Meggie, and if Sabin de Gifford can't see that, the fault is in her.'

Slowly she nodded. He was right; she knew it.

338

Suddenly she realized exactly where she wanted to be. Putting her heels to the mare's sides, she said, 'Race you home.'

POSTSCRIPT

Midwinter 1211

Jehan de Ferronier reached down and patted the neck of his horse. 'Not far now, Auban,' he said, speaking in Breton since Auban was a Breton horse. 'It's been a long road, and both of us are hungry and weary, but soon we'll be able to rest.' The horse responded to his voice with a shake of his head, making the long, pale-coloured mane fly out in an arc which released a cloud of dust. Jehan, waving the dust away from his face, gave a short laugh. 'Yes,' he added, 'and we're both filthy. I forgot to mention that.'

He turned round in the saddle, looking back into the west. The sun would soon be setting – this was, after all, the shortest day of the year – but he reckoned enough daylight remained for him to reach his destination. The thought of yet another night curled up under some hedgerow that provided inadequate shelter from the cold was all but unendurable. Once or twice, at the start of his journey, he had treated himself and Auban to a night in an inn, but now he felt he must save every coin of the money that remained in his purse.

He thought – he *hoped* – he was going to be needing it.

* * *

He had been in Wales, where he had sought out and joined the group of fellow Bretons who had gone to add their strength to the Welshmen fighting under Llewellyn ap Iorwerth. Neither Jehan nor any of his companions had any personal allegiance to the Welsh lord; none had even met him before arriving in Wales. It was simply a case that *my enemy's enemy is my friend.* Llewellyn was fighting King John for reasons of his own – most of Jehan's fellow fighters had only the haziest idea of what these reasons were – and Jehan's Bretons were willing to put their strength of arms behind anyone who fought the king of England.

Their own reason for fighting him was crystal clear, and it amounted almost to a holy crusade: King John had murdered his own nephew, and that precious young man had been the Bretons' beloved Arthur, son of Constance of Brittany and King John's brother, Geoffrey. The rumour – so widely believed that, in most men's minds, it had turned into gospel truth – was that, at Easter 1203 in Rouen, John himself had crushed the life out of the young man, then weighted the body with a stone and thrown it out of a window into the Seine.

Jehan and his Bretons had found a confused and constantly changing state of affairs in Wales. The problem, as Jehan saw it, was that the majority of the Welsh lords were primarily – some of them solely – concerned with themselves and their own small fiefdoms, and, accordingly, they tended to switch their loyalty

341

depending on which of the two protagonists, Llewellyn or John, was in the ascendancy. John's initial attack had been an abject failure, leading the Welsh lords to flock to Llewellyn, but his second advance – better-planned, better-executed – had been devastatingly successful. When Jehan had left Wales, rumour had it that Llewellyn was in the middle of forming new and powerful allegiances with other Welsh lords, and that their uprising against John, when it happened, would have the support of no less a figure than Pope Innocent himself.

Less widely broadcast – in fact, Jehan had only heard it as the merest whisper – was the suspicion that Llewellyn was in touch with the French king, Philip Augustus, and together they were planning a massive counterstroke against John.

Jehan had not been the only Breton to leave Wales late that autumn, as the season slowly and irrevocably turned to winter. As the brave stand against King John had deteriorated into a squabble between rival Welsh lords, many of Jehan's companions had also decided they'd had enough. Most of them were only there, in that mountainous, incomprehensible land so far from home, because they had believed they would be offered the chance to take a swing at the man who had murdered their Duke Arthur; because, with any luck, they might witness the royal head severed from the royal shoulders. Sitting in a dirty, damp, cold camp, with inadequate and pretty disgusting food and, most days, nothing to do, most of the Bretons had decided they would be better off back home. *We can always come back*, they reassured each other as they packed up their meagre possessions and prepared to leave. *When the fight begins anew, we'll be here!*

Jehan knew they meant it; knew they sincerely believed the brave proclamations. And, in truth, the mass departures suited him, for nobody thought to comment when he, too, announced he was off.

He said farewell to the last of his fellow Bretons – a group of seven who came from a small town near to Duke Arthur's former stronghold in Nantes – as the road they had been travelling on diverged. His friends headed south, to the coast and a boat to take them home. Jehan went on eastwards, giving as his reason his urgent need to find a town or a village with a decent blacksmith to attend to Auban, who had cast a shoe and was beginning to favour his off hind leg.

Nobody questioned him, and the farewells were affectionate and sincere, with many calls of, 'See you in the spring, when the fight resumes!'

As he headed off on his long road, Jehan felt a moment's regret at his duplicity. Auban did indeed need the attentions of a blacksmith, but only because Jehan had himself removed the shoe. But he'd needed an excuse for not proceeding with his companions, and that was the best he'd been able to come up with.

He had two reasons for not returning to Brittany, and he was prepared to share neither of them with the men with whom he had been living and fighting for the past couple of months. The first was personal: he had promised Meggie

343

he would join her in the Wealden Forest before winter made travel impossible. He knew he had left it very late, for the temperature had been steadily dropping and he was sure it would be snowing before long. The second reason was involved with the campaign he had just left behind in Wales.

Although Jehan had been careful not to say so out loud, he sensed that he was more deeply committed in his opposition to King John of England than many, if not most, of his Breton companions. He had nodded in agreement with the comments that suggested there was no point in remaining in Wales, while in his heart he had been angry with those who made them. *The struggle is not over*, he wanted to shout. *We should take the initiative, and ally ourselves to Llewellyn himself, offering our swords and reiterating our reasons for joining the fight! We should tell him what to do!*

He had done nothing.

Other than, in the privacy of his own head, to formulate a plan of his own.

Yes, he would be returning to the south-east of England anyway, to honour his commitment to Meggie. It was fortunate, therefore, that the south-east was precisely where the king now resided – where, or so they said, he would be spending the next few weeks.

It made a lot more sense, really, for a man who wanted to kill him to be in the same vicinity...

He was on the very last leg of the long journey. To his right, the dark, shadowy forest loomed like a sleeping giant. Ahead, the road wound around the bulge of its northern perimeter. Presently he passed Hawkenlye Abbey, where, as the light began to fail, lamps were being lit.

He urged Auban forward, for suddenly he had need of haste.

He turned into the forest, casting in his memory and trying to picture the twists and turns of the track. After a while, he relaxed, and a smile spread across his face. It was all coming back to him; he knew he would find the way.

And, sooner than he expected, the clearing opened up before him.

Meggie was tidying the little hut, preparing to close up for the night and go down to the abbey. Once again, she was helping Sister Liese with a patient in the infirmary, and it made sense for her to sleep at Hawkenlye rather than walk back to the House in the Woods. Looking round the beloved hut, she sighed. She had tried over and over again to persuade Josse that she was as safe within its stout walls as anywhere on earth, but still he was not happy about her sleeping there alone. 'When you have company – if Tiphaine, for example, is staying with you – then that's different,' he had said. 'Otherwise please, Meggie, do as I ask and go down to the abbey at nightfall.'

Because the habit of obeying him was strong in her – and far more importantly, because she loved him and did not want him to worry about her – Meggie had given her word and she kept it. But, denied of the precious solitude of the hut

345

overnight, instead she regularly escaped to it during the day. Whenever she was not needed in the infirmary – which, in fact, was quite often, since her contact with her patient involved talking to him and listening to him rather than actually nursing him – she slipped out of the abbey, up the long slope, in under the trees and along the track to the hut.

Now, as she finished her tidying, she reflected that she needed her time alone, more than ever, just at the moment, for her heart was uneasy. She remembered something one of her instructors over at Folles Pensées had told her: *Little is more exhausting to the human spirit than a mental conflict that cannot be resolved.*

The truth of that wise old man's words was proved to her now. The one benefit – she smiled grimly to herself – was that, having experienced the condition herself, she might more easily be able to help fellow sufferers.

Her conflict was simple: she had met a man who was universally loathed, yet she was drawn to him. Not for the first time, she had allowed physical sensation to take over, seducing her into feeling deeply attracted to someone who, she knew very well, would use her and discard her with no more regard for her than if she had been a hound that would no longer run. Perhaps less, for he was said to treat his hunting dogs with particular care and affection.

For what felt like the hundredth time, she fought to suppress her vivid memories of that meeting in the glade. Yet again, she failed. *What if you had done as you so badly wanted to, and yielded?* she demanded of herself. *What do you think would have happened? Do not fool yourself with dreams of some sort of lasting commitment. Would you even want that, you idiot?*

Of course not. Her life was here, in this beloved place, and, beyond it, with her family. And her future was with Jehan, who loved her and who treated her with respect, as his equal. *Who is coming back to me*, she reminded herself, *and already overdue.*

Amid the bigger anxiety, another worry niggled its way into her mind: *What if he's not coming?*

'Stop it,' she said aloud.

What troubled her most was that, despite every resolve, every promise she had made to herself, still she had found her footsteps returning to the glade where she had come across the king. He hadn't been there, and she told herself she was very relieved. But then, drawn to the other place where she had encountered him, she had seen him, standing outside St Edmund's Chapel. He had carried a cloth-wrapped parcel in his arms. Some warm, luxurious garment? Some vastly expensive, beautifully soft furs? She did not know. But she had been quite sure it had been for her.

You saved his life, she thought. *Without your warning, he would have gone unsuspecting to Benedict de Vitré's funeral feast, and now he would be dead. He probably wanted to present a gift to say thank you.*

Did kings do that? Did they ever feel the need to reward faithful, loyal service with gifts?

347

Kings probably didn't, she reflected. Men did, though, especially when the recipient was a woman they desired.

It had taken all her strength to turn back into the shelter and safety of the forest and softly walk away.

She had won that particular battle; the greater one – of stopping herself from thinking about him – was still going on. 'It's because I know what is in store for him,' she whispered out loud, as if explaining herself to someone; perhaps the silent, unseen but constant presence of her mother. 'I shared Lilas's visions of his future, you see, and I know he hasn't got many years left.' She paused, for she was fighting tears. 'And I know how he is going to die.'

Despite everything – despite the king's selfishness and thoughtless cruelty; his savage treatment of his subjects; the deep intransigence that had made this stupid quarrel with the Pope go on for so long, so that the whole land suffered; the fact that England would undoubtedly be better off without him – still, the thought of his fate made her sad.

She stood for some time, quite still, letting her sadness and her distress abate. Then she raised her head, squared her shoulders and took a deep breath. It was time to go. She took one last look around the tidy space, then turned and opened the door.